MIKE NORRIS

Reap Sleep Rock Repeat

ETERNAL ALCOVE

PUBLISHING

Cover art by Angga 'Pixelogan' Pratama
Editing by Natalie Gray Proofreading

This book was professionally typeset on Reedsy.
Find out more at reedsy.com

To my wonderful wife Kayleigh and our beautiful daughters Eleanor and Imogen. Thank you for believing in me for all those years I didn't...

And a special shout out to my lifelong friend, Death Anxiety. Without you, I would never have had the idea for this book!

Contents

Acknowledgement

Ten years ago, I met my favourite author, WWE Hall of Famer Mick Foley. After several minutes of chatting about his two fantastic novels 'Tietam Brown' and 'Scooter', I walked away inspired and determined that I would one day write a book of my own. Thank you, Mick, for inspiring me to put pen to paper... or fingers to keyboard.

When my wife Kayleigh met me three years earlier, I was a geeky neurotic mess of a man. I still am, but thanks to her, I am now armed with self-confidence that I never had before. Thank you for being my badass cheerleader and helping me to reach heights I never dreamed I'd reach. This book wouldn't exist if it weren't for you.

Thank you to my mum Bev, my older sister Sarah and my friends Emma and Lisa for reading this book in its earliest stages. Thank you for harassing me to write more chapters because you were so concerned for Ben's wellbeing. Your excitement and enthusiasm helped me to achieve my lifelong dream of writing a novel.

Finally, a special thanks to you for reading this book. The thought you're about to give several hours of your life to immerse yourself in this story is mind-blowing. God help you!

Prologue

Was that it? Toby Daniels couldn't help but feel cheated. For centuries, humans have debated the precise moment of death. Does it hurt? Does it take seconds, or is it a long, drawn-out process? Is there life after death? Well, Toby suddenly felt qualified to answer some of those questions. He was dead, and yet he felt no pain. This was particularly odd, being he was lying on an operating table. Perhaps it was the anaesthetic. He was dead, and yet death hadn't been the big song and dance he'd expected it to be. It just sort of happened. *Is death the end?* he found himself wondering. The fact that he was even asking himself that question made it quite obvious that death was not the end, far from it.

How did Toby know he was dead? It was just a feeling, in the same way happiness is, or sadness. Although he had never been dead before, its feeling was unmistakable. He concluded that the feeling of "death" was some strange hybrid of hunger and embarrassment. It felt very new, but there was no denying it.

Despite the sheer panic going on around him, Toby felt detached from the chaos, almost like he wasn't in the room. He guessed that for the surgeons trying to save him, all that was left on the operating table at this time was a body. One doctor tried to restart his heart, and Toby felt a strange sensation. He didn't feel like his heart hung in the balance. In fact, he didn't feel any connection to any part of his body at

1

all. That was when Toby realised he was no longer in his body. He was standing next to it.

Staring down at himself, Toby's previous feeling of detachment began to drown under a sea of fear. Surgeons rushed around and even through him with such distress and fervour that their anxiety was bound to transfer to Toby himself.

"Oh my God!" he said out loud. "I'm dead! I know I am. What on earth do I do now?" Now it had been established that death wasn't the end, Toby wondered what he was supposed to do next. Was he a ghost? Would he spend his days roaming the Earth aimlessly? Was there a Heaven? Was there a Hell? Was there anywhere to go?

Then, Toby felt an icy chill on his shoulder. In the same instinctual way he had known he was dead, he knew that chill could only mean one thing. He slowly turned around to face the answer to all his questions.

"Tobias Jordan Daniels?" The answer was exactly as Toby had imagined, yet conversely, like nothing he could comprehend. A tall figure stood before him. Withered and perished from an eternity collecting souls, he still commanded an impressive presence within the operating room. His cloak wasn't just black; it was blacker than night. So black that a whole universe could have burst out from the darkness at any moment. Hidden beneath his dark hood was a face void of anything but grey. It looked frail and broken, sapped of anything that had once made it beautiful. It seemed almost fraudulent to call this a face. It was nothing more than a husk. Then there was the scythe. That was just how Toby had imagined. "Tobias Jordan Daniels?" the figure repeated. Toby noticed how the voice made every bone in his body shiver. He managed to utter a short reply.

"Yes, sir?"

"Tobias Daniels. Born 27th June 1995 in Morpeth, Northumberland. Died 6th June 2011. Day 6,189. 16 years, 11 months, and 11 days. Death by surgical incompetence." Toby was speechless. He'd had his entire life summarised in a few short sentences. It was also quite the insensitive way to confirm his suspicions that he was, in fact, dead.

"There must be some mistake," Toby found the courage to say. "I'm sixteen. My life has only just begun!"

The withered man looked deep into the eyes of the newly deceased teenager and flashed a dusty smile, "My friend, you may be young, but in your short time on this planet, you did everything that was expected of you. You may not see it, but you lived a full life."

"But what about my family," Toby asked. "And my friends? How was my life fuller than theirs?"

The man smirked once more. Toby sensed he had heard all these questions before, "I don't make the decision of whom I reap," he began. "I merely carry out the spiritual act. All I can say is that you have been deemed ready to move on to the AfterLife. You have done what was set out for you." Without a further word, the Reaper turned his back and drifted towards and out of the door. Toby wanted to follow him. Every single part of his being ached to walk alongside him. While truly terrifying, it was the most natural thing in the world.

When Toby stepped through the theatre doors, he was no longer in the hospital but on a cold, dark, empty street. His eyes adjusted from the bright lights of the theatre to the dusk before him. What he saw next caught him completely off guard. His new acquaintance stood before him, opening the door to an old-fashioned, Victorian-era steam bus. It looked like the sort of thing one would see in a history textbook or straight out of a museum.

"Climb aboard, Mr Daniels," the Reaper smiled. "I will take you where you need to go." Toby slowly walked towards the entrance of the bus. Each step towards the archaic vehicle brought him closer to a foul, musty stench, threatening to override all his senses completely. The street was eerily quiet, and Toby could hear creak after creak as he cautiously climbed the five steps up and onto the bus. He turned to his right and looked down the aisle. The entire bus was dismal and damp. The darkness of the street outside seeped through the dirty windows and polluted the whole deck. Huddled in random seats around the bus were others. Some were old, and some were young, but there was one thing they all shared. They were scared, and they weren't going anywhere.

Toby found an isolated area and sat down. He didn't particularly like sitting next to others on a bus when he was alive, and this attitude had undoubtedly carried over into his AfterLife. The Reaper solemnly entered the bus and settled himself into the driver's seat.

"Next stop: The AfterLife!" With that cry from the Reaper, the bus spluttered into life and drove towards a new beginning.

1

What had started as the most raucous of New Year parties had slowly quietened down through the early hours of January 1st, 2022. Big Ben chimed on TV on the hour, and the party had kicked into full swing. Three hours later, amongst the passed-out partygoers and discarded plastic cups were the all-nighters. The music had changed from the usual party anthems to a peaceful and subdued playlist. The six revellers who were still conscious sat in the lounge, deep in the kind of philosophical conversation only had by drunk people at 3 am. Among them was Benjamin May.

Ben was rarely out this late. He wasn't often out at all. An introvert in the truest sense of the word, Ben kept himself to himself and had spent most of the night avoiding conversation from even his closest friends. Ben's avoidance of others may have offered him some short-term relief, but he would feel incredibly isolated. He often wondered why his friends continued to bother with him. The natural conclusion he always came to was that it was only a matter of time before they gave up making an effort and moved on with their lives. Ben had struggled for years to reach out and be a part of the group and his New Year's resolution was to be more sociable. This party seemed like the perfect place to start. However, it had taken his flatmate Jamie a considerable amount of effort to persuade him to join his friends in the festivities.

"I don't feel like it's for me," Ben had protested hours earlier. "You know I'm not the partying type!"

"Don't worry so much, Ben!" Jamie retorted. "It's going to be really chilled out. A few drinks and a bit of music. It's not as if we're going to a rave." Ben was still unsure. After all, he'd dropped out of so many get-togethers over the past couple of years that he wasn't sure anyone would even want to see him.

"I'll cramp everyone's style," Ben replied. "You know I'm not good in that kind of situation." Jamie saw the look on Ben's face. The same look he always got when he backed out of something, the perfect blend of self-loathing and anxiety.

Jamie sat down opposite Ben and smiled. "You won't be cramping anyone's style. Plus, I'll be there the whole time, so we can come home if it gets too much." Ben thought long and hard about what was the best thing to do. He took great comfort from the idea that he had an out whenever he wanted it.

"Promise?" asked Ben.

"I promise," Jamie replied. "Besides, no one should be alone for New Year."

Just because Ben had decided to come to the party, it didn't mean he had been able to shake that horrible feeling of impending doom. He knew most people in the room, but that didn't stop him from feeling those ever-familiar butterflies. To Ben, butterflies didn't accurately describe the churning in his stomach. They were more like birds. Giant birds of prey causing havoc in his digestive system. Ben looked across at his friend Stevie, who he had known for years. They'd been in every class together through school, and now at the age of twenty-seven, they were still great friends. So why did the thought of spending time with Stevie and others make him feel so nauseous? The doctor had called it "social anxiety disorder" and suggested that Ben see a counsellor who could help him understand why he didn't like talking to people. Ben had thought that talking to a stranger about why he didn't like talking to people seemed to be a nonsensical way of dealing with the problem. Ben wished he could be like Stevie, who was babbling on about some abstract concept he'd written about for his philosophy dissertation. Had the group been talking about something else like music or literature, Ben thought he might have felt more at ease, but philosophy? He didn't want to sound like an idiot. The birds of prey stopped swooping long enough for Ben to realise that the rest of the group was now looking right at him!

"So what do you think, Ben?" asked Kara. Kara was a nice girl. Ben had met her through Stevie, and she was always very friendly. She had also studied philosophy, and with a few drinks inside her, she was ready to engage in spirited debate all night. Ben did not have a good understanding of the discussion when it began. Still, once he had ventured deep into his anxieties, he had lost the thread of the conversation or any idea of what his friends had been talking about.

"Sorry, Kara," Ben replied hesitantly, "I completely zoned out. I guess I'm just tired." Kara smiled and nodded.

"Well, it is three in the morning," she chuckled. Sensing Ben's anxiety, Jamie leaned over to the wireless speaker to find music more to his friend's taste. He replaced the painful wailing of an anonymous singer-songwriter in favour of "Planet Caravan" by Black Sabbath. This dreamy, psychedelic track was one Jamie knew his friend enjoyed.

"We were talking about the meaning of life," slurred Richard, another group member. Ben noticed that, as usual, Richard was far drunker than the rest of the party but harmless enough. "I mean, it's mind-blowing that we are all here. Together. In this house, you know?" No. Ben did not know. "It's like some cosmic force has brought us all here tonight. But ... why?" Kara laughed at how drunk Richard was as he got to work on yet another beer.

"I guess what Richard's trying to ask is why are we all here?" she continued.

"Because we were all invited?" Ben replied slowly. The meaning of life was an interesting concept, but Richard's drunken ramblings had gone entirely over his head. Everyone laughed at Ben's reply. He wasn't sure whether they were laughing at him or with him.

"Not so much here tonight, Ben," Richard replied over the laughter. "I mean the bigger picture. Why are we here? What has God or science or whatever put us here to do?" Ben thought hard about what Richard had said. He sat and thought about why he was here and what life was all about. The conclusion he came to made him rather sad.

"If I'm honest, mate, I don't know why I'm here," Ben sighed.

"I guess none of us truly know, do we?" Stevie interjected. "I mean, we've all got theories, but they're just that – theories."

"I see what you mean," Ben replied. "I guess what I mean is that I don't know my reason for being." The rest of the group looked across at him. Ben was suddenly very aware of the five sets of eyes staring at him. He knew these were his friends, who showed genuine interest in what he had to say, but it still made him feel uncomfortable. "I guess I always felt that the meaning of life is to make the most of it and become what you believe you can be. Take a soldier, for example. Their life has meaning because they want to fight for their country. I don't know what I can be or even what I want to be," Ben continued.

"Your meaning doesn't need to be defined by your career," countered Jamie. "Money, prestige, and all that crap isn't necessarily that important in the grand scheme of things. After all, we don't take anything with us."

"Or do we?" piped Richard, his eyes as wide as saucers. Ben's birds of prey started to take flight once again. He scolded himself for not considering the inevitability that a discussion about the meaning of life would segue naturally into a discussion about death. It was the one topic that made Ben feel very uncomfortable. "We don't know that death's the end, you know? There could be some kind of cosmic force or something." Richard's continued ramblings about cosmic forces and such drivel made Ben wish he'd never opened his mouth. A slightly sharper voice came from another side of the conversation. Nathan had been quiet so far, but now he had something to say.

"Oh, come on, Richard!" snapped Nathan. "There's no cosmic force or angels on fluffy clouds. When you're dead, that's it; you're dead. You stop breathing, you rot in the ground, and that's the end of it." Nathan's nihilistic words caused Ben's chest to tighten. His lungs felt as heavy as dumbbells. The thought of death being the end often kept Ben up at night as all kinds of questions ran through his head. What if death really is the end? What if you search your whole life looking for meaning, but in the end, it's a huge con? Ben hadn't studied philosophy like his friends but had taken a psychology class at college years earlier. He learned that the sheer panic he experienced around the finality of death is known as "death anxiety" and had read some fascinating existential theory from a gentleman called Irvin Yalom. At least, it would have been fascinating if it hadn't made him feel sick. That sickness was repeating eight years on, and the birds of prey in Ben's stomach had evolved into pterodactyls!

"What makes us as humans so bloody special?" bleated Nathan. "Dogs don't think there's a Heaven. Neither do cats or bloody platypuses. We're so up our own arses as a species that we believe we're worth more than our time on this planet!" Nathan continued to rant, but all Ben heard was the sound of blood rushing to his head. Everyone in front of him sounded muffled, and his heartbeat began to ring so loud he worried it would burst out of his chest. Suddenly the room that had previously seemed quite unremarkable felt as if it was getting smaller by the minute, and the walls around him reached in closer and closer. Ben's mind raced in desperation, hoping to find an answer to the unanswerable. In his panic, Ben conceded maybe he was being "up himself" like the rest of the human race but concluded that surely there had to be something more. He couldn't bear the thought of anything to the contrary.

Before he knew it, Ben found himself standing up and heading for the door. He knew he had to get out before the walls came in and swallowed him up completely. From the corner of his eye, he saw Jamie looking very concerned, his voice just about making it through the cacophony of muffles.

"Are you alright, mate?" Jamie asked. Ben managed to squeeze out enough words before he left the room intact.

"I just need some air."

2

T he rain sprayed softly onto the pavement. Ben walked quickly
through the fog and mist of a typical January night. *So much
for being more sociable*, he thought. Ben felt so stupid for
running out of the party and was sure everyone would laugh at what an
idiot he'd been. *Stupid old Ben*, he imagined them saying. *Why do we
even invite him to stuff anyway?* The longer he fixated on the thought
of his friends mocking him, the more anxious he felt and the louder
his self-loathing thundered in his head. *You're an idiot, Ben. What on
earth is wrong with you? You should have just stayed home.* The venom
and self-hatred inside him caused his chest to tighten, almost ready to
explode. If Ben could have heard his common sense through the panic
and despair, it would have told him to turn around and go back to the
house, but he was far too embarrassed to even think about returning.

The street was eerily silent. There wasn't another soul about, and
the only light came from two lamp posts that dimly lit the pavement
below. Ben stopped at the foot of the street and glanced at a bench that
just missed the light of the lamp posts on either side. It seemed as good
a place as any to sit down and collect his thoughts. The seat was damp
from the rain, but Ben didn't mind. Anything was better than being in
that room talking about death. With each drop of rain beating on Ben's
head, the world slowed down to a more manageable pace, his chest
relaxed, and the mental torment faded. Ben sat with his eyes closed,

willing the panic to pass before he tried to find his way home. Several minutes passed before he felt a vibrating pulse from his pocket. Ben reached for his phone to see two texts from Jamie and a missed call.

You ok, Ben? Where did you go?
I can ring us a taxi if you want to go home.

Reading back the messages, Ben started to think about how worried Jamie would be following his abrupt departure. Even so, he didn't know he had the courage to go back. He considered ringing Jamie and suggesting they get a taxi together. However, that ran the risk of returning to the party to meet him. Ben knew he didn't want to see the rest of his friends for a while. A month maybe. Perhaps even two. Ben found life much easier when left to his own devices, even if the cost was him slowly becoming more isolated and cut off from the world. He always had Jamie to look out for him. Still, on this night, Ben's lack of self-worth and abundance of social guilt led him to decide to leave Jamie to enjoy the party rather than come away for his sake. Ben quickly replied to Jamie's messages so as not to worry him.

I'm ok. See you at home.

Ben pressed send on his phone when something caught his eye across the street. The only lights in the street shone on either side of the same bench he sat on, leaving the other side of the road in darkness. Ben took a few seconds to make out a lone figure crouched down in the corner of a bus shelter. There wasn't much more Ben could make out from where he sat. Amidst his own uncertainty of the situation, and despite his better judgement, Ben felt an unexplainable urge to go over. He wondered if this person needed help. There were only the two of them out in the dead of night. If this person was in trouble, who else would help them? Ben's heart beat deep into his chest. He stood up and walked across the road towards the bus shelter; something inside him instinctively told him it was the right thing to do. There was just something about this moment. The fact that he was there when no one else was. He was meant to approach this person.

Ben got closer, and the figure became clearer through the mist. He saw a young woman roughly around his age shivering in a heap on the bus stop floor. Ben noticed that the girl was wet from head to toe. The rain began to intensify, and a shower of droplets poured from the roof of the shelter and splashed onto her shoulders. She had no coat, and consequently, her dress was drenched.

"Excuse me?" Ben asked. "Are you alright?" The young woman looked up at Ben as he stepped into the shelter. Her long black hair was soggy and wildly brushed against her face. The dismal January weather had smudged her make-up, but even with ruined mascara, Ben couldn't help but notice how beautiful her eyes were. A vibrant shade of green that stood out amongst the drab and dull New Year's morning. "I saw you from the other side of the road," Ben continued. "I was worried you might be hurt."

Sitting in the corner of the shelter as the rain beat on the roof, the young woman didn't respond, instead looking back, frozen in fear. Ben felt a pang of guilt for making her feel this way. "I'm sorry if I've scared you," Ben said. "I just want to help."

"I'll be fine," the girl responded quietly.

"You know the buses don't run here at this time of night?" Ben asked.

"I know," she replied. "I'm just waiting. Once this rain stops, I'm going to head home. Please, just leave me alone." Ben reluctantly went to turn and walk away. The girl was upset, and as much as he wanted to help, he didn't want to add to what appeared to be a difficult night for her. Ben looked down at the floor and noticed the girl wasn't wearing shoes. Rain bounced violently off her bare feet, and Ben noticed small, bloody cuts and scratches on each one. He flinched at the sight of the rainwater diluting the blood, which caused it to run down her feet.

"I can't leave you like this! What happened to your feet?"

"Well, it's kind of my own fault," she sighed as she lifted the soles of her feet, revealing further cuts and bleeding. "I lost my shoes in town and ended up stepping on broken glass. A shitty end to a shitty night!"

"Bloody hell!" gasped Ben. "Let me help you get to a hospital or something. Is there any glass in there?"

"No, I don't think so," the woman answered. "I don't want to go to the hospital. I'll get myself sorted at home."

"Can I at least help you get home?" Ben asked. "Is it far? I don't mind getting you a taxi or—"

"No, it isn't far," she interrupted. She went quiet for a moment, almost as if she was weighing up the situation. Ben knew at that moment to stay silent. The woman looked up at him, and her eyes softened, only for a moment but long enough for Ben to notice. "I'll warn you, though, it might take us a while. My feet are killing me." Ben looked down at her soles once more and winced. He held out his hand and helped her cautiously to her feet.

"Good thing I've got all night then, isn't it? Hi, I'm Ben."

"Thank you. I'm Lucy."

Lucy and Ben slowly walked down the street, and although they had just met, something about it felt completely normal to both of them. Ben somehow overcame his usual nerves and misgivings about meeting new people. Lucy also felt safe walking through the streets with a stranger. Something felt right about the whole thing. As it turned out, Lucy's shitty night had been just that. Like Ben, she hadn't wanted to go out for New Year's Eve in the first place but had ended up in Durham for drinks. A friend who'd had far too much to drink had decided to try his luck, and when she turned him down, he became aggressive. With her other friends either nowhere to be seen or too drunk to help, Lucy had no choice but to run away. She had even abandoned her shoes when they were only slowing her down. Without noticing the smashed glass bottles and pint glasses on the ground, Lucy had run through the shards and cut her feet to shreds. The next thing she knew, she was huddled at that bus stop, cold, scared and alone. The events of Lucy's night put Ben's freak out at the party into a whole new perspective. Here was someone who had been in actual danger tonight, and he had stormed out of a friend's house because he didn't like the conversation. Soon Lucy asked him the question he'd been dreading.

"So we've covered why I'm out here alone. How about you?"

Ben's butterflies started up again. He had only known Lucy for a few minutes but had already decided that he didn't want her to think badly of him. "I'm almost embarrassed," he replied as he struggled to find words that didn't make him sound like a complete idiot. "I was at a party tonight, and I—" He hesitated for a moment. "I had to leave before I had a panic attack."

Lucy looked back, genuinely concerned. "Why would you be embarrassed by that? I've had panic attacks too. I wouldn't wish them on anyone."

Ben sighed, "It's complicated. Everyone was drunk, talking about the meaning of life and if there's anything after we … you know." Ben was relieved that despite looking confused, Lucy didn't appear to be judging him. "I struggle with that kind of thing," he continued. "I had a friend who passed away when we were sixteen. It was so sudden, and I never really dealt with it, so I just—" Ben never talked about this stuff to anyone, yet here he was, baring his soul to a complete stranger. "I'm sorry, this is nothing compared to what you've been through tonight."

"It's ok," Lucy smiled. "It's nice to talk about something else, to be honest." After a moment's thought, she continued, "Let me guess. Was it one of those moments where everyone was sat around thinking they were so insightful because they'd had a few drinks, and it was two in the morning?" Ben started to chuckle.

"It doesn't help when three of them studied philosophy," he laughed.

"Oh bloody hell, no wonder you walked out!" shrieked Lucy in amusement and just like that, the conversation moved on. Ben's butterflies melted away, and for the first time in a long time, he felt a wave of calm and contentment. Contentment and acceptance.

A t that very moment, a few miles down the road, lives hung in the balance. Only while on one plane of existence, emergency services were doing all they could to save lives; on another, there was only one being responsible for making sure that everything went as it should, and he was late.

"Shit, shit, shit," he grumbled as he raced towards the crash scene. "I can't believe I'm late again. A Reaper should never be late." As a guide into the AfterLife, it was essential that a Reaper was present from the very moment a person passed over; otherwise, they may become disoriented and confused. Worst of all, they may not even realise they are dead, which could cause all sorts of problems. On a day like this, the results of a late Reaper could be catastrophic. Tom pushed his foot down on the accelerator, and the bus engine spluttered loudly. As a card-carrying member of the AfterLife (and he genuinely did have a card), he did not need to worry about the rest of the traffic on the road. The sun was only just starting to rise, but the roadways were surprisingly busy. However, the other cars were mere spectres on the road to Tom, and he could quickly drive through each vehicle with ease. Even after all this time, Tom enjoyed the novelty of moving right through people without them having any idea other than a quick shiver down their spine. But on this day, all Tom could think about was how late he was and how each passing second only made him later. Suddenly, Tom knew what he had to do. He shuffled around in his glove box in frustration.

"Drastic times call for drastic measures," Tom thought out loud as he grasped the cassette he was looking for. Crudely labelled "Reap Sleep Rock Repeat", the mix tape was Tom's go-to soundtrack when things weren't going right. He pushed the cassette into the player, and "Peel Out" began to bellow from the speakers. Meat Loaf's song of reckless abandon on the road may not have had the notoriety of his iconic single "Bat Out of Hell", but Tom felt "Peel Out" was just as good, if not better. He pulled back his hood with one hand while he turned up the volume with the other. The song burst into life, and Tom slammed down the accelerator with all his strength. He'd get to his passengers no matter what.

Just over three miles down the motorway, there was much panic and chaos. One man was more alarmed than most. It would be easy to understand the shock of a significant accident causing such a terrified reaction. The mass hysteria of people rushing around trying to save lives would highlight the true gravity of the situation for anyone. However, this particular gentleman had expressed such a strong reaction to proceedings because he was staring at his own bloodied and lifeless body slumped over in the front seat of his car. How had this happened? Moments earlier, he'd been driving home from an epic office party contemplating whether it was too late to order a kebab. Now all of a sudden, he was dead. He couldn't be a partner in Newcastle's most influential law firm if he was dead. Putting aside the gruesome visual of his own corpse, being dead so far seemed like a major inconvenience.

A sharp voice broke him from his gaze. "Twenty-two-year-old female suspected internal bleeding and fractured ribcage," the voice stated as the man turned to face its owner. They were already in front of him. Two paramedics were pushing a gurney with an unconscious woman straight towards him, and it was too late for him to move out of their way. Just at the moment of impact, the group went through uninterrupted. There was no collision. There was not even any kind of physical interaction. It was almost as if everyone had walked right through him.

"Hey, buddy," he yelled. "I'm a partner in Forster Forster and Davis. Show me some respect!" He felt immediately stupid after his rant when he realised no one could hear him. Surveying the wreckage across all three lanes, he felt like everything was happening around him, almost despite his presence or lack thereof. Was this a dream, or was he really dead, and if he was indeed dead, then what on earth was he supposed to do next? He looked back towards the wreck that was once his £40,000 pride and joy. He'd never so much as scuffed a bumper; now, it was a write-off. As thick, ugly, black smoke billowed into the sky, he once again had to remind himself of his current predicament and that his insurance could no longer go through the roof as he was no longer around to pay it. There was so much of his materialistic life that had suddenly become utterly irrelevant upon his death.

The man looked across the road at the wreckage. In the middle of it all, amongst the mechanical mess and carnage, stood a young woman. She was shaking and had tears streaming down her face. Against the backdrop of vehicular mayhem, the woman seemed much more prominent than everything around her. The mangled cars and frenzied paramedics seemed dull and blurry in comparison. This girl was somehow brighter.

"Excuse me!" shouted the man. "Can you see me?" The woman looked up, her eyes drenched in tears. "Can you hear me?"

"Yes! Yes, I can see you!" gasped the woman, her voice drowning in relief. She ran towards him as the chaos continued around them. She stopped no less than two paces in front of him. "Am I ... dead?" Her tears had brought so many feelings rushing through the man. Sadness.

Anger. Confusion. Suddenly he felt tears streaming down his face. No matter what happened next, at least he wasn't alone.

"I believe we are," he replied. "I thought I was the only one." He offered his hand for his new friend to shake. "My name is Barry. Barry Forster." The woman threw her arms around him; her body shook with fear and grief.

"I'm Gemma."

As Gemma held on to Barry as tightly as she could, she heard a faint roar of an engine in the distance. The noise grew louder until both recognised the jarring sound of a heavy metal guitar piercing the air. Gemma let go of Barry and looked down the motorway. To their complete disbelief, a bright yellow school bus shone in the night, racing towards the crash scene. The sound of the guitar and Wagnerian harmonies grew louder as the bus drove closer and closer. Barry worried it was going to cause another accident.

"NO!" screamed Barry running towards the wreckage. "Stop! You're going to—" Barry never finished his sentence. Instead, he stood in awe as the bus skidded through the mess of tyre tracks and smoking cars and swung into an emergency stop. The music stopped, and the door flung open. A mysterious cloaked figure leapt out of the vehicle and scrambled through his pockets. Tom had finally made it. He could only hope the damage hadn't already been done.

"A pen, a pen! Where did I put my pen?" Tom hissed to himself. He looked up to see Barry and Gemma frozen to the spot in fear. Tom composed himself, brushed his cloak and cleared his throat. "No need to be frightened," Tom began. "Yes, you are dead, and yes, I'm here to guide you into the AfterLife." Following Tom's succinct summary of events, there was an awkward silence soon broken by a blood-curdling scream. It was Gemma, and her whole body was shaking once again.

"Your face ... It's nothing but bone!" she screamed. "You're the Grim Reaper, aren't you?" That had done it! Tom was sick of being compared to Grim. While it was true that Grim had managed to infiltrate popular culture, it didn't mean that he was capable of gathering up everyone who died. For centuries, there had been many Reapers who worked together to get the job done. However, Tom had to concede that Grim would have definitely not been late.

"Wrong," Tom replied in answer to Gemma's question. "My name is Tom. However, you are correct that I am a Reaper, and I'd ask you not to scream at the state of my face as it's rather hurtful." Gemma bashfully looked away as Tom flicked through sheets of paper on a clipboard. "Barry Christopher Forster and Gemma Kirsty Lane?" Both Barry and Gemma nodded sheepishly. "I have all your information somewhere," Tom continued, frantically flicking through the sheets on his clipboard. "I haven't got it to hand at the moment, but needless to say, you've died in a car accident ... as you can see." Tom looked over the pile-up and whistled. "As crashes go, that's a nasty one." Barry finally broke his silence.

"So what happens now?"

"Oh, that's simple," Tom replied. "You get on the bus."

4

The bus pulled into the Pathway at a sedate pace. Gone was the screech of heavy metal guitars from the speakers. The Pathway was far too solemn for such anarchy. Even Tom knew that. After all, the Pathway was the crossroads of the dead. It was where the good would go to Heaven and the bad ... well, no one liked to speak about that. Who went where was of no consequence to Tom. His only job was to safely collect and deposit the newly deceased for the decision to be made. As a result, the fact that Tom was a good forty-five minutes later than expected was of great concern. Soul collecting was a significant yet very time-constrained occupation, and Tom was certain that the Council of Reapers would not take his tardiness kindly. Every wasted minute could potentially leave a freshly deceased person without a Reaper, thereby creating a lost soul. The Council didn't like lost souls; there was far too much paperwork.

"Come on, everyone!" cried Tom to his passengers. "Time to get off." Some started to rise from their seats; others were frozen in fear. What united them all was the look on their faces as they gazed out the sooty windows of the bus, surveying the murky wasteland that stretched for miles around. It wasn't so much that there was anything to see. What was perhaps the most disturbing thing was that there was nothing natural out there at all. The land outside Tom's bus was completely barren. There were no trees or hills, not so much as a blade of grass.

The ground looked like it had never seen water or even direct sunlight. An ugly fog hung in the air with a hideous stench that polluted the night sky, so thick it even blocked out the moon and the stars. This was death, and it was genuinely terrifying.

"We're already late, dudes!" shouted Tom, snapping everyone out of their trance-like state. One by one, Tom's passengers hesitantly filed out of the bus. In front of them, an ominous, rusty gate loomed menacingly over the atmosphere, its shadow diminishing any remaining light. The structure shot so high it proudly burst out of the mist, its apex obscured from view. Tom craned his neck to take it in. The Pathway gates always amazed and intimidated him in equal measure. One day he hoped he would get to the other side and see what death was supposed to be like.

"Coach number?" a monotone voice croaked as Tom approached the gates. The fog obscured his vision, but the voice was all too familiar.

Winston had sat at the Gates to the AfterLife for as long as anyone could remember. Many moons ago, death wasn't nearly as organised and meticulous as it had since become. There was a time when death was a simple process; it just sort of happened. Nowadays, everything had to be recorded. What time did a person die? What was the underlying cause of death? What was their National Insurance number? Winston had sat at those gates for so long that no one quite knew when he'd arrived, let alone how he'd got there. Rumour had it amongst the Reapers that Winston had actually been present when the first mortal died. Some believed he was the first mortal and had to find something to do with his eternity. No matter how Winston had ended up outside the Gates to the AfterLife, one thing was clear. He was a Gatekeeper, and he was very good at it.

Winston's role as Gatekeeper required him to get everyone signed in so they could be judged. As each bus arrived, packed to the rafters with the newly deceased, Winston would ensure that he could account for every last soul. Once he had checked everyone in, Winston would leave them to stand before the Council for judgement, and he would entrust the Reaper with their next assignment. If, for whatever reason, a soul was missing, then it was back on the road for the Reaper. Winston didn't suffer fools kindly and knew when the Reapers tried to pull the wool over his eyes. He never missed a beat.

"Coach number 2112", Tom replied. Tom had got to pick his coach number and couldn't resist paying tribute to his favourite Rush album.

"2112?" Winston answered back. "You are late." As Tom got close, the smog cleared to show the unimpressed look on Winston's face. Winston may have been an excellent Gatekeeper, but he wasn't the most intimidating fellow. It would be kind to describe Winston as short. It would be more indicative of his size to inform you that the chair in which he sat outside the Gates to the AfterLife was a glorified highchair. The years had not been kind to Winston on the Pathway, and the lack of regular exercise had left him rather dumpy and fat. Couple this with the baby-like pout that adorned his face, and he didn't exactly fit the bill for what one may expect of a Gatekeeper. Perhaps there was a genuine reason for all the fog after all. "Never in my entire career have I known a Reaper to be forty-five minutes late. This is most egregious!"

"I'm sorry, Winston," Tom pleaded. "The bus broke down, man. I've been saying for years that I could do with an upgrade. This thing's on the fritz!"

"Yes, well, you can take that up with the Council," Winston fussed. "They want to see you."

"Oh, man. Surely you could do me a solid Winnie? Tell them about my ride!"

"Sorry, 2112. Grim has asked to see you personally." A shiver rushed down Tom's spine. The fact that Grim wanted to deal with this meant that he was in big trouble. As Winston waddled over to the bus with his clipboard, Tom tapped him on the shoulder.

"Did he seem mad?" Tom asked. "I need to know what I'm letting myself in for after I've checked this lot in."

"Check this lot in?" Winston scoffed, "2112, the Council wishes to see you immediately. I shall check your passengers in. If I were you, I'd get into that boardroom quick, sharp!"

Tom glanced across the murk and fog of the Pathway. On the opposite side of the desolate wasteland was a small, rickety, old hut. The uninitiated may have missed it engulfed in the mist, but an experienced Reaper such as Tom knew it was there. The shack, known colloquially as City Hall, had fallen into disrepair over the years. The smog had discoloured the walls and seeped through the felt roof, leaving it damp and muggy. The door was hanging off one rusty hinge while the windows were blacked out and full of cobwebs. Compared to the awe-inspiring view of the gates, this old shack looked unassuming. However, the conversations and decisions made inside this broken-down shell of a building would form the very structure of one's AfterLife. Unless a Reaper were a member of the Council of Reapers, he would tend to avoid City Hall as much as possible. Going in was bad enough; being summoned was terrifying. Tom took a deep breath and tentatively stepped inside.

Tom closed the remnants of the door behind him and rubbed his eyes as he adjusted to the light. While the outside looked run down and dishevelled, the inside of City Hall was dull and corporate. As Tom walked down a corridor that felt far too long for a building that looked so small from the outside, he glanced at the paintings that adorned the walls. Every member of the Council from its inception to the present day was immortalised in oil. A prerequisite for membership required a Reaper reaped for a set number of years before settling into retirement and a seat on the Council. Some had sat on the Council longer than they had been a Reaper, while others got bored and stepped down, happy to live an AfterLife of pure monotony. Others were impeached or left in scandalous fashion. No matter the path they took, every member had their place on the wall.

Many great Reapers of the past stared back at Tom as he walked down the hallowed corridors. He marvelled at the paintings of Godfrey Marmaduke, who famously reaped the whole of England during the bubonic plague without any assistance, and Sebastian Le Coeur, the first Reaper to use a bus to transport the deceased. As Tom reached the end of the corridor, he looked above the two double doors leading to the conference room. There was one more painting that hung pride of place – the Grim Reaper.

Grim was the First Reaper. Tom had previously had a life of his own. He hadn't done much with it, but he fondly remembered his time on Earth. Grim had never walked the Earth other than to gather the dead. He had dedicated his entire existence to reaping the world of anyone whose pulse had inconveniently gone missing. As time went on and the planet's population rose, it became clear that one Reaper wouldn't cut it. Grim decided that his solitary quest needed to become a more extensive operation. Grim recruited his Reapers from the ranks of the very people he collected. The criteria for the perfect Reaper were not particularly clear. Tom wasn't sure why the Council had chosen him but knew their decision had not been made lightly. He began to wonder if Grim and his Council were regretting their decision.

Tom stared at Grim's painting at the head of the corridor. While none of the images were easy on the eye, Grim's was particularly gruesome. It looked uncannily like an Iron Maiden album cover. Grim stood proudly, a sea of bodies strewn around him. His scythe gleamed with a streak of blood in his right hand while his left lifted a severed head high into the air in some kind of sick victory pose. That wasn't what frightened Tom about this painting. The scattered corpses and the dismembered head seemed more unnecessary than scary. What disturbed Tom the most was Grim's face, or lack thereof. It was common knowledge that no one had ever seen beneath Grim's cowl. There were hushed whispers around City Hall that Grim didn't even have a face under his hood, and the painting captured this perfectly. The artist hadn't even tried to use any colour. Even in a work of art, looking at Grim was like staring into the deepest of black holes. There was no colour, only abyss. Tom composed himself, cleared his throat and knocked on the door.

5

"Enter!" an authoritative voice boomed back. Tom grabbed the ornate gold handle and pushed. The door opened, and Tom felt a chill that sunk deep into his bones. The boardroom was never an ideal place to be. It was where the Council of Reapers thrashed out all the major decisions of the AfterLife. For the Council to summon Tom for an audience with them wasn't good news at all. Unlike the rest of City Hall, the boardroom itself was extremely grand. Chandeliers shone from above as the light bounced off the diamonds studded across the enormous table which hosted the Council. The table seemed to stretch back for miles. The Council members, their faces obscured by their hoods, looked away from Tom towards the end of the table. The light shone in Tom's eyes. He shielded them from the glare, and the authoritative voice that had demanded his entry boomed out once again.

"Thomas Frederick Hudson!"

In complete unison, the Council turned their heads and faced Tom. It was a movement that was sudden and startling. Every member of the Council stared at him. Other than his own death, this was the most scared that Tom had ever been. Some Council members were hidden under their hoods; others gave away a piercing stare that shot right through him. Nevertheless, Tom knew everyone in that boardroom was giving him their undivided attention. The voice boomed again.

"Thomas Frederick Hudson!"

Words were not forthcoming. Tom tried to speak, but his throat was empty. All he could feel was an ever-increasing sense of fear rising from the soles of his feet to the very top of his head. He stood motionless in fear.

"Mr Hudson, failure to respond to the Council of Reapers is deemed very disrespectful indeed. We are all peers here, so I will give you one more chance. Are you Mr Thomas Frederick Hudson?" At the very last moment, the fear engulfing Tom's vocal cords released its firm grip, allowing him to address the Council with an affirmative one-syllable word.

"Aye."

A ghoulish figure at the very end of the table stood up and made a swift motion with his hand. The other Council members turned in unison and gazed straight ahead. Tom tried to look into the darkness beneath his hood and saw nothing. This was unmistakably the Grim Reaper. The room fell quiet. All Tom could hear were the ominous footsteps of Grim as he advanced slowly to the foot of the table. "I ... I meant no disrespect, Mr Grim dude ... I mean, sir," Tom began. "I was just in awe of this beautiful boardroom you have." As Tom stuttered his way through an apology, he heard a light tapping in the corner of the room. His eyes darted to a darkly lit table at the back left-hand corner of the boardroom. A small man tapped away at a typewriter, presumably taking minutes during the most nerve-wracking moment of Tom's AfterLife.

"The Council has no time for your sycophancy Mr Hudson!" Grim responded sharply yet calmly. "I'm sure you are aware of why you are here." Tom nodded slowly. Words seemed to have escaped him once again. "Mr Hudson, do you mind if we drop the formalities?" Grim asked. "I know that the other Reapers call you Tom. May I have that same courtesy?" Tom nodded once again. "Tom ..." Grim continued.

"I haven't reaped for 500 years. Some may say I've become more of an administrator than a Reaper. That being said, even I know that to be late for a reaping is unacceptable!" The last word rattled through the room as the chandelier lights shook above them. Grim stepped right up to Tom and towered over him by a good foot. The darkness beneath Grim's hood was as black as hate. "I'm going to give you a small opportunity to explain yourself to the Council before we deliberate as to how to plan to deal with this ... episode."

Grim stepped back and walked slowly towards his seat. "Start anytime, Tom," he said as he returned to the head of the table. "The floor, as they say, is yours." Tom didn't know what Grim meant by "dealing" with him, but he knew it couldn't be good. Tom had one chance and one chance only to get out of whatever unspeakable punishment was heading his way. Tom cleared his throat and tried to talk his way out of being "dealt with".

"Well—" Tom began timidly. "While I'm totally stoked to have a bus for my reaping, it's ... well ... sometimes it can be a bit—"

"A bit what, Tom?" interrupted Grim in an accusatory tone. Tom gulped once more. He decided he might as well go out in a blaze of glory.

"Shit, sir," Tom replied. "My bus is a piece of shit." The Council turned in unison to face him once more. Maybe going out in a blaze of glory was overrated. "I'm sorry to be so blunt, sir," Tom continued, "but it has been falling apart for the last few months. I think I may be the eighth Reaper who has driven it, and while it is great for getting more people in, it's no good when it breaks down on the side of the AfterLife, and I haven't got a mechanic on board." There was a brief silence as Grim took in what Tom had to say.

"Are you aware that there are some Reapers who still collect on foot?" Grim asked calmly.

"My son has to reap with a pink bicycle with a wicker basket on the front!" another voice from the Council piped up angrily.

"I understand that," Tom conceded. "And as I said before, I'm stoked that I was given a bus in the first place! I guess I'm saying that I wouldn't have been forty-five minutes late today if my bus hadn't broken down for the sixth time this month."

"You guess you're saying?" Grim asked, picking up on Tom's uncertainty. Sensing that despite his reservations that this could potentially go in his favour, Tom straightened himself up and cleared his throat one more time.

"I'm positive, sir. I'm positive that if I could get a new bus or even just get this one fixed that I'll never be late again!"

Silence fell upon the room as the Council thought about what Tom had just said. Even the clicking of the typewriter had stopped. Suddenly Grim rose from his seat and clapped his hands together. "I'm pretty sure we can accommodate our good friend Tom and get him a new method of transportation for his duties, can't we?" Grim cheered gleefully.

"But, sir!" a voice from the Council cried out. "With all the respect in the world, we don't have enough in our budget for—"

"Nonsense!" Grim interrupted as he bounded towards Tom. "A Reaper must be provided with all the tools he needs to do his job." Grim put his arm around Tom's shoulder and addressed the Council. Despite it seeming like a warm gesture, it felt empty and disconcerting. "This Reaper has explained that his bus is unreliable. To be the Council we claim to be, we must repair or replace it, no ifs, ands or buts." The Council murmured, some in agreement, others less so. However, Grim's word was always final. Tom felt Grim's grip get tighter. Grim leaned over and whispered in his ear, each breath sharp and ice-cold on his skin. "Besides Mr Hudson, if the Council goes to all this trouble and your tardiness continues, I will come down on you so hard you'll wish you'd never died!"

Grim released his grip and walked back to his seat. "You'll have your new bus within fourteen days. Please dismiss yourself, Tom. The Council has other items on our agenda to discuss." Tom slowly slinked out of the boardroom, relieved that he got out in one piece but also shell-shocked by Grim's threat. Gazing at the grotesque portrait one more time, he realised that he needed to up his game. What Grim said wasn't a threat; it was a promise.

6

L ife is so unpredictable that we rarely know when one moment
with someone will be the last time we see them. An emotional
farewell to a co-worker or an ex-partner doesn't eliminate
the chance of seeing them walking down the street in a few months. On
the other side of the coin, even the most important people in our lives
can leave before we get the chance to say a proper goodbye. We can be
left feeling guilty about what we could have said. What we should have
said.

Ben remembered his final moments with Toby. It may have been
over ten years, but some memories never fade. Neither knew it would
be the last time they saw each other, let alone that Toby's time left on
this plane was short. Their final evening together was similar to many
other nights they'd spent over the years. Ben and Toby spent hours
digging through albums and listening to the rock and metal Gods they
worshipped so passionately. While messiahs, the likes of Osbourne
and Kilmister, usually took centre stage, occasionally, one of the boys
would introduce a new band to the mix. Their final meeting was one of
those nights.

"They're called Black Stone Cherry," Toby told Ben excitedly. "This
is only available via import, and I managed to get the last one in town
this afternoon. It's called 'Between the Devil & The Deep Blue Sea'.
Their third album, apparently." Ben took the CD from his friend and

surveyed the album's minimalist artwork, which included a compass surveying choppy waters. Rather than the swashbuckling shanties he expected to hear from a nautical-themed album, Ben was surprised to hear crunching, southern rock burst from the speakers. It was just the kind of heavy, riff-laden music Ben and Toby could geek out on for hours. The opening track "White Trash Millionaire" powered on, and while Ben loved the whiskey-soaked vocals and melodic guitar solos, his ears kept returning to the drums. Charged and deliberate, Ben could feel the pounding percussion thundering in his chest. The song screeched to a southern-fried halt. Ben's jaw dropped, and for a moment, neither he nor Toby said a word.

"Who is that drummer?" Ben asked in disbelief as the song ended. "He's unbelievable!"

"I know, right?" replied Toby as he flicked through the album booklet with the CD and shoved it in Ben's face. "His name's John Fred Young, and I think he's my new hero!" Ben looked down at the band photo in the booklet. Standing behind the other three band members, John Fred was slightly hidden from view. However, with his long curly hair inviting comparisons to Animal from the Muppets, he looked every inch a rock and roll icon. To two impressionable sixteen-year-old boys, John Fred Young was already a legend. Rock and heavy metal weren't exactly the most modern music tastes in 2011, but that didn't weaken its power to bond these two friends. For Ben and Toby, bands like Black Stone Cherry proved that rock wasn't dead.

"You can lend it over the weekend," Toby relented at the end of the night as Ben got ready to head home. "But please don't forget to bring it to school on Monday."

There was no emotional goodbye. No hug at the door or an admission of how much they meant to each other. Why would there be if neither of them knew how significant this moment was? Ben grabbed his coat and made his way out the door.

"See you soon!"

Ben never heard Toby's reply. The growl of James Hetfield replaced whatever Toby had to say as Metallica's *Death Magnetic* played through Ben's headphones. *If I'd known I'd never see him again*, Ben often thought, *I'd have waited.* The rational part of Ben's brain knew that Toby's death wasn't his fault. How could he be blamed for an appendectomy gone wrong? However, it couldn't stop him from thinking that maybe if he had been more present in that final moment, maybe, just maybe, things would be different.

Toby's death hugely affected Ben. He'd never exactly been a social butterfly, but Ben retreated further into himself once Toby had gone. When many of his friends stopped calling, he presumed they'd had enough of him. The truth was they knew that any invitation extended his way would be turned down, and none of them knew what to say. Ben didn't want to see anyone while at the same time wishing he wasn't alone. Unlike the anxiety he would experience later in life, which was sudden and urgent, depression slowly crept up on Ben and submerged him. Ben was lost, and in some ways, he had never truly found his way back.

That was why his friendship with Lucy was so important. From that first meeting under the bus shelter late at night, Ben and Lucy spent time together almost daily. Ben had always prided himself on having an impressive music collection. However, Lucy's spare room boasted enough vinyl to get lost in for days. Ben's love of rock and metal was well catered for, but Lucy also enjoyed the likes of Fleetwood Mac, Joni Mitchell and Neil Young. It was easy to lose hours sitting in Lucy's spare room, and it was the first time since Toby died that Ben had someone to share his love of music with.

Ben noticed that, for the most part, when he was around Lucy, the knot in his stomach was gone. The tightness in his chest was a distant memory. Ben didn't feel like life was an effort for the first time in years. He could be himself and was starting to find his way back. When he didn't overthink and enjoyed the moment, all was right with the world. However, there would be the odd instance, perhaps when Lucy was cleaning the dust off the next album or how her eyes lit up when she spoke about something that excited her. They may seem inconsequential to some, but to Ben, it was those seemingly random moments that he realised he wanted more.

Ben wasn't naive enough to think he was in love. He'd only known Lucy for two weeks, and although it already felt like she'd always been around, he knew it was too soon for him to love someone. But he couldn't deny there was something there. Some kind of connection. Who knew what that would mean a year or even six months from now, but right now, Ben knew he liked how it felt and that it was something worth exploring. But surely having someone like Lucy in his life at all was better than risking ruining what was already a wonderful friendship? As his train of thought continued, the knot in his stomach would return, and instead of being in the moment and enjoying Lucy's company, he was too busy playing out various worst-case scenarios.

One night as Ben was looking through Lucy's record collection, he spotted a sleeve that was very familiar to him. He had never been able to return Toby's album, and as the years went by, it remained a link between them that no one could take away. As Ben pulled the LP off its shelf and examined the compass on the cover, he noticed Lucy returning to the room.

"I didn't even know you could get this Black Stone Cherry album on vinyl," Ben said as he thought back to the first time he'd sat and listened to it with Toby.

"It's so great," Lucy replied. "They released it on coloured vinyl ahead of the next tour." Ben's mind couldn't help but return to that final night with Toby, and an overwhelming sadness washed over him. "Are you ok?" Lucy asked as Ben felt the colour drain from his face. He took a moment to compose himself.

"I'm fine," Ben said quietly. "It might sound strange, but this album means a lot to me." Without saying a word, Lucy took the album out of Ben's hands and placed it on the turntable. They sat and listened to it in full, much like he had with Toby ten years earlier. It made him think about how quickly life can change. The first time he'd heard these songs was the last time he saw his friend. The decade had flown in the blink of an eye, and Ben didn't want to waste any more of his life. He knew he owed it to himself to see where things could go with Lucy and decided at that moment that he would do just that.

The final track reached its end, and Lucy returned the vinyl record to its sleeve and placed it back on the shelf amongst her vast music collection.

"I had a suspicion you were cool, Ben, but being a Black Stone Cherry fan confirms it," joked Lucy. Ben tried in vain not to blush. "That's got me right in the mood for Saturday night."

"What's happening on Saturday?" Ben asked.

"You don't know? Black Stone Cherry! They're playing in Newcastle!" Ben smiled as Lucy's eyes lit up at the mere mention of seeing the band live. Lucy opened a drawer on her desk and flashed a pair of tickets to the show. "You should come with me!" she cried. A wave of panic coursed through Ben's body. It was as if the deep blue sea was crashing inside his stomach. The idea of going to a concert with Lucy was exhilarating, but he could barely control his anxiety around half a dozen people, let alone several thousand. Ben had always loved live music, but as the years rolled by, he had retreated into himself. Consequently, it had been at least two years since he had experienced the thrill of a concert. Ben thought about who had introduced him to Black Stone Cherry in the first place. Losing Toby had been out of his control, but pushing people and life away since then was his fault alone. He swallowed hard and listened to his heart.

"I mean, I'd love to, if you're sure?" Ben replied. The words had barely left his mouth when Lucy whooped and threw her arms around him. The stormy waves inside subsided. Ben was sure he'd made the right decision.

"Great! Oh, Ben, we'll have such an amazing time." Lucy released her embrace, and for a brief moment, time stood still. The two looked into each other's eyes, blind to the fact that they both wanted the same thing. With their friendship at such an early stage, neither one wanted to overstep or complicate things. To avoid any awkwardness, Lucy changed the subject. "Now, time for one of my favourites."

Lucy grabbed a tattered, old album and put the disc on the turntable. The dulcet tones of James Taylor drifted out of the speakers as he sang one of his most loved songs, "Fire and Rain". Ben wasn't hugely familiar with JT. He felt more at home listening to Corey Taylor than James Taylor, and the confessional lyrics about death, loss and loneliness hit a bit too close to home for him, especially since revisiting the Black Stone Cherry album after all these years. Worried that bashing her favourite song might hurt Lucy's feelings, Ben tried a different approach.

"It's nice," he lied.

Lucy smirked to herself, knowing Ben wasn't being entirely truthful. "Oh, come on," she laughed. "You're allowed to not like stuff."

Ben blushed, realising he'd been caught out. "I don't hate it!" Ben insisted. "It's just not what I'd usually listen to."

Lucy grinned at Ben's backpedalling. "It doesn't always need to be shredding guitars and drum solos," she teased. "One day, you'll listen to this song and kick yourself for not realising sooner how perfect it is."

Ben and Lucy spent another hour and a half listening to more Black Stone Cherry and planning how they'd get to the gig that weekend. As the clock ushered in the early morning hours, Ben reluctantly got ready to leave but consoled himself with the fact that at least the show was only a few days away. He had no way of knowing he'd never get there. He didn't know this would be the last time he'd see Lucy before he died. How could he? Life is so unpredictable sometimes.

There was no emotional goodbye. No hug at the door or an admission of how much they meant to each other. Why would there be if neither of them knew how significant this moment was? Ben grabbed his coat and made his way out the door.

7

"Shaune Timothy Caldwell," Tom began. "Born 21st April 1984 in Bewdley, Worcestershire. Died 14th March 2022. Day 14,026. Thirty-eight years, four months and twenty-five days. Death by … sexual misadventure." Tom surveyed the room, and the array of seemingly random objects spread across Shaune's bed. Tom shuddered to think precisely how Shaune had planned to use the light bulb before his heart stopped, but he felt it was still a good idea to be professional. Tom had reaped for decades and often thought he had seen it all, but there were always days like this that proved him wrong. Shaune stood sheepishly in front of him, as naked as the day he was born, barely making eye contact. The gravity of the situation hadn't truly hit him yet.

"I don't know if this is a hidden camera show or something, but my wife will be back any minute!" Shaune said quietly, with both hands covering his modesty. "So, could we move this along, please?"

"As I mentioned before, Shaune, I'm afraid you're dead, dude," Tom replied. "No hidden cameras. This is the real deal."

Shaune sobbed and dropped to his knees. He had so many questions and didn't know where to start. "I don't understand," he managed to utter through ugly snorts. "How on earth have I died?"

"Well, in all honesty, Shaune, I don't think whoever made your ornament of a giraffe designed it for that purpose," was all Tom could think to say. Shaune's wails of anguish were a good indicator that this wasn't the most tactful response he could have given. Shaune sat crouched on the floor sobbing, and Tom realised that his new charge wasn't taking his death very well at all. Helping new souls adjust to their passing was an important part of a Reaper's job. Death is a scary and jarring experience. Therefore, while ensuring the dead get to the Pathway in good time, it's also crucial for a Reaper to make sure they arrive acceptant and at peace with the beginning of their AfterLife. Tom dropped to one knee and put a hand on Shaune's shoulder. The hand-on-the-shoulder technique was Tom's tried and tested method to get people past their initial shock and onto the bus.

"Shaune," he began. "I know this is scary, dude. Trust me; I've been where you are. The dying bit, not whatever you were doing just before the dying bit." Shaune looked across the room at his body on the bed. If he wasn't already deceased, Shaune might have died from embarrassment. "This is the good bit," Tom continued. "We spend years toiling away without any idea of what comes next. Now you find out, dude. It's one hell of an adventure!"

The colour drained from Shaune's face and was replaced with a look of sheer terror. "Oh my God! What if I go to Hell? Am I going to Hell?" Shaune cried, shivering like a leaf. This was a common question. Almost everyone who died was terrified of an AfterLife of fire and brimstone. The truth was the Council of Reapers judged very few people to be evil or immoral enough to spend eternity in Hell, mainly due to budget cuts. As the Earth's population exploded over the last couple of centuries, what was deemed bad enough to warrant an audience with Lucifer had to be relaxed. There was simply no room for everyone who deserved to be there if they followed the Ten Commandments or other such religious scripture to the letter.

Furthermore, as those living life grew from millions into billions, Grim demanded more resources to reap the dead. This left Heaven and Hell with little finances or capability to accommodate the influx of fresh souls entering the AfterLife on a daily basis. The Architect of the AfterLife ensured that those not evil enough to be consigned to Hell or pure enough to enter Heaven were given some job or responsibility in the AfterLife. The true irony of death was that, for many, it had become just as mundane as life.

Tom often felt bad referring to death as an "adventure". While it had its marvellous moments, even he had to admit he didn't think he would be doing shift work for the rest of eternity. He was smart enough to know that letting people know their most likely future was an AfterLife of monotony wasn't the most effective way to get them on his bus. As Tom reassured Shaune that he wouldn't go to Hell for acts he'd committed with his rolling pin, he heard a familiar pinging sound. The Council had issued all Reapers with pagers around five years earlier. Any technology needed to be obsolete before it could make its way into the AfterLife. The pagers were a stroke of genius as Reapers could be contacted immediately with any changes to their reaping schedule that day. Tom slyly glanced at the message.

Death Postponement: Sarah Louise Lowe. New expiration date: 26/02/2024

Tom breathed a sigh of relief. His next collection had been cancelled, leaving him more time to process Shaune and get him onto the bus. However, there was another bump in the road he hadn't considered.

"Can I at least get dressed before we go?" Shaune asked. "I can't exactly go wherever you're taking me with my balls out, can I?" Shaune made a valid point, but there wasn't much Tom could do to resolve the issue.

"The problem is that we're on a different plane of reality now, dude," Tom explained, "and nothing that isn't already on your person can come with us."

"Well, that's ridiculous!" Shaune spluttered as he walked towards his wardrobe. "My clothes are right here. I'll just—" As Shaune reached for the handle of the wardrobe door, his hand went straight through it, almost as if everything in front of him was an apparition. Further attempts yielded the same result, and try as he might, Shaune could not grasp the doorknob to open the wardrobe and get to his clothes. Tom felt a mixture of amusement and annoyance. Watching a naked man flail around trying to open a cupboard in an entirely different realm of existence was hilarious. On the other hand, Tom couldn't help but think that that same naked man would spend several hours sitting on his bus and that his bits would be in direct contact with his upholstery.

"You know what?" Tom interrupted just as Shaune was about to run headfirst into his wardrobe like a battering ram. "I may have a spare cloak on the bus. This can be a messy job sometimes." Shaune smiled meekly and followed Tom out of his bedroom door.

Rather than the upstairs landing that usually led out of his bedroom, Shaune found himself on the street in front of Tom's school bus. Now that Sarah Lowe had temporarily dodged a bullet, Shaune would be the only passenger; for now, at least. Although safe in the knowledge that no one could see him, it felt extremely unnatural to walk down the street outside his house with no clothes. Once again, Shaune covered his modesty and stepped onto the bus as Tom took his seat at the wheel.

"Can I ask you one more question?" Shaune asked as Tom grabbed a cloak sprawled over the back of his seat and passed it to him. "Was it always meant to end this way? I mean, was I always going to die today? Here? Now?"

Tom looked up and smiled. He always forgot how threatening his smile looked these days, considering he had a skull for a face. "It certainly seems that way, bro," Tom replied. "I've been dead for longer than I ever lived, and while I have so many answers about life and death, I have a ton more questions too." Tom motioned to the empty seats behind him. "Go grab yourself a seat. I'll get you where you need to be as quickly as I can."

Shaune slowly wrapped Tom's spare cloak around him. It was unfathomably cold, but he figured he would warm up soon. He grabbed a seat a couple of rows back. Wiping the thick, grey layer of dust from the window to his left, he could see the world going by without him. One of his neighbours walked his dog without a care in the world. A taxi driver pulled over to pick up his next passenger. It slowly dawned on Shaune that he would never see any of this again. A tear streamed down Shaune's face as he heard Tom start the engine, and the few working lights inside the bus flickered dimly. Years of having the road to himself had made Tom carefree behind the wheel, and the bus lurched forward with little restraint.

As the bus careered out of Shaune's street, Tom fumbled around in his glove box, looking for the appropriate soundtrack for their journey to the Pathway. Tom took his eyes off the road, and Shaune heard a tremendous clatter from outside the bus. Against all the laws of the AfterLife, Tom's bus had knocked over an empty rubbish bin as it verged right out of the street. Had Shaune been dead for more than ten minutes, he may have had a better understanding of the significance of this event. The bus and the rubbish bin were on different sides of life and death. The two of them should never have been able to make contact, yet somehow they had. However, Shaune had only just finished spending two full minutes trying to open his wardrobe door. He certainly didn't have a firm handle on the physics of the AfterLife. Instead, Shaune's main concern at that time was the reckless nature of Tom's driving.

"Hey! Watch where you're going! You just hit a—"

"Chill out, dude," Tom replied, completely oblivious to the collision. "This baby will get us there in no time!"

8

The clock ticked loudly, making the silence engulfing the room even more deafening. Ben hated visiting his parents. Nothing had changed in the eight years since he'd lived there, and the family pictures on the wall were woefully out of date. Ben hadn't worn braces since he was seventeen, but there he was, gurning back at himself from the fireplace with them on full display. He hated that photo. His mother loved it because she always said it captured how silly he was back then. How he "used to be". Ben may have been smiling in that photograph, but his eyes told a different story. Seventeen was a difficult age for him.

But that's not why he hated seeing his family. There always seemed to be a stench of disappointment in the air, as if Ben hadn't amounted to what they wanted. It was easy to ignore his mum. If Ben had inherited his anxiety from anywhere, she was the main suspect and would never dream of inviting conflict. Ben's dad was different. He wasn't the most subtle of men and would interrogate Ben on why he couldn't get a proper job or hadn't settled down yet. These conversations didn't help Ben's confidence and reinforced his own thoughts that he was a failure. His dad was also not afraid to sit through an uncomfortable silence. In those moments, it was just the two of them and the ticking clock.

"Here's your drink, love," his mother said, entering the room with mugs of tea. As she passed over Ben's cup, she quickly shuffled back to the sofa to sit next to her husband. "So, who did you say you were going to see tonight, Benny?" Ben took a small sip of tea and set his mug down next to him.

"Black Stone Cherry," Ben replied. "A rock band from Kentucky. They're really good."

"Can't be any worse than that noise you used to play when you lived here," snorted his dad. Ben ignored him. He'd said far worse before and would again before it was all said and done. "Is that how you're spending your money these days?" Dad continued. "I thought you'd be saving up for a nicer place."

"I'm fine where I am, Dad," Ben replied sharply. He could never get through to his dad that it was much more challenging to buy a house or get a well-paid job than it had been in his day. He'd given up on that crusade a long time ago. "I actually met someone ..." Ben found himself saying. Where had that even come from? Ben hadn't visited his parents intending to talk about Lucy. He still had no idea what was happening between them. Perhaps there was a part of him still striving for his father's approval. Ben's mother's face beamed at the news.

"You met someone? Tell us more, Benny. What's she like?"

"Her name's Lucy," Ben interrupted gently. "We met on New Years', and we're just getting to know each other. Don't make a massive thing out of it."

"I won't," mumbled his dad under his breath as he flicked through his phone. Ben had become a master of ignoring his dad's passive-aggressive ways, but he couldn't resist biting this time. Maybe it was because it was about Lucy, or perhaps it was simply a case of one time too many. Either way, Ben needed to stand up for himself for once.

"Sorry, Dad, I didn't catch that," said Ben, barely hiding his agitation. "Wanna try that one again?"

"I said I won't, Ben," replied his dad in a condescending tone. "I'd love to see you settle down and grow up, but I'm not holding my breath!"

"Gerald!" snapped Ben's mum. She hated any kind of conflict, whether she was involved in it or otherwise.

"I'm just looking out for the boy Cheryl," responded her husband sternly as he turned his attention back to Ben. "It's always the same story. There's a job or a girl you've met, and then you somehow blow it for yourself. It's exhausting to witness," he continued as he searched through his pockets for cigarettes and a lighter. "I just don't understand why you have so little self-confidence. One day you'll look back on your life and realise you let it pass you by."

Ben felt a lump in his throat, and loathing seethed inside him. The voices of self-doubt that constantly plagued his head had changed their focus. If only for a moment, they knew who was to blame. Why do you think I hate myself? You've taken all my confidence. It's your fault, Dad! Ben stood up before his thoughts overwhelmed him.

"You don't understand why I have no confidence in myself?" Ben asked in disbelief. "I tell you I've met someone, and you tell me it won't last because I suck at life?" Ben's eyes started to well up as years of resentment began to flow. His dad sat silent and unimpressed. "It would be great if you were just supportive sometimes," Ben continued. "Even when Toby died you—"

"Not this again!" shouted Gerald. Even by his low standards, his next words were particularly cold. "Benjamin! It's unfortunate that your little friend died, but it happens to us all, and the sooner you get over it, the sooner you can—"

Ben couldn't remember throwing the mug. His father's words had made him so angry that the rest had been a blur. As it smashed against the wall and shattered into several pieces, hot tea splashed on the side of the sofa, narrowly missing its target. Ben had never been a violent person, and his actions shocked him. He looked at his mum, who was close to tears, shell-shocked at the events which had just transpired.

At least his dad had finally shut up.

"I'm sorry, Mum," Ben said softly as he walked to the door. "I should go." He turned to his dad on the way out. "Don't call me for a while." With that, Ben walked out the door and left his childhood home for the final time in his life.

Ben wandered into the street, stunned at what had just taken place. His mind spun, wondering why he had chosen that moment to challenge his dad like that. He asked himself what had caused him to react aggressively when they talked about Toby. Ben shook with adrenaline, wishing he wasn't in this frame of mind before meeting Lucy at the concert. Then conversely, he wondered if this had been the perfect time to confront his dad after all. Still riding on the wave of defiance he had used to stand up for himself, Ben could go to the show and spend the evening with Lucy without his usual self-critical voices polluting his thoughts. The rain beat hard on the cobbled pavement, and Ben decided that those thoughts could disappear down the drains with the rainwater. Maybe they'd return in the morning, but for now, Ben wouldn't let his father's negativity dominate his life. Tonight he planned to enjoy great music with a good friend, and with any luck, it may even become something more.

But Ben would never get to the concert. His life was mere moments from ending. He started to walk across the road towards his fate.

Tom continued his journey back to the Pathway. As "Rock You Like A Hurricane" by Scorpions blasted out the speakers of the bus, it tore dangerously down the streets. The rain was heavier than usual, leaving the roads eerily quiet. Tom was disappointed he couldn't show Shaune his driving-through-cars trick. But as the rain hammered the school bus roof and he sang along with Germany's premier hard rock band, he thought to himself that being a Reaper definitely had its perks.

Tom closed his eyes and tried his hardest to nail the challenging solo from "Hurricane" with his trusty air guitar. He may have picked up some bad driving habits after many years in the AfterLife, but with all obstructions and potential hazards being a lifetime away, it was easy to let standards slip. He had spent many an hour getting lost in the music of the great bands of yesteryear, giving zero attention to the road ahead. Tom opened his eyes as the solo ended, and the song slowed down for a beat. There in front of him, no more than fifty metres away, was a figure walking across the road, directly in the path of the bus! Although Tom had driven through as many living people as he had their cars, the urgency of the moment caught him off guard. He instinctively slammed his foot on the brake and the bus ground to a sudden halt. It wasn't enough. Tom heard a stomach-churning thud, and the bus shook violently. Whoever had previously been in the path of the bus was nowhere to be seen. Tom felt sick to the pit of his stomach.

The fury of a bus travelling seventy-nine miles an hour burst through the very fabric of the AfterLife and smashed into Ben without restraint. Without warning, Ben felt an intense force crush into his right side. He felt a more heavy and more violent pressure than anything he'd ever experienced in his entire life. Time slowed to a crawl. Ben turned his head, but the road was as empty as it had been when he had started to cross seconds earlier. Ben heard a sickening snap in his right shoulder as the unearthly collision sent his body flying several feet down the road. His head bounced off the wet tarmac, and Ben landed in a muddled heap of fractured bones and blood.

Ben lay unable to move, staring upwards at the stars above him. The falling rainwater stung the cuts on his face, and the light from the moon overwhelmed the night sky. It became so unbearable he had no choice but to close his eyes.

Life faded away.

9

Tom sat at the wheel motionless. Every ounce of his experience and training told him that what had just happened was impossible. But as Tom stared at the young man lying in a lifeless heap several feet ahead of him, it was undeniable that the impossible had happened. Tom's mind went into overdrive, considering every conceivable angle. How could an object in the AfterLife interact physically with something that was living? The only possibility Tom could come up with was that whoever he hit with his bus must already be dead. If this were, in fact, someone who had already died, it would explain how they ended up bouncing so dramatically off the front of his bus. Perhaps this person was a lost soul who'd reacted to their death so badly that they'd run away. Tom wasn't aware of any Reaper having lost a passenger before, but he reasoned there was a first time for everything. It was bad news, but the situation was still redeemable. There was just the small matter of apologising to this poor soul for knocking him over. Tom took a deep breath, climbed out of the driver's seat and headed for the door.

The rain didn't burn anymore. That was the first thing Ben noticed. Seconds earlier, each raindrop had stung mercilessly as they splashed onto the scratches and cuts all over his face. At first, he presumed that the excruciating pain through the rest of his body had taken over anything else he was feeling. Then he realised that the pain was gone too. No pain in his shoulder. No pain anywhere!

Ben opened his eyes. The moonlight that previously shone so brightly no longer overwhelmed the night sky. For a brief moment, Ben felt a sense of calm and tranquillity wash over him as he looked up at the stars, thankful that the agony he'd just felt had drifted away. Slowly, he used his hands to sit up and dragged his knees towards him. While his joints felt stiff, they didn't hurt when he moved them. It didn't escape him that this wouldn't have been possible only a minute earlier. As Ben began to question whether the last few minutes had even occurred, an oily chug broke his train of thought. When Ben had started to cross the road, and even as he'd been thrown off his feet, the street had been ominously silent. Now the oily chugging sound filled the entire area. It sounded like the noise was coming from a car engine, yet there hadn't been a vehicle in sight when he was hurt.

Ben looked down the road to see a bright yellow bus sitting in the same spot he had been walking when the impact hit. He knew that he would have remembered such a distinctive vehicle even amongst all the chaos. It was the kind of bus he'd only ever seen in cheesy movies about American high schools. The words "SCHOOL BUS" adorned the front above the windscreen, albeit faded and worn after years of neglect. He glanced at the windows down each side; he saw that most of them were sodden with dust and dirt, obviously untouched for some time. Then there was the grill at the front. With enough speed and force behind it, it looked like it could cause a lot of damage. It made no sense for a bus like this to be there on a miserable winter's night.

Ben stared at the bus as he replayed the accident over in his mind. Was it possible that just a few seconds earlier, that same school bus had struck him down? A sense of embarrassment swathed over him. He'd never had so much as a near miss with a moving vehicle, let alone a full-blown collision. Ben remembered turning his head and not seeing anything on the road. A bus so out of place would have been hard to miss. Perhaps he'd been so consumed with thoughts of Lucy and his dad that he hadn't been paying attention. Ben started to rethink the situation as his embarrassment quickly turned to anger. He'd had spent a lifetime taking responsibility for things that weren't his fault. He may have been distracted after arguing with his father, but Ben was positive that there were no cars around when he'd started to cross the road, and there had undoubtedly been no bright yellow buses. The driver had obviously been speeding like a maniac!

Ben leapt to his feet with a vigour not usually reserved for a man who'd just been hit by a bus. His anger at the situation took over his rational mind. He didn't question how his bones were no longer broken or why the crippling pain he'd felt was a distant memory. Ben was too angry and ready to confront the careless bus driver to realise that none of this made sense. He found himself sprinting towards the bus just before the side doors burst open. A figure in a dark grey cowl rushed out in an utter panic, unbecoming of his intimidating appearance.

"Oh my God, dude!" Tom exclaimed. "I think I hit you with my bus!" Ben was so incredulous that the driver's unorthodox dress sense barely registered with him.

"You think?" screeched Ben. "Were you not watching where you were going?"

"I'm sorry, man, I didn't see you!" Tom replied. "How long have you been away from your Reaper?"

"My Reaper?" Ben spluttered. "What are you—" Ben never finished his sentence. At that point, he had taken a good look at his inadvertent assailant. What stared back at him from under that grey cowl was a face withered down to nothing but bone. Ben struggled to catch his breath. This man's head was little more than a skull, a skull tinged with a sickly yellow of decay earned from generations of exposure to the elements. If he had eyes, then Ben couldn't see them, but Ben knew the man was looking back at him. The darkness emanating from his eye sockets spoke to the depths of Ben's soul. Ben stood frozen to the spot in fear, unable to speak.

Tom had heard about this before. Some people could become so distressed by their death that they became disoriented and hysterical. He pulled out his notebook and grabbed a pen from his pocket.

"Tell you what, dude," Tom started in an effort to break the silence. "Just give me your name, and I'll let the Pathway know I found you. I don't have your details 'cos I'm not your Reaper."

"What happened to your face?" Ben managed to ask. He hadn't heard a word Tom had said. The anger he'd felt as he'd sprinted to the bus was gone. All he felt was horror and dread. The look of terror plastered on Ben's face helped Tom realise that he should tread lightly.

"It happens to all of us in this line of work," Tom explained. "Your Reaper will look the same. Did he introduce himself?"

"Reaper?" Ben replied anxiously. "You said that before. As in the Grim Reaper? What the hell is going on?" Tom looked at the young man in front of him. A big part of his job was encountering people at their most scared and vulnerable. Tom had never seen anyone so confused out of the hundreds of thousands of souls he'd met since becoming a Reaper. He'd never seen anyone so terrified.

"Dude," Tom began gently. "Death is scary. There's no other experience like it! But I think on this occasion, something has gone seriously wrong. I need to know everything that's happened since you died so I can find out where you need to be." A hushed silence fell as Ben contemplated what Tom had said. Both felt unease at what would happen next.

"Can I ask one question?" Ben managed to whisper.

"Totally, dude," Tom replied. "Shoot."

"I'M DEAD?"

That had done it. Watching Ben's face turn a whiter shade of pale,

Tom concluded that he'd handled the situation rather poorly. His next move wasn't any better.

"You mean you didn't know?" Tom responded unhelpfully. In his defence, every soul Tom had ever met was at least aware of their death, even if they were terrified by it. Ben turned away to try and get some semblance of privacy to collect his thoughts. Tom placed a supportive hand on his shoulder. It worked with crying naked men, and he hoped it would work here. Ben felt a chill that bled through his entire body. It was unlike anything he'd ever felt before, but it told him an undeniable truth. Benjamin May was dead, and he hadn't even had a chance to put up a fight.

"I don't understand," Ben finally sighed. "One minute I was walking ... I'd just left my parents' house. Then I just—" Ben looked wearily down the road. "I didn't even see you coming!" Tom swallowed hard. He'd been clinging desperately to his theory of Ben fleeing another Reaper, but as their conversation unfolded, it was becoming clear that this hadn't happened. Tom's eyes scanned the road. The night had grown darker, but he saw it just a few metres away. Confirmation that the impossible had indeed taken place. He knew Ben wasn't ready to see his own corpse. It was likely he never would be.

"My name is Tom," he said, interrupting Ben's gaze. "I'm a Reaper, and I'm supposed to be able to tell you what's going on." He sighed before continuing. "But I'm sorry, I have no clue, dude. All I know is that you've died here tonight and that I was responsible. I don't understand how it happened." Ben looked back at Tom and sensed his turmoil. After a life filled with self-judgement and anxiety, it felt all too familiar.

"I'm Ben," he replied as he tried to avoid making it obvious how much he was staring at Tom's skull. "So, what do I do now?" he asked. Tom had always had a carefree approach to his job, but that didn't mean he didn't carry a tremendous sense of responsibility for every soul he reaped. As he was the reason Ben stood before him deceased, that responsibility was amplified tenfold.

"Well, I guess I'm your Reaper. The first step is to get on my bus. I guess we'll work out the rest together."

Tom fumbled with his keys and forced the bus doors open. Ben hesitated momentarily. Nothing felt real, and part of him hoped he would wake up any minute. He looked down the street he'd grown up on, the same street where he had seen his life end. A profound feeling of sadness swept over him. Tom noticed Ben's eyes welling up with tears.

"I'll get you where you belong," Tom said resolutely. "That's a promise."

Ben walked slowly down the aisle and found himself a seat. He spotted a middle-aged gentleman sitting across from him, wrapped in a cowl similar to Tom's. Shaune was still on his way to the Pathway and had witnessed everything. The bus fired into life and slowly picked up speed. Tom drove more cautiously than usual, ensuring he paid more attention to the road. Shaune turned and introduced himself, just long enough for Ben to miss his bloodied and lifeless body lying on the side of the road as they passed.

"Hi, I'm Shaune. Tom just saw my balls."

10

A low, ever-present hum of the engine and the rattling of the rusted window locks were all that could be heard as Ben sat on the bus that ended his life. The dusty vehicle slowly journeyed back with its passengers to the AfterLife. Slow and steady was the objective despite how out of character for Tom that was. He had no idea how he'd managed to hit Ben when he was supposed to be on an entirely different plane of existence. However, he wasn't going to take any chances. Usually with a CD turned up to eleven and an apt skill for driving on two wheels around corners, Tom was positively sedate as he adhered to the Highway Code as if he had an examiner in the seat across from him. Of course, this would make him late, but that would be of little consequence when he revealed he'd managed to kill someone! But there was little that could be done at this point. All Tom could do was drive.

Ben hadn't looked up since he sat down. With his head in his hands and his eyes closed, Ben had tried to will himself awake. *This must be a dream*, he thought to himself. *That's the only thing that makes sense. If I sit here long enough, I'll wake up, and this will all be over.* Ben thought about his parents. Of all the ways to end a final conversation with the people that brought you into the world, Ben regretted how out of hand things had gotten. He replayed that moment over and over in his head, knowing he would never be able to make it right. While his father's words had been wounding, Ben wished he could revisit that moment and not react with violence. The memory became so vivid in his mind that Ben pulled his hands away from his face and sat bolt upright.

The hum continued as Ben's eyes adjusted to the dim, murky light aboard the bus. The entire interior looked weathered and forgotten, right down to the faded advertisements above the windows, which were starting to peel off at the corners. Even in his indescribable state, he did wonder how an ad for haemorrhoid cream with the tagline "Pile it on your piles" found its way onto a school bus. Two LED strips ran the length of the entire vehicle from Tom's cab at the front all the way to a selection of shabby, neglected seats at the back. The left side flickered erratically, in dire need of replacement. The right side struggled to fare much better, with what light given off feeling artificial and cold. Ben thought back to his college days when the sterile lights in the classroom gave him migraines. What he'd give to be back in that room rather than here.

Ben looked across at the only other passenger on the bus. The man who had introduced himself as Shaune sat in a foetal-like position with Tom's cowl wrapped around him. Ben watched as his reluctant travel companion rocked backwards and forwards in his seat while talking to himself intermittently.

"This isn't real. Just stay calm. It'll be ok. This isn't real. Just stay calm. It'll be ok."

Of course, Ben could relate to Shaune. Although he knew nothing about him (other than the fact that Tom had, for some reason, seen his testicles), they were going through one of the most significant moments in their lives ... or rather, their deaths together. However, Ben sensed now was not the time to get acquainted. Instead, Ben got to his feet and slowly walked to the front of the bus.

"So, where are you taking us?" Ben's words broke Tom's concentration on the road for the first time since their journey began. Tom dared not look away for fear he might hit something or someone else. There was also the small matter of the intense ball of guilt deep in the pit of his stomach, which he hoped he could keep at bay as long as he didn't look directly at the human being he'd smushed with the grill of his bus. Instead, he kept his gaze ahead as he slowed down for a red light.

"It's easier if I show you when we get there," replied Tom, aware this was not going to be a sufficient answer. Ben's mind began to catastrophise. He'd spent his adult life trying to avoid contemplating death, and now he was about to get some answers. If life after death exists, then Ben reasoned Heaven and Hell must exist too. Ben didn't think he'd been amoral enough to go to Hell, but how could he be the judge of that? Ben recalled that time he'd stolen a Mars Bar from the corner shop when he was four. Then he remembered calling his classmate "fatty" when she'd sat next to him on a school trip. It was the true definition of a Freudian slip, but Ben wasn't sure if that would be taken into account. What would Hell be like? Were they on their way right now? What if Hell is a bus journey that never ends? A bus journey with a practically naked, crying man and a skeleton driving like an OAP whose licence should have been revoked years ago. Ben started to hyperventilate.

"Tell me we're not in Hell. Tell me that's not what this is!"

Sensing the rising panic, Tom flicked the bus's indicator for the first time in his reaping career and pulled over to the side of the road. No one else may have been on the road, but Tom wasn't taking any chances.

"Dude," Tom started gently. "Deep breaths, dude." Reapers were taught how to teach their passengers diaphragmatic breathing and progressive muscle relaxation, as panic attacks were common. Ben mirrored Tom's deep breathing and gained a sense of balance. He appreciated the irony that most of his previous panic attacks were exacerbated by the thought that he was dying. Having a panic attack when dead admittedly eliminated such concerns. "We're not going to Hell," Tom continued. "This bus is heading to the AfterLife." He paused for a minute, contemplating Ben's future. "Until we get there, I'm not really sure where you'll go. This has never happened before."

"You weren't supposed to hit me, right?" Ben asked.

"Not only that," Tom replied, "It should be physically impossible!" Ben's look of pure confusion lent itself to further elaboration. Tom scrunched up the arm of his robe into his bony hand and used it to wipe the dust off the windscreen in front of him. "See this road?" Tom began. "It might look like I'm driving down some road in the middle of Darlington, but we've passed over. It's like drawing on tracing paper. The AfterLife sits on top, but it should never interfere with what's underneath." Recognition flashed across Ben's face. Tom was pretty impressed with that on-the-spot analogy.

"So this is all going on above us?" Ben asked as he pieced together what Tom was telling him.

"I guess that's one way of putting it," Tom replied as he pulled back out onto the road, confident that Ben's anxiety had passed for now. "It's just a whole other plane of existence. That's the best way I can explain it."

"So you hitting me tonight was almost like the tracing paper ripped?" Ben theorised.

"Dude!" Tom cried happily. "That is totally what it's like. I should be a theologist or something!" Quickly remembering the gravity of the situation, Tom settled down. "I'm sure someone at the AfterLife will have the answers. All I know is we never interfere in someone's death. We're just there to reap and deliver."

As Tom uttered those last words, the road in front faded into darkness. Tom flicked a switch on his dashboard that dimmed the flickering lights aboard the bus to a mere glimmer.

"You might wanna sit down for this bit, dude," Tom warned Ben. "It's trippy, but it's a hell of a ride." Nervously Ben chose the seat facing Tom's cab directly opposite and sat down. Tom lowered his hood to expose his head in its whole, skeletal glory. As he did, the darkness outside burst into an overwhelming light. Tom reached into his glove box and pulled out his ever-trusty cassette. "Even on a night like this, the right soundtrack is essential". Tom popped the tape in, and a strange, unsettling voice crackled through the speakers. After several seconds of inane narration, Ben felt the need to interrupt.

"What on earth is this?" Ben asked dismissively. Tom looked back with a judgemental expression on his face.

"You mean you've never heard Zappa before?" the Reaper replied in disbelief. Ben blushed. He had always had a deep love and encyclopaedic knowledge of rock music. Still, he had never felt ready to dive into the heady world of Frank Zappa.

The strange monologue made way for a simple yet haunting guitar solo that took the air out of Ben's chest from the very first note. Perfectly timed with the opening moments of "Watermelon In Easter Hay", the white light outside burst into a kaleidoscope of colour, flooding through the windows and lighting up the entire interior of the bus. A flicker of green would quickly make way for a sparkle of blue, straight into a flare of red. Wisps of light danced around each other and then evaporated into the air. All the windows and doors aboard were locked, but a lush breeze drifted through the entire bus. Even Shaune sat up from his foetal position and smiled as beams of colour prismed around him.

Ben found himself lost in the moment, his eyes dancing in all directions at the light show around him. The flashes of colour almost appeared to interpret the story of the song. Zappa's guitar struck a chord deep in Ben's soul. It was undeniably beautiful, but there was a desperation about it. Ben resonated with the loneliness ringing out of every note. It was an all too familiar feeling, but this time he felt comfort that someone understood it enough to translate it into music. He sighed and uncharacteristically let any tension he felt drift away. It was the most ethereal experience Ben would ever have in life or death.

Nearly ten minutes later, "Watermelon In Easter Hay" reached its crescendo. The final notes rang out, and almost in response, the wisps of light and colour began to fade away. Ben closed his eyes and took in the moment. When he was younger, Ben used to look forward to Bonfire Night. It was his favourite night of the year. After each fireworks display, Ben would go home to bed, close his eyes, and see fireworks bursting and shimmering in the darkness as he fell asleep. This was just like that. A sense of calm washed over Ben, if only for a brief moment.

11

The beautiful carousel of colour faded away as the drab, mundane sight of the AfterLife appeared on the horizon. A cold shudder went down Ben's spine, and his old friend Anxiety reminded him of its presence with a jolt of fear. As Ben looked ahead, he could see a selection of buses parked side by side, no two the same. Old Victorian carriages alongside long-distance coaches. Red double-deckers tower over airport shuttle buses. Tom pulled up beside an open-top bus with dozens of frightened passengers on the top deck packed in like tourists, Ben looked at him with confusion.

"Is this a bus depot?" Tom nodded affirmatively.

"The Depot of the Dead, we call it," Tom replied. "Not every Reaper gets a bus, to be honest. More trouble than they're worth, I say. I'd sooner have a taxi!" As Tom turned off the ignition, he sat up, pulled out his notepad, walked over to Shaune and ushered him to the front of the bus. "It's pretty busy this time of day. I'm usually back before the rush. Don't be afraid to push your way through!"

Tom led Ben and Shaune off the bus into the throng of Reapers and their passengers. Ben felt suffocated, joining the crush of bodies trying to make their way out of the Depot of the Dead. He could hear a smattering of different languages among the hubbub as the Reapers tried to coordinate their tribes.

"Gehe zum Pathway!" yelled one Reaper as he shoved a passenger towards the exit.

"Làm thủ tục tại Pathway", cried another as he hastily motioned in the same direction.

"I must brush up on my Vietnamese before they send me there next," Tom thought aloud. The Reaper guided his cohort out of the Depot, noticeably far less aggressively than the rest of the Reapers. As they reached the exit, the Pathway loomed ominously in front of them. Shaune gulped at the mere sight of it. The hallowed gates dominated the landscape, even with seventy-five people in front of them. While Ben had already established that the gathering had an international feel, none of the other passengers appeared to have grasped the very British tradition of queuing. The Reapers encouraged their passengers to push in front of each other, trying their hardest to get to the head of the crowd. In fact, about a hundred yards from where they stood, Ben noticed two Reapers looking very close to coming to blows as they brandished their scythes menacingly.

"This is always your problem, Victor!" screamed one. "You think your time is more important than mine."

"I've got my Reaper's insurance to renew. The deadline's today, you cretin!" Victor retorted. Usually, Tom hated waiting in the queues for the Pathway and rarely did he have to. Tom's shifts usually meant he would get back to check in his passengers before the real rush happened. With how carefully he'd driven tonight following the accident, he had ended up a good two hours late. However, he knew that despite hitting the peak check-in time at the Pathway, they wouldn't be waiting long.

"2112!" a familiar voice yelled over the chaotic throng of bodies. Suddenly Tom wished the wait could have been just a little bit longer. The entire queue stopped whatever they were doing as the Reapers turned to face Tom. Even Victor and his adversary abandoned their scuffle. This time it was Tom's turn to gulp as he guided Ben and Shaune past the Reapers and their passengers to the very front of the

Pathway, where Winston sat incredulously. As Tom sheepishly flashed the heavy metal horns to greet him, Winston took off his glasses and cleaned them with a cloth. "It was only last week that you were brought before the Council for your tardiness," Winston began. "I would have thought you would be making an exceptional effort to keep to time."

Tom attempted to explain. "Winston. Dude. I—"

"TWO HOURS LATE!" screamed Winston as the congregation tittered. Although it was clear for all to see that Tom was in serious trouble, the sight of a pouty little manchild such as Winston screaming was undoubtedly hilarious. Winston had often lamented the fact no one would take him seriously. "Two hours late with only one passenger to reap! You had better have an unbelievably good explanation for this," he continued. Tom moved in closer in an attempt to make sure the other Reapers didn't hear.

"I do, sir," Tom replied. "There was a problem with the bus. It …interfered with the living plane and killed this dude here." He finished his sentence and motioned to Ben to indicate that he was the dude he was referencing. Winston rubbed his glasses again as, for the first time, he realised that Tom had two passengers with him. For a few seconds, his eyes darted between Ben and his BlackBerry (which had been obsolete on Earth for many years). He tapped frantically on the device as his eyebrows lifted to the very top of his dumpy, little head. An audible gasp rang out from the crowd as Winston leapt out of his chair for the first time in hundreds of years. No one present had ever seen it happen before. For as long as any of them had reaped, Winston had guarded the Pathway. Never in anyone's mind could they comprehend he would leave his post. Winston's feet touched the floor, and Tom went to catch him as the Gatekeeper's legs gave way. Winston swatted him aside.

"I'm ok. I'm ok," he growled as he got to his feet and marched to a small outhouse located next to the Pathway. With the mist and fog,

Tom had never spotted it before in all his years of reaping. "Come, Mr Hudson, let's discuss this in private."

The door shut with a bang. Winston waddled over to a desk as another gentleman stood from his chair.

"Sir? You're out of your chair. Does this mean—?"

"Yes, there's been an Anomaly!" Winston interrupted. He gestured towards Shaune. "Take this man in the gown and get him processed." The man quickly grabbed Shaune by the arm to lead him back outside. Shaune turned to return the cowl to Tom and inadvertently exposed himself to the entire room. A brief, awkward silence ensued, which Tom broke to spare Shaune's blushes.

"You keep it, buddy!"

With Shaune out of the room, Winston started to tap frantically on a keyboard as a modem dial-up tone crackled through an archaic pair of speakers.

"Are you certain?" Winston asked as he anxiously typed away.

"Absolutely, dude," answered Tom. "One minute, I was driving along, listening to Scorpions, living my best death and the next, he was just there."

"And you're certain he's not a lost soul?" Winston replied.

"Have you had anyone report someone missing?" Tom countered. Winston tutted to himself, almost irritated that he'd made such a suggestion.

"You, boy," he turned his attention to Ben. "What is your knowledge of this?" Ben took several seconds to answer, his face not unlike a deer in headlights.

"I don't know what to tell you, sir," Ben began. Winston's eyes grew wider as Ben continued to speak. "I'd just left my parents' house. I crossed the road. There was nothing there. Then there was. It came literally from nowhere!"

"My boy, that is quite impossible," Winston spluttered as he ripped a sheet of paper from his printer and threw it erratically in the general direction of a wastepaper bin.

"But it's happened," Tom replied, "And I was hoping you'd know what to do, Winnie!" Winston sat, his bottom lip pouting as he tried to come to terms with the situation.

"And what of your bus?" Winston asked, breaking the silence. "Has it interfered with anything else?"

"That's why I was so late, dude," Tom reasoned. "I didn't dare drive through anything in case I caused even more damage!" As Winston sat pouting and stroking his chin, Tom felt a rush of panic through every bone in what was left of his body. "Grim! Aww, Winnie, you can't tell Grim. Please, dude, he will kill me all over again!" A flash of sympathy flickered in Winston's eyes. He knew first-hand what a tyrant Grim could be, and he didn't want Grim to know anything about this until he'd had time to process it himself.

"Grim must be informed about this," Winston warned. "But … there is no sense getting him all riled up before we know exactly what's happened here." Winston grabbed all the sheets of paper he had printed, including the one that had missed the waste bin by a good foot and shuffled them into one pile. As he fed them into an antiquated paper shredder, he turned the handle slowly in the hope that as the paper ripped, it would somehow be quieter. "I will get the Depot of the Dead to look over your bus and see if they can spot anything amiss. We'll just say we're bringing its MOT forward." Winston sat back in his chair and popped a pipe in his mouth. "Meanwhile, you just lay low until I send for you."

"And what about Ben?" asked Tom. "We can't send him through the Pathway, can we?" Winston raised one eyebrow and frowned.

"I said, lay low. You ran the boy over. He's going to have to stay with you!"

12

"Make yourself at home, dude," said Tom as he ushered Ben down a flight of stairs leading to his basement flat. Surprisingly spacious, Tom's home was at the very bottom of a colossal high-rise, home to all the Reapers in the AfterLife. Ben craned his neck upward, unable to see the very top of the building as fog and mist obscured it from sight. Tom had explained that it was a perk of the job that Reapers lived in the complex rent-free. For the most part, each flat was nothing more than a studio apartment with a sofa bed, shower, oven, and sink. However, as Tom was in the depths below ground, he had plenty of room to work with. While dark due to the lack of windows, Tom had lit his digs up with lava lamps throughout the entire apartment. He also ensured there was plenty of room for creature comforts and souvenirs from his reaping adventures. Ben sat down on a tatty-looking sofa with a throw over it. He noticed Tom rearrange a couple of trinkets and place a wooden ornament of a giraffe in their place. Tom chuckled to himself and sat in a leather recliner opposite.

"So what happens now?" asked Ben after a brief silence that almost descended into awkwardness. Tom sighed.

"Well, I guess Winnie will look over my ride and see if he can work out what happened here."

"But what about me?" Ben replied. "How am I supposed to get

home?" If Tom had a face, it would have drained of all colour at this point. In truth, the Reaper had no idea how to fix what had happened. No one, to his knowledge, had ever left the AfterLife and returned to their life on Earth. There was the occasional chatter amongst the Reapers around clerical errors, also known as "near-death experiences". Yet even those who had experienced a near-death experience didn't so much as make it on the bus. Ben had already been dead for several hours and had travelled to the AfterLife. Tom couldn't see how Ben had any chance of getting home. Rather than voice his concerns, he thought it better to try and reassure his new house guest.

"You somehow got here. I'll somehow get you home. I promise." Ben smiled meekly, knowing deep down that Tom wasn't in a position to make such a guarantee.

Tom stood up to remove his cowl and switched on the remaining lava lamps dotted around the room. Ben was amused to see that beneath his dark, intimidating cowl, Tom was wearing Hawaiian shorts that barely reached his knees and a faded Motörhead t-shirt. The shirt got Ben thinking. First, Tom had played Frank Zappa on the bus as they made their way into the AfterLife. Now he was wearing a Motörhead t-shirt. Ben wondered if a love of rock music could be some common ground between the two of them.

"Cool shirt, man," Ben said as Tom scrunched up his cowl before dropping it into a basin ready to wash. "You know I saw Motörhead a couple of times before Lemmy died." Tom's head turned towards Ben, and his jaw opened wide.

"Dude! You like Motörhead?" Tom bounded over to the sofa like an excitable Alsatian and pulled Ben out of his seat. The Reaper dragged Ben across the room to a wall full of mismatched photo frames of various shapes and sizes. He grabbed one urgently and took it down from the wall. "Check it out. I met Lemmy, dude! Best day of my entire death! Ben took the picture from Tom's hands and looked closer. Sure enough, it was a selfie taken by Tom standing next to the legendary founder of Motörhead. Tom was not quite in focus as he feigned downing a bottle of Jack Daniels, but Lemmy, with a wild look in his eye and a middle finger to the camera, looked much sharper. This was the strangest of all the things Ben had seen so far. Ben started to ask a question.

"So you—"

"I was his Reaper, dude!" Tom interrupted, excited to divulge further. "I had to call in so many favours to get that assignment."

Ben looked up at the other frames on the wall. A who's who of rock 'n' roll stared back at him, all posing for a selfie with a certain heavy metal-loving Reaper. One photo immortalised Tom's meeting with Ronnie James Dio, with both men flashing heavy metal horns in sync. Another saw Meat Loaf pretending to throttle Tom with Meat's hands firmly around Tom's neck.

"Ooh, that's a good one!" Tom yelped with joy. "So I walked in the room, and Meat Loaf's all, 'I guess if you're here, that means I'm dead?' and so I said, you took the words right out of my mouth, Mr Loaf!" Tom fell about laughing, and Ben started to question if Meat Loaf really was pretending to throttle Tom in that picture after all. As Tom composed himself, Ben spotted a photograph of David Bowie looking less than pleased as Tom wore the iconic Ziggy Stardust face paint next to him. The Thin White Duke may not have been impressed, but Ben certainly was.

"So you were there for the deaths of all these rock stars?" asked Ben.

"They call me the Rock 'N' Roll Reaper," Tom boasted. "Deaths are supposed to be dished out randomly, but I know a couple of dudes." Ben looked further up the wall. Literally, any music legend he could think of who had passed away was represented. One particular photo caught his eye.

"Paul McCartney?" Ben asked accusingly. "Paul McCartney's not dead!" Tom grabbed the photo off the wall and passed it to Ben to get a closer look.

"Oh, isn't he?" Tom replied knowingly as he flashed a cheesy grin. Ben passed the photo back to Tom, who hooked it gently back on the wall.

"You must have been doing this for years," Ben reasoned, stepping back to take in the most morbid hall of fame he'd ever seen.

"Try decades, dude," Tom laughed. "None of this music was around when I was alive. I'm just glad I discovered it in death."

"So you were alive at one point?" asked Ben. It had never dawned on him that Tom might have once been mortal.

"Totally," Tom nodded. "I was a soldier. I fought the Nazis in World War II." Tom's disclosure took Ben by surprise. The skeleton in the funky Hawaiian shorts, didn't exactly look like your average war veteran. Furthermore, littering every other sentence with words like "dude" and "bro" didn't fit with Ben's perception of a soldier from the 1940s.

"Is that how you ..." Ben tailed off before finishing his sentence. Even though Tom had been the reason for his death, it seemed rude to ask him about his own.

"Died?" Tom hesitated for a moment. "It's a long story. I won't bore you with it." He didn't elaborate further, and Ben sensed it was a subject he'd rather not get into. "But as I got into reaping, I used to hear the awesome music of all these guys." Tom wandered over to his cassette player and pressed play. "It's kept me going. Reaping is a pretty lonely existence at times." Tom and Ben returned to their seats as Iron Maiden's *Seventh Son of A Seventh Son* blasted through the speakers. Ben could relate to the loneliness Tom talked about. The difference was that Ben had knowingly isolated himself for most of his adult life. If Ben's life was over, as it seemed very likely it was, he was determined not to make the same mistakes in death. He glanced over at the album art of *Seventh Son*, which Tom had propped up on top of the CD player.

Referencing the other worldly appearance of Maiden's mascot Eddie on the cover, Ben cheekily asked, "So, is this your cousin?"

Tom paused for a moment before slapping his knee and laughing raucously. "Awww, dude. We're gonna have fun. We're gonna have so much fun!"

The night rolled on and Tom shared tales of his time reaping the dead while Ben shared what he thought were far less exciting stories about his life. However, Tom listened to every one intently; especially those about the bands Ben had seen and the festivals he'd been to. He may have met his musical heroes, but he'd never felt the euphoria of watching them play live. What Ben worried was mundane was more exciting to Tom than all his reaping stories combined. With a captive audience, Ben forgot about his predicament for a while but suddenly caught himself.

"It's been a while since I've gone to a gig," Ben began, "but I can't wait to see Lucy's face when she—" Ben stopped talking. Tom hung his head in shame, realising that what Ben was talking about was never going to happen and knowing that he was the reason it never could. Ben's face drained itself of colour. It wasn't missing the show that had stopped him dead in his tracks.

"Lucy!" Ben gasped, "I was meant to meet her at the gig. Oh my God, I stood her up!" Ben's anxiety went into overdrive. This was meant to be the moment they became more than friends, but he never even made it to the building.

Never good at saying the right thing in times of turmoil, Tom chose his words wisely. "To be fair, dude ... you had an excellent reason." Ben shot a dirty look that sent the message that Tom's words hadn't landed as intended.

"I hope she's ok," Ben whispered sadly as he slumped back in his seat. "There's just something about her. Something special." Ben buried his head in his hands and sighed. "I just wish I could see her again."

Tom sat solemnly in silence, watching his friend's torment. Suddenly a kernel of an idea flashed through his head. "You know what, dude? Maybe you can!"

13

Winston chose to stand down Tom's reaping duties while the Depot of the Dead prioritised his bus service. While to the mechanics, it was just another service, they were unknowingly investigating potential reasons for the Anomaly; the word Winston was using to refer to the accident. Winston had reasoned Grim would be too concerned with matters at City Hall that things could be resolved without him ever finding out. He likely hadn't banked on Tom commandeering an out-of-commission vehicle for an impromptu trip back to Life.

The Benz Patent-Motorwagen was the first car ever built back in the late 1800s and would, for a time, become Grim's preferred method of transportation. As the AfterLife acquired all manner of vehicles over the passing decades, that original Motorwagen sat in a nondescript corner of the Depot, gathering dust. No one had given it a second glance for years. No one, of course, until Tom Hudson, AKA The Rock 'N' Roll Reaper.

"Do you really think we should be doing this?" asked Ben nervously.

"You wanna see this Lucy girl, right?" Tom replied as he wiped the dust off the driver's seat. "Aww, man, there's not even a tape deck," he moaned. Tom shoved his mixtape in his cloak pocket, furious that a vehicle patented in 1886 could not cater to his musical preferences. Ben frowned and clambered aboard the Motorwagen, as if he was trying to mount a Shetland pony. Tom stared blankly at the controls. There was no steering wheel of any kind; in its place, a tiller was used to angle the wheels in whichever direction the driver wanted to go. Tom cocked his head in a manner that Ben did not find at all comforting. "Here goes nothing," Tom shrugged and started the ignition. The Motorwagen purred to life, but amongst the hubbub of Reapers and their passengers, no one so much as glanced over. Tom tentatively guided the tiller to drive the Motorwagen out of the nearest exit. With the hustle and bustle proving a sort of audio camouflage, Tom took a sharp intake of breath as he drove discreetly out of the Depot. "That's what I'm talking about!" whooped Tom once they were out of earshot. "Next stop, Lucy's house!" The power of Tom's words was greatly diminished by the Motorwagen travelling at a snail's pace. The archaic vehicle rolled so slowly that a Reaper out for his morning jog sauntered past the pair with ease. Tom sighed in frustration. "This might take a while."

It took fifteen hours into their journey for Ben to start to recognise his surroundings. While the Motorwagen in its prime could hit heady speeds of up to 9mph, time had not been kind to it. Furthermore, the Motorwagen wasn't a hugely comfortable ride, meaning sleep wasn't an option. Instead, he and Tom whiled away the hours debating such topics as "pineapple on pizza" and "David Lee Roth or Sammy Hagar". The Motorwagen trundled laboriously across mile after mile of motorway, each looking as nondescript as the last. With no discernable landmarks or signs of progress, the journey felt every bit as long as its excruciating fifteen hours. By the time Tom pulled off onto the junction heading into Durham, Ben was at his absolute limit. As the sun began to set, Ben noticed that Tom had turned into the same street where they had first met, the very spot where he died.

The Motorwagen rolled past Ben's parents' house first. He had only been there a day earlier, but childhood memories of playing in the street ran through his mind. He wondered how his parents had reacted to his death. Did they even know? Ben had stormed out of the house that night. They may have presumed he was cooling off and didn't want to speak to them. The Motorwagen travelled further down the street, and an unfamiliar road sign came into view. The words made Ben feel sick to his stomach.

FATAL ACCIDENT. SERIOUS COLLISION OCCURRED HERE. 14/03/22 APPROX 18:45. PLEASE CONTACT DURHAM CONSTABULARY WITH ANY INFORMATION.

Next to the sign appealing for witnesses, bouquets of flowers lay on the side of the road. No one was around right now, but footprints in the mud nearby indicated many had been there to pay their respects throughout the day. Tom stopped the Motorwagen as the two climbed down to look closer. Ben approached the area and knelt to read the kind words people had written attached to the floral tributes left in his memory. Family, friends, and even people he'd never met had been moved enough to pay their respects. Ben took his time to read each handwritten note and felt a lump in his throat. Everything he had experienced since that fateful collision had been such a whirlwind that this was the first time he could take in the true impact of his death. Ben sat in the street and read how much his passing had affected those around him. The reality brought him close to tears.

The sound of footsteps brought Ben back into the moment. He looked behind him and saw Lucy walking solemnly, her head lowered. She stopped inches away and knelt beside him. The two sat side by side, separated across two divergent planes of reality. Ben had wanted to see her so badly, but it didn't feel like he had expected. Lucy sat within touching distance, but she may as well have been thousands of miles away. Ben felt as if he was watching a simulation of Lucy rather than the real thing. After coming all this way, Ben wished that he couldn't see her just as she couldn't see him. Ignorance is bliss.

Lucy sat silently with her eyes closed. Ben watched as she pulled out what looked like a scrap of paper from her coat pocket. As a gentle rain started to patter over them, Lucy unfolded what Ben could see was her ticket to the show they were meant to enjoy together. Lucy had waited all evening for him to show up. She remembered how angry she'd been that he never came. She stared at the ticket for a moment before tucking it into one of the bouquets to stop it from blowing away in the wind.

"I'm sorry I doubted you."

The detachment Ben had previously felt disappeared. Things were starting to feel very real. He placed his hand in his jacket pocket. He pulled out his own ticket and looked over to Lucy, who was now quietly weeping.

Ben turned to Tom. "We shouldn't be here. This is too much for me."

Silently Tom climbed back aboard the Motorwagen and tried to start the ignition. The engine chugged pathetically and fell silent. Tom tried a second time to no avail.

"Oh man," gulped Tom. Ben felt a jolt of panic through his entire soul.

"You're not telling me—"

"Dude. This ride ain't starting."

All the anxiety and frustration building up inside Ben spilt over. He was mere metres from the house he'd grown up in, yet Ben had never felt further away from normality. Ben turned around and screamed at the top of his voice. As he did, he instinctively kicked a glass bottle on the kerbside. The bottle flew through the air and hit the tarmac on the road with a crash. As shards of glass took flight, Lucy turned around and appeared to look directly at Ben. Startled, Lucy walked over to the side of the road and looked around. No one else had walked by since Tom and Ben had parked up. As far as Lucy was concerned, she was alone. She stared at the broken bottle with confusion before glancing back towards the floral tribute and walking away. Ben watched as Lucy left, hoping she would look back one more time. He turned to Tom desperately.

"Did she see me?" he shouted as Tom stared at the broken bottle in shock.

"She didn't see you, dude ... but she definitely saw that!"

After repeated attempts to bring the Motorwagen back to life, Tom had to do the unthinkable and page for the RRA. Reaper Roadside Assistance was always on call for any Reapers who broke down outside the AfterLife. With the reliance on vehicles that had been written off in their natural life, the RRA were very busy and were only to be called by exception. Tom knew he had no choice. It would have taken nearly a day to get home if the Motorwagen was still operational. Walking would take a lot longer. Tom knew the effect of spending too long outside the AfterLife. Decades of journeys back and forth reaping the dead had left his body withered to the bone. Ben's circumstances may have been unique, but Tom didn't know what effect prolonged time walking the Earth could have. Knowing that calling the RRA after stealing a vehicle and bringing Ben along for the ride was career suicide, he also knew that, at this point, it was the safest option. As the RRA tow truck arrived, Tom spotted a familiar face sitting in the passenger seat.

"Lay low. That's all I asked you to do!"

Winston leaving his seat at the Pathway was one thing. Leaving the AfterLife was quite another. Tom gulped hard as the gravity of the situation hit home.

"Winnie," Tom began.

To his surprise, Ben cut in to interject. "Sir. With all due respect, this is all my fault. I asked Tom to bring me here. He warned me, but I insisted anyway," he lied. "I told him he owed me for hitting me with his bus. I didn't think a ride out would cause so much trouble." Winston's hard stare softened slightly. This felt like uncharted territory for him. He couldn't even begin to comprehend what Ben must be going through. "Ok, you two, hop in. Hopefully, I can get us all back before we get into any trouble."

The ride back, while infinitely quicker than the Motorwagen, felt like an eternity as everyone sat silently for the entire trip. Ben may have seen Lucy, but her leaving in confusion and fear wasn't quite how he'd hoped he would remember her. Once again, he unfolded the concert ticket and took it out of his pocket. Ben stared at it for what felt like hours as he realised it was the only link to Lucy he had left. A symbol of what could have been.

Tom stared blankly out the window as life flew by. As he did, he replayed what he'd seen over and over in his mind. Ben's foot connecting with the bottle should have been impossible, but then Ben's death had not exactly been standard. Bringing Ben back from the AfterLife was supposed to offer closure but ended up creating more questions than answers. Tom hoped Winston could tidy up his mess and share some insight into what was happening.

It was late as the tow truck pulled into the Depot of the Dead. Unlike the hustle and bustle that had welcomed Ben earlier, this time the Depot was uncharacteristically quiet. Tom and Ben started to climb out of the tow truck and Winston took a moment to thank the driver for his help. Tom's feet hit the ground when a chilling voice echoed throughout the Depot.

"Mr Hudson. How delightful to see you again." Grim had arrived, and the jig was up.

14

"**B**enjamin Michael May!" thundered the teacher as an entire classroom of children cowered at every crashing syllable that left his mouth. Nine years old was old enough to know that his teacher's tone meant trouble, even if he wasn't 100% sure what he had done. The scrapes and screeching of twenty other chairs broke Ben from pondering as his entire class turned around to look at the object of their teacher's ire.

Mr Boddington was the last of a dying breed of teachers. Well-versed in the art of caning a child, it had been a good few years since he'd legally been allowed to do so. Behind closed doors, he had lamented such drastic changes in the discipline of school children, citing his concerns about childhood development. In reality, all Boddington cared about was the pent-up stress and anger released whenever he struck a child as hard as he could. How could it be fair to take away his only outlet? Alas, this kind of "character building" had become a thing of the past. Without physical violence, all Boddington had to stroke his pathetic, little ego was fear. The fear of a nine-year-old boy who sat frozen in his chair at the mere bellow of his name.

"Yes sir?" gulped Ben in almost a whisper. He didn't know how unkind the years had been to Mr Boddington. However, the days since his discharge from the Air Force had weathered him. What stood before his classroom of students was a bulbous, balding old man with an unkempt moustache that gave him an uncanny resemblance to a walrus. But to Ben, that was all hidden behind a facsimile of power. A booming voice and a pinpoint glare could do wonders.

"Benjamin, I asked the class to do questions one through three in their English textbooks, did I not?" As the voice boomed around the classroom, Ben did everything in his power not to wince. He hated his full name and would have much rather everyone shortened it.

"I did, sir," Ben replied. "I answered all the questions."

"Yes. Yes, you did, didn't you?" Boddington gobbled accusingly as little splatters of spit bounced around on the moustache hair that had outgrown his top lip. His eyes lit up greedily in the knowledge he was one step ahead of a primary school child. "Benjamin, at what point did I ask you to complete question four?" he asked with a tone that belied innocence.

Ben walked right into the trap. "You didn't, sir, but I—"

"No!" yelled Boddington as the other children sat like statues, relieved that they were not today's target. "I certainly did not ask you to complete question four!" Boddington grabbed a handkerchief from his breast pocket and wiped the spittle off his facial hair as he resumed his seat at the front of the class. "So why don't you explain to me and all your peers why you think you know better than me?"

Ben was confused. "I'm sorry, sir, I don't understand."

"You must know better than me to answer question four when I haven't asked you to answer question four," Boddington replied with agitation. "So you tell me. You tell us all, boy! What makes you think you know better than me?" Ben thought back to the work Boddington had set the class. Even at nine years old, Ben was aware that these were not questions but more a series of exercises linked together. Part one had been to write down his favourite animal and give it a name. Ben had always loved watching elephants on TV and decided to call his pachyderm Ernie. The second part of the exercise was to pick a location where you wouldn't usually find an animal like Ernie. In all the nature documentaries he'd watched with his dad, one place Ben had never seen an elephant was inside a haunted house. The third (but not final) part was to choose a feeling for his animal. Ben decided that Ernie would be nervous; after all, Ben knew very well what it was like to be nervous. The controversial "question four" involved bringing the three elements together to write a short story.

"I don't think I know better, sir," Ben began. "I saw that we had to write a story, and I like writing stories." Mr Boddington grabbed Ben's exercise book from the top of the pile that he had stacked haphazardly on his desk. After flicking through to the right page, he mumbled to himself as he read down to the relevant passage.

"Benjamin, if you had time to do all this in the time I set you, then you obviously didn't complete the work properly," Boddington replied. Ben disagreed but kept this to himself. Dreaming up a nervous elephant in a haunted house was unlikely to take more than a few seconds. The room fell silent short of Boddington's inane mumbling as he read Ben's short story. After several seconds, Boddington stood up and walked towards the waste bin next to his blackboard. As he ripped the offending page out of Ben's exercise book, there was an audible gasp from several of Ben's classmates. "Silence!" screeched Boddington, secretly enjoying the reaction he'd received.

Boddington walked over to Ben's desk and slammed the book down in front of him, now one page lighter. His next word would shape Ben in a way not even his joke of a teacher could comprehend. "Unremarkable."

Ben felt unremarkable. He felt the size of a small pin as his teacher had ripped the creativity out of him along with the page of his book.

"Let that be a lesson to everyone," Boddington droned as Ben swallowed his harsh dose of reality. "No one is special. No one is remarkable. Stay in line, do what has been asked of you and do not deviate from the norm!"

***

As Ben stood before the Council of Reapers deep in the depths of City Hall, the sound of his full name echoing throughout the regal auditorium had brought Mr Boddington back to the forefront of his mind. That same level of distaste his teacher held for him could be heard in the voice that had uttered his name for the benefit of the Council. However, at this point, Ben was not being spoken to but rather spoken about, which in many respects felt a step down from the one-sided discussion he'd had with his teacher many years earlier.

"The Council has convened for this emergency meeting to discuss Mr May, henceforth known as the Anomaly." The Anomaly? The words stung as Ben attempted to process them. At least there was a morsel of respect in being full-named. "I shall now pass over to our Commander in Chief, and leader of this committee, Sir Grim: the Architect of the AfterLife." As Grim stood to address the Council, the entire auditorium went cold. Ben glanced subtly to his left to gauge Tom's reaction. Both they and Winston stood together in what was known colloquially as the "Hot Box". Ben didn't need to ask why. Usually affable and friendly, Tom did not so much as acknowledge Ben, knowing the Council would be watching his every movement. Ben darted his eyes to Winston on his right and looked at his arm. Goosebumps. Ben pushed down his anxiety and waited for Grim to speak.

"My esteemed gentlemen," Grim began. "A truly unique situation stands before us, with the fallout already quite significant." Grim motioned to the Hot Box, thrilled by the attention bestowed upon him. "We have before us today an Anomaly. An Anomaly thrust into the AfterLife before his scheduled expiration." He gave a brief pause for dramatic effect. "An Anomaly thrust into the AfterLife through the actions of a Reaper." Grim's words caused a rush of murmurs and whispers to ripple throughout the Council. Rumour had gotten out about a Reaper somehow killing a living being, but this was the first time someone had confirmed it. Grim waited for the chatter to die down. "Two further transgressions have come to light from this inconceivable event, which I would like to deal with individually," Grim continued as he waved his bony arm towards Tom, who stood deathly still in the Hot Box. "First to discuss; an operation by the very assailant of the Anomaly to cover his tracks and return his fatality back to whence he came!" The Council once again burst into life. Ben knew that was never the purpose of their trip, no matter how misguided it was. In an almost unconscious action, Ben found himself correcting the leader of the AfterLife.

"That wasn't how it happened!" Ben interrupted firmly. The Council's chattering devolved into audible shock and awe.

"What is happening?"

"How dare he interrupt the Architect!"

"This is most abhorrent!" A Reaper sat to the right of the Hot Box wearing a resplendent red gown, turned his attention to Ben following his outburst.

"This meeting is about you, not for you," he growled. "You will not get an opportunity to address the Architect, let alone in such a confrontational manner!" Grim gently waved away such a suggestion dismissively.

"Mr Speaker, while I admire your sycophancy, the Anomaly has piqued my interest." Grim moved closer to the Hot Box, seemingly gliding across the room as a shiver ran down Ben's spine. "Please, enlighten me on your perspective on yesterday's events." Ben looked over to Tom, whose jaw was agape. No one had ever spoken to the Grim Reaper in such a way before. It was clear Ben was on his own.

"I was on my way to see someone when I ... met Tom." Ben still struggled with vocalising the truth that he was dead. "Because of what happened with Tom's bus when we met, I knew how guilty he felt. So, I used that guilt to persuade him to take me back so that I could see this person one last time." Looking for Lucy had been all Tom's idea, but Ben knew it had come from a good place. He didn't want Tom or Winston to get into any more trouble if he could avoid it. Ben continued to speak and could feel his courage build. He had no idea where it came from, but he was ready to fight for himself. At that moment, he felt remarkable. "But even if Tom was trying to take me back for good, how do you know that wasn't the right thing to do?"

The Council erupted in anger. Reapers leapt to their feet, some climbing on the tables in front of them. A quill flew through the air, missing Ben's face by a couple of inches as the offending Reaper was berated by his colleagues for his misconduct. The red-gowned Reaper, who had been the first to jump to his feet, stormed to the front of the Hot Box.

"How dare you question the Architect's knowledge of what is appropriate here? Your fate has yet to be sealed!" His fate? Ben's confidence drained away along with all the colour in his face.

Before any discussion could continue, Grim silenced the room. "Everyone, please desist!" With Grim's command, the rowdy Reapers meekly climbed down from their tables. Grim turned to the Reaper in the red gown and whispered to him. Grim turned back to Ben and nodded in respect. "It takes courage to speak your mind in such a way, and for that, I applaud you. Therefore I am giving you one further opportunity. Please explain yourself."

"I don't know why I'm here," Ben started, hoping the right words would come to him as a room of skeletons stared back at him. "But standing before you today, I know I shouldn't be. Even you calling me an Anomaly must mean my circumstances are unusual. My arrival here is not Tom's fault," he continued, and as he did, Tom felt the weight of guilt he carried dissipate ever so slightly. "If I am an Anomaly, as you call me," Ben summarised, "And you don't know how this happened, then surely I deserve a chance to go back and live my life." As Ben sat down, he heard affirmative murmuring from the Council. He hoped that meant he had made his argument rather eloquently. Even Winston had let a hint of a wry smile cross his face. Grim stood before them, clearly deep in thought.

"Should a mortal dispute their expiration, item 347 of the Reaper's Constitution dictates said mortal has a right to appeal within 48 hours of their passing." Grim looked at an imposing grandfather clock in the corner of the auditorium. "As you have met this deadline, you can exercise this option, but I must warn you that no mortal has ever had their expiration overturned." Grim returned to his chair in the centre of the room and sat down. "Please speak with the secretary at the conclusion of this meeting to exercise this right." Ben felt a rush of emotion. For the first time, there was a chance, no matter how small, that he could live again. As Ben's mind raced at the very possibility, Grim's voice brought him back to reality.

"While preparations are made for the appeal, I wish to reflect on the actions of Mr Hudson in light of the articulate words of the Anomaly. Mr Hudson, your reaping licence will be revoked until the full version of events comes to light. I trust there will be no further attempts to abscond with your charge?" Tom hung his head in resignation as Grim ended the hearing. "The Council is now adjourned. I wish to speak with our Gatekeeper alone regarding his personal transgressions." As the Council filed out, Ben and Tom were ushered out of the Hot Box towards the exit. Ben looked back at Winston, his wry smile now a thing of the past. As Tom caught the attention of the secretary to confirm the appeal, Ben couldn't help but feel concerned for Winston. An audience with Grim in front of the Council of Reapers had been terrifying. He couldn't comprehend what the experience must be like behind closed doors.

15

The door to the auditorium slowly creaked shut. Only Grim and Winston remained. While Winston's presence in the Hot Box was enough for those in attendance to know something was amiss, none of the Council of Reapers was privy to the extent of his involvement with the Anomaly. Once the sound of the Council chattering through the walls faded away, Grim turned to address his old friend, having chosen to give him the respect of a private audience.

"Winston, how long have we known each other?" asked Grim. Winston sat silently with his eyes focused ahead. Sensing he wasn't going to get an answer, Grim continued. "Centuries. Millennia even. I remember the early days before the army of Reapers that work so diligently in my name. The days before our beloved City Hall was even built. In those early days, all that stood here in the AfterLife was you and me." Winston's eyes flashed with recognition. He couldn't deny that those early days had been far easier for both of them. "What happened to us?" Grim asked with a tone that almost conveyed genuine sadness. "How did we get to this point?"

"You let everything get out of hand," Winston responded slowly.

"I wasn't the one complicit in covering up a Reaper's mistakes or deceiving this entire Council," Grim seethed. Winston stood up and looked into the abyss beneath Grim's hood. This was a conversation centuries in the making.

"I only did what I did because you have taken this too far!" Winston groaned. "Those early days you look back on so fondly only worked because our intentions were pure. You reaped the Earth, and I checked them in. There was no political agenda or ulterior motives. I knew that you would somehow make everything about you the moment you learned about this."

"I have no idea what you're suggesting," Grim replied dismissively.

"Don't tell me that the moment you found out about this young man, you didn't instantly think about how badly this reflects on you. That you worried that people would wonder how the so-called Architect of the AfterLife let this happen on his watch." Winston's words struck deeply with Grim, but he would never show weakness in confirming they were true. "Tom told you he was having problems with his bus," Winston continued. "You could have resolved it there and then but instead, you ask him to wait 14 days and make it seem like some benevolent gesture. We're still waiting for the Depot of the Dead to service that bus, but if it fails that service and it's deemed that that bus wasn't road safe, I'm afraid that man's blood is on your hands."

"So now you were trying to protect me?" scoffed Grim. "How self-sacrificing of you. Please, regale me with further stories of how this was all for my benefit."

"I'm not protecting you," Winston replied firmly. "I'm protecting that young man! I have pulled through every record I can find. I've poured over every last page. I can tell you he is not supposed to be here, and I'm scared of what lengths you will go to to hide that." After a tense silence, Grim shook his head slowly as he walked towards the door. As he did, he offered his final words on the subject.

"The Anomaly has been offered and appears to be exercising his right to appeal his expiration," Grim concluded. "But I'll be damned if this one freak of incongruity destroys everything you and I built." Grim opened the door and surveyed the corridors to make sure they were still alone before he stepped out. "I won't allow it."

While Ben's very fate was being discussed behind closed doors, he and Tom tried their best to avoid the throng of people who had heard that the unthinkable had happened. As they left the hearing and emerged on the steps of City Hall, a horde representing a true cross-section of the AfterLife was there to greet them. The Reapers and various other sorts who had arrived hoping to get a glimpse of the Anomaly grabbed and pulled at Ben as he and Tom tried to navigate their way through the crowd. Cameras whirred loudly while disapproving voices yelled obscenities. Tom wrapped an arm around Ben and guided him through the hostile crowd. Tom looked at Ben in shock.

"Who knew you'd end up such a celebrity dude!" he said with exasperation as he gestured for Ben to follow him past the Pathway back towards the high-rise. "I think the best thing for both of us is to lay low at—" The word "home" never left Tom's mouth as both he and Ben walked upon a crowd twice the size of the mob they'd left behind at City Hall, blocking the way into Tom's home. While they hadn't spotted the pair yet, they appeared to have worked themselves into a bloodthirsty frenzy. Ben saw that many had crude signs thrust into the air emblazoned with phrases such as "What makes you so special?", "Anomalies belong in Hell" and "Reap what you sow!" Neither Ben nor Tom fancied their chances of taking on that crowd to get inside. As Ben looked on at the increasingly aggressive group, he felt a violent tug that nearly knocked him off his feet. Ben turned to see Tom sprinting down a side street. Still holding his hand, Ben had no choice but to follow. They ran down the dark, dishevelled passageway. Ben could see a dead end and no way through. Tom rapped on the door of an anonymous-looking building before assuring him, "We'll be safe here."

Tom was right that they would be safe at the Eternal Alcove. Like the speakeasies that died away after the Prohibition Era, the Alcove was a place away from the prying eyes of authority. Even with the near-dictatorial hold that Grim held over the AfterLife, the Architect appeared to have no knowledge of the Alcove's existence. For that reason, the misfits of the AfterLife could all come together, safe in the knowledge that the Alcove was their safe place. Tom grabbed a Reaper cloak from a nearby coat rack and draped it around Ben. It was an unspoken rule that those who needed to fade away the most could grab a gown with no questions asked. Ben appreciated the anonymity.

The bar inside the Eternal Alcove was already busy, that's if "already" was the appropriate word. Since Ben had set foot in the AfterLife, a murky, grey fog hung in the sky, devoid of any indication of night or day. Ben realised he had taken for granted the reassurance he got from the sun rising and setting when he was alive. As he took a seat in the darkest corner of the room, he felt it could just as easily be first thing in the morning or the middle of the night. After a brief pit stop at the bar, Tom walked over to Ben empty-handed. For a moment, Ben worried that even here, he would receive a hostile reception.

"The barman's name is Gulliver. He prepares a drink he thinks is best suited to you," Tom explained as he shuffled onto his seat. "He'll be along in a second." Ben looked across the bar. Sure enough, Gulliver was hard at work preparing two drinks. Even with everything Ben had seen since his passing, the sight of a skeleton in a full waistcoat juggling and throwing around various bottles may have been the strangest thing he had encountered yet! That being said, the presence of a thin, twirly moustache and two perfectly styled eyebrows on Gulliver's face was nothing short of impressive. Upon completing their drinks, Gulliver spotted his two customers and presented two fancy cocktail glasses, which were totally out of keeping with the decor of the Alcove. With a flourish of his cocktail shaker, he poured his perfectly crafted beverage across the two glasses.

"One ounce of Calvados, one ounce of cognac and just half an ounce of sweet vermouth," Gulliver announced. "I give to you – the Corpse Reviver!" With a cheesy grin, he presented his eerily appropriate cocktail to the table. Ben's face turned scarlet with embarrassment as Gulliver wiggled his eyebrows knowingly.

"Get out of here, dude!" Tom hissed at Gulliver in hushed tones. Sensing the mood at the table was no longer welcoming, Gulliver backed away, offering apologetic jazz hands as he went until the awkwardness had subsided. Tom took a sip of the offending beverage. "I have to say, though, that guy really knows how to make a drink," he said quietly to himself as Ben idly played with the umbrella Gulliver had placed in his Corpse Reviver.

"I'm sorry about your licence," mumbled Ben miserably as he pulled the hood of his cloak further over his head. He hadn't enjoyed the reception he had received from the residents of the AfterLife, and he didn't wish to attract any more attention.

"Not your fault, dude," Tom replied as he took another swig of Gulliver's finest. "To be honest, I knew this was coming. Besides, you've got the appeal coming. I'll likely get my licence back when you win."

"You heard what Grim said," Ben sighed. "No one has ever won their appeal."

"No one else has ever been in your position," Tom countered. "I've been to a couple of those appeals. It's usually people who were arseholes in real life. Serial complainers. They never won because it was always their time. We know it wasn't your time and all we need to do is prove it!" Ben appreciated Tom's optimism. That initial flash of hope back at City Hall had evaporated as the day progressed, but as he sipped his admittedly enjoyable cocktail, Ben promised himself he would try his hardest to win the appeal and avoid being too pessimistic about his chances. Ben agreed with Tom's suggestion to stay in the Eternal Alcove until the heat died down. A timid apology from Gulliver and an assertion from Tom that his intuition had been spot on led to the decision to take up residence on two stools opposite the bar.

All three drank the hours away. Without livers or any other vital organs, Tom and Gulliver could happily drink without concern for long-term repercussions. However, they could still feel the short-term effects of alcohol and were both feeling rather merry. Ben learned that despite being dead, he too was still very able to get inebriated.

"So I thought it would be a good idea to go and see her," slurred Tom after his seventh Corpse Reviver. "I hit him with my bus ... the least I can do, right?"

"Of course! Of course!" garbled Gulliver in reply before looking at the pair quizzically. "Why did you hit him with your bus again?"

"Oh, I didn't mean to, obviously," replied Tom as he rocked back and forth on his stool. "However, I must also say that he is a very nice guy, so I'm kind of glad that I did." Ben smiled for a moment. While Tom had essentially admitted he was glad to have murdered him, the sentiment was heartfelt. As it happened, Ben thought Tom was a very nice guy too.

"So, did you see her?" Gulliver asked as he accidentally smashed a bottle of cognac on the floor mid-juggle.

"Well, we did, but it didn't go so well," Ben answered, with a bellyful of spirits leaving him no longer concerned with his anonymity.

"And then Grim caught us when we got back to the AfterLife," Tom cut in, finishing Ben's sentence.

"Of course he did," a female voice came from across the bar. "How did you think that plan was even going to work?" Tom looked around the bar, trying to find the source of the voice but being three sheets to the wind, he gave up far too quickly.

"Who said that?" he asked. "What was wrong with my plan?" In response, a slender figure halfway down the bar lifted themselves off their seat and walked over. Wrapped in an old cloak similar to Ben's from the coat rack, whoever this was looked as if they had tried to avoid attention until now.

"You take a vehicle that's been out of action for over 100 years to go cruising for chicks, and you wonder what you did wrong? Oh, and it just so happened to be the Grim Reaper's most treasured Motorwagen. What did you expect?" Ben looked closer at their new acquaintance. A flash of red hair peeking out of the top of her hood and a pair of intense, green eyes revealed that this wasn't a Reaper. Suddenly those green eyes locked on to Ben's, aware that he had been staring at her. "You're the Anomaly, right?"

"My name is Ben," he replied, sobering up quicker than a hiccup.

"I'm Jade, and if you don't mind me saying so, I think I can help you."

16

Jade led the way to a part of the AfterLife even Tom wasn't hugely familiar with. The dull metropolis that was home to the Depot of the Dead and the Pathway was a daily sight for the experienced Reaper. He couldn't help but feel excited as he tried to keep up with their mysterious new acquaintance. While Tom already considered Ben a friend, his untimely death had caused all kinds of problems so far. Now it was time for some adventure. With permission from Gulliver, Ben still wore the cloak he'd acquired from the Eternal Alcove, which made it far easier for him to walk amongst the citizens of the AfterLife without consequence. Jade still chose to wear her cloak as she grunted anonymously at Reapers going about their daily deaths. Jade hadn't made it clear back at the Alcove how she could help Ben, but after his previous adventure on the Motorwagen, he reasoned this random stranger in a bar couldn't make things much worse.

The ominous City Hall shrunk away from view just as Tom started to get an idea of who this person might be and where she was taking them. He looked down to see the cobbles below his feet make way for green and vibrant grass. Without the benefit of a nose, Tom was unable to smell how much fresher the air around them had become. Ben, however, could and took a deep and satisfying breath in. He took a moment and surveyed the rolling hills and subtle streams that formed the landscape in front of him.

REAP SLEEP ROCK REPEAT

"What a beautiful place," Ben smiled as Tom came one step closer to realisation.

Not stopping or slowing down a jot, Jade kept walking and said, "Yeah, it's not bad. No good pubs, though." The trio continued to wander through the lush greenery for several minutes. Tom noticed Jade was following the flow of a stream to their left. He saw it widen until what was once a trickle of water soon became a calm and gentle river. The river mouth came into view, and all the streams on the horizon combined into one far-reaching lake stretching out for miles. The final stages of the journey confirmed Tom's suspicions. What they were walking towards wasn't a lake at all but a moat that wrapped around the entire boundary of an enormous villa.

"Aww damn," Tom moaned with disappointment. "Don't tell me you're a freakin' angel?" Jade didn't answer and continued walking towards the villa. Ben dropped behind slightly to catch Tom privately.

"What's the problem with angels?" Ben whispered as the party approached the moat.

"They're so full of themselves, dude," Tom replied, making no attempt to lower his voice. "It's like their work is more important than ours!" Feigning ignorance to Tom's petty opinions, Jade stood at the moat's edge, allowing Ben to see the villa in its full glory. Majestic in stature, it added to the beauty of the land around it without being overstated. Ben could spot swimming pools and what looked like tennis courts dotted around the outskirts of the property. Compared to the lifeless high-rise designated to the Reapers, this villa sure looked like a desirable place to live.

Jade lowered her hood and removed her cloak. As she did, a pair of dazzling wings revealed themselves from the confines of the cloak. Both were so immense that it seemed unfathomable that she'd been able to keep them concealed in such limited space. Rather than the traditional expectation of an angel's wings, Jade's were closer to that of a butterfly, only more radiant and nuanced. Colours bled into each other and burst into shades unlike anything Ben had ever seen, delicate but powerful simultaneously. As he got lost in the sheer art of Jade's wings, he wondered why on earth one would feel the need to hide something so beautiful. Tom's reaction started to provide some insight.

"Urgh! Why didn't you tell us you were an angel?"

"Because if I did, I knew you wouldn't come with me," Jade replied nonchalantly. She walked behind Ben and casually wrapped her arms around his waist. "There's no bridge across, so I'm gonna need to help you out here." Ben looked into the moat with trepidation. While as calm as the streams that merged to create it, Ben couldn't help but notice how deep it looked.

"Are you sure that's a good idea?" Ben gulped.

"Looking after people is what I do," Jade reassured him. With a graceful wave of her wings, Jade lifted off the ground, taking all of Ben's weight as they made their gradual ascent.

"What about me?" Tom asked incredulously. "How am I supposed to get over?" Jade smiled insincerely.

"You're a Reaper. You'll figure it out. After all, my work's far too important to help right now."

Jade lurched forward towards the villa, leaving Tom behind and carrying Ben effortlessly across the entire length of the moat. Rather than land at the villa entrance, Jade turned her body upward and took flight, clearing the impressive building by several hundred feet. For a man who had spent his entire life anxious and afraid, the idea of being high up in the air with only a stranger between him and a long fall should have filled him with fear. However, any semblance of fear Ben felt seconds earlier had been replaced by wonderment and awe as he was able to view the entire landscape from above. The beautiful scenery stretched out for miles as far as he could see. No other buildings or landmarks were in sight — a true scene of tranquillity. As Jade made her descent down towards the villa, Ben had to take a moment to catch his breath. No matter what Tom's opinion was of angels after an experience like that, Ben already trusted Jade implicitly.

Ben followed Jade through the halls of the villa. He had forgotten that Tom was still trying to navigate his way across the moat. Instead, his mind was filled with all manner of questions, with one most prominent in his mind.

"So if you are an angel, then this must be—"

"Heaven? No, this isn't Heaven," Jade interrupted. "We didn't go through the Pathway. Wait a minute while I sign us in." Jade then turned to a very pleasant-looking angel staffing a desk as they stood in what appeared to be a lobby of some sort. As Jade scribbled a signature on a sheet of paper, she looked up at her fellow angel and said, "There's another guy with us. You can't miss him. He's a Reaper, likely soaked to the bone." The angel held her hands together and graciously bowed at Jade, then once more for Ben's benefit.

"Thank you, and have a pleasant day!"

"Sure, yeah ok ..." mumbled Jade as she led Ben down a corridor towards a pair of double doors. With a quick turn of a key, the doors opened slowly to reveal a spacious and luxurious living space. While also confined to obsolete technology, the Angels made the most of what they had, with Jade's quarters looking like a Tudor palace. However, Ben reasoned that Henry VIII probably didn't have a patio area with a swimming pool. As the sun shone through the windows and lit up the entire room, Ben felt a million miles away from the dirge of City Hall. If this wasn't Heaven, then where were they?

"So you are an angel, but we're not in Heaven?" Ben asked as Jade untied some distinctly un-angel-like boots. After the miles they'd walked from the Alcove, the trekking boots were a solid choice.

"To be more exact, I'm a Guardian Angel," revealed Jade as she kicked her boots towards the double doors they'd just walked through. "We're more hardcore anyway. It's much more interesting." Jade sat down and began explaining to Ben the Angels' role in the AfterLife. "So those who get to Heaven are the good ones, right? We lived our best life, and Heaven is our reward. But the only problem is, well ..." She struggled to find the right words.

"What?"

"It's boring. Heaven is so boring!" Jade groaned. "Everyone gets to be an angel, and we all sit on clouds and read. If you're really unlucky, you get a harp. I can't play a bloody harp! Do you know what a harp sounds like when it's not played properly?" Ben couldn't give her an answer, shell-shocked that he'd just been told that the ultimate concept of nirvana was a snooze fest. "Calm down. Take that look off your face," Jade continued as she noticed Ben's skin turn a whiter shade of pale. "Most people think it's as amazing as everyone hopes, and there are some cool parts. It's just not for me, you know?" Ben wasn't sure whether Jade meant what she said or whether she'd said that to avoid having to deal with an existential breakdown. "So one day," she digressed, "there's an advert that comes out that they're looking for Guardian Angels. You're out in the thick of it, you've got something to do, and there's no harps in sight. So here I am!"

"And all the Angels here are Guardian Angels?" guessed Ben, beginning to understand the whole operation.

"Exactly," Jade confirmed as she stood up and motioned around the room. "Welcome to Borrowed Heaven ... although if you get to Heaven at some point, don't tell them we call it that. They wouldn't take too kindly that we've 'borrowed' it."

Jade's situation may have made more sense, but Ben still had no idea where he came into things and, more importantly, how she could help him. He thought back to their initial meeting at the bar. She had presumably been sitting within earshot for some time yet only introduced herself when Tom relayed their disastrous trip to find Lucy. Perhaps Lucy had a Guardian Angel. Maybe Jade knew who it was.

"When you overheard Tom and I in the Eternal Alcove, do you know a better way I can see Lucy? Check that she's ok?" Ben avoided eye contact as he gazed down at his shoes. "I haven't known her long, but she's pretty special to me."

"I get that he was trying to help, but your Reaper friend is a moron," replied Jade. "Grim watches their every move. He was always going to know you were out there. We Guardian Angels are a whole different concern. He has nothing to do with us. We come and go as we please."

"So, does Lucy have a Guardian Angel?" Ben asked. "Could I see her?"

"I'd need a lot more information about her to find out for sure, but either way, nothing is stopping us from heading out to see her regardless." With the knowledge that he may get another chance to see Lucy and erase the image of her walking away scared and uncertain, Ben could feel the excitement building inside of him. There was only one question that still played on his mind.

"Why are you offering to help me when you don't even know me?" As Ben asked the question, Jade took a long pause and looked deeply into his eyes.

"I saw you and your Reaper outside City Hall," she replied. "The way everyone was so angry and out to get you. You didn't choose for any of this to happen." Ben smiled meekly, his eyes struggling to hide immense sadness at the whole situation. "Besides," Jade continued, "it'll give you something to do instead of sitting around waiting for your appeal." Ben had an overwhelming urge to wrap his arms around her with gratitude for her kindness. However, sensing Jade was more inclined to grab you for flight rather than a hug, Ben settled for a simple yet heartfelt thank you. "It's no trouble at all," Jade insisted. "Call it a favour for a friend."

Suddenly the double doors parted, and a sopping-wet skeleton squelched dejectedly into the room. Utterly defeated, Tom stood dripping from head to toe as he wrung his cloak out like a flannel causing a puddle of dirty moat water to form in front of him.

Acknowledging his drenched Hawaiian shorts clinging to his soggy pelvis, Jade laughed and quipped apologetically, "Well, you're certainly dressed for the occasion. Welcome to Borrowed Heaven!"

17

Unlike Tom's previous clandestine operation, Jade was completely upfront with her fellow Guardian Angels. She relayed her wish to allow Ben to check in on Lucy before his appeal. Being the caring, virtuous individuals they were, the rest of the Angels saw the good intentions in Jade's actions.

"That sounds wonderful, Jade," beamed Imogen, the General of the Guardian Angels. With her peaceful demeanour and unwavering positivity, Imogen didn't seem like any general Ben had come across before. "What a compassionate and altruistic Guardian you are." Jade waved off Imogen's praise. Ben couldn't tell if this was due to embarrassment or Jade's confessed difficulties fitting in with the angel lifestyle. "But I must ask that you take Peyton with you," Imogen continued. "She has yet to make her maiden voyage as a Guardian Angel, and she can carry our esteemed guest Thomas here." Even with his attitude towards Angels, Tom melted at the very mention of his name. Imogen was such a positive and radiant presence that she completely enchanted the Reaper. Imogen gently grabbed Ben's hands and sincerely wished him the best of luck on his travels. "I will pray for your safe return Benjamin," Imogen pledged as Tom awkwardly cut in. He grabbed her hands and held them in front of him in much the same way.

"And I will ensure that no harm will come to your Angels, dude ... I mean, ma'am." As Tom flashed his toothiest grin, Ben felt second-hand humiliation for him. Imogen waved the group away, oblivious to Tom's ever-increasing crush on her. As they headed out of Imogen's quarters to meet with the apprentice tasked with joining them on their journey, Tom turned to Jade and whispered in her ear.

"So, any chance I can get her page number?"

Jade led her friends out to the entrance of the villa. Just ahead, a young angel was lost in her own world as she intensely star-jumped on a verge of grass ahead. As her count between jumps reached triple figures, it was clear she had been there for quite some time. The sight of Jade with Ben and Tom in tow brought her back to reality.

"Jade!" the angel squealed as she began to star-jump even more furiously than before. Picking up pace, she no longer jumped on the spot, instead using each jump as an opportunity to make her way closer towards the others. "General Imogen says I can come with you on your trip to Life!"

"Hey, Peyton," Jade replied coolly before she made introductions. "This is Ben, and this is his Reaper Tom. You may have heard about this Anomaly stuff going down at City Hall. That would be these guys." Peyton's eyes widened like saucers.

"Oh my gosh, that is so exciting!" Peyton exclaimed, giddy with adrenaline. "The only other celebrity I ever met was Claudia Winkleman, but that was before I died."

"We need you to carry our Reaper Tom here," Jade interrupted, sensing the Claudia Winkleman story would waste time they didn't have. "Think you can keep up?" Peyton continued her star jumps with ferocious enthusiasm to prove she was ready for the task. Tom looked quizzically at the apprentice. As she tied back her hair that covered all the colours of the rainbow, Tom couldn't help but notice that Peyton was a little on the short side. Was she really expected to carry him all the way there and back?

"I dunno if this will work," Tom grumbled.

Jade sighed. "What's the problem now?"

"Well, I don't know if you can tell, but my bones are pretty dense, dude, and this girl only comes up to my ribcage!" Rather than seeing Tom's complaint as an insult, Peyton immediately relished the challenge.

"I was born to ... I mean, I died to do this," Peyton insisted as she spread her arms out and signalled for Tom to come closer. "Let's do it!"

Moments later, Ben once again felt the exhilaration of flying high above Borrowed Heaven and the gorgeous valleys surrounding it. Jade fluttered her wings sparingly, letting the light breeze lift both her and Ben to greater heights. What should have been another euphoric moment for Ben was marred by Tom screaming at the top of his lungs somewhere behind them.

"Stop wriggling!" scolded Peyton as Tom hung precariously by one foot over the ever-changing terrain below. Peyton flapped with all her might and tried to pull her reluctant cargo upward. "How are you so heavy?" she groaned.

"I told you I have dense bones," complained Tom. "You can't judge me. I have osteopetrosis!" The pair continued to bicker and gripe at each other, with Tom becoming increasingly nauseous, swaying upside down in the wind. With no stomach to speak of, Tom retched loudly in place of vomiting. From his perilous point of view, Tom started to see the sights below evolve into something more familiar.

"Stop messing around now!" Jade shouted back for Tom's benefit. "The fog near the Pathway reaches even these heights. Make sure you hold him tight, Peyton!" Peyton wrestled Tom into a full nelson and wrapped her legs around his to ensure he wasn't going anywhere.

The awe-inspiring Pathway came into view. With how tall the gates looked from the ground, Ben found it jarring to be able to see the summit. The top of each stake culminated in a very sharp point, each piercing through the fog with conviction. Ben looked back to make sure Tom wasn't likely to fall to see him still firmly grappled in place. Ben attempted to see what lay on the other side of the forbidding entrance when, just as Jade forewarned, the fog continued to build and obscured the ground below. Whatever lay behind the Pathway would have to remain a mystery for now.

The flight continued as the Guardian Angels flew over the Depot of the Dead. Tom wondered how his bus was doing. It had been a while since Winston took it to be evaluated following the accident. Now that Grim had involved himself in proceedings, Tom knew that the outcome of his bus's service would considerably impact the success of Ben's appeal.

***

Several thousand feet below them, the all-important service was finally close to completion. One of the mechanics recoiled with disgust as he collected the litter of energy drink cans, crisp packets and mouldy fruit strewn across Tom's cab. His two colleagues stood in deep discussion. Winston had insisted on a complete and thorough service of the bus, with the team essentially deconstructing the entire vehicle and rebuilding it from scratch. The findings were being evaluated when a sudden, crisp chill filled the air.

"Mr Grim, sir!" The senior technician stood to attention for the Architect of the AfterLife. "We don't often see you down at the Depot, sir. What brings you here?"

"I understand that Tom Hudson's vessel has had a full-service today," replied Grim in his usual unsettling yet charming tone. "Are you the engineer leading the investigation?"

"Norman Wells, sir," confirmed the technician, introducing himself. Norman extended his hand for a handshake, but Grim, with no time for formalities, ignored the gesture.

"I trust you have completed the work to the highest standard?" Grim asked, his demeanour becoming increasingly patronising.

"That it has, sir. We were just about to take our findings to Mr Winston at the Pathway as requested," Norman explained, brandishing a rather weighty envelope which contained the report he and his colleagues had spent all day compiling.

"No need to bother Winston with this. I'm on my way to the Pathway myself. I'm more than happy to take it for you," offered Grim trying his hardest to mask his illicit intentions.

"I'm sorry, but Mr Winston has asked us to deliver this report to him and him alone, sir," Norman replied.

"Mr Winston isn't the Architect of the AfterLife, is he?" growled Grim, revealing a side of himself seldom seen by others. Grim thrived on control. For hundreds of years, things had always gone his way, and because they did, Grim could expertly manipulate any situation to get what he wanted. However, the Anomaly was different. This was a situation out of his control, and that could cost him dearly. He imagined the report in Norman's hand revealing that Tom's bus wasn't roadworthy, that the bus Grim should have written off straight away caused the Anomaly. That could affect the appeal, leading to the Anomaly returning to his life and telling everyone that there is life after death. Grim would be driven out of City Hall, and his death's work would be for nought.

Grim's anxieties catastrophised, and as they did, they manifested into anger. The darkness beneath his cowl started to take the form of a furious spiral. The deepest of blacks emerged from the circle's centre, first a small point slowly building to a ball of black mass. As it grew in size, its darkness grew in equal measure. A whirlpool of gloom spun erratically, sucking in lighter shades as it made revolution after revolution. Norman stood frozen in horror. While to Grim, this was a physical and involuntary manifestation of his uncertainty and lack of control, to Norman, it was the closest thing he'd ever seen to pure evil. Norman handed over the report intended for Winston. With the report in Grim's hands, the violent helix started to cease, with the whirlpool retreating and the darkness taking a more natural shade of black. Silently, Grim turned around and retreated from the Depot. Even he did not like his frame of mind when he lost control.

Grim rushed across the street from the Depot of the Dead to City Hall, avoiding the gaze of anyone else who crossed his path along the way. Upon reaching his office adjacent to the Council room, he checked the corridors impatiently and locked the door. Grim sat down with the envelope on the desk in front of him, aware that its contents could be the beginning of the end. He grabbed his monogrammed letter opener from his top drawer and ripped the top of the envelope with one swift movement. However, as he went to pull the report out, he stopped. Instead, Grim grabbed a lighter and struck it against the rough stonework of the office wall. Fire met paper, and Grim watched the flames gently dance and burn the potentially incriminating evidence to cinders. As the fiery blaze continued, Grim tossed it into his waste bin in the corner of the room. The fire spread to the rest of the rubbish in the basket, giving the entire office an intimate glow.

A wave of calm washed over the Architect. He was in control once again.

18

Ben thought of Lucy until the Guardian Angels landed outside a cafe in the centre of Durham City. He had no idea what day it was after spending so much time in the AfterLife. It was like experiencing the ultimate jet lag. Jade tapped a stylus on a cumbersome tablet device before placing it back into a satchel.

She turned to Ben, "If my coordinates are right, Lucy's right in there drinking coffee." Ben felt a wave of apprehension. The last time he'd been in this position, it hadn't gone so well. He swallowed hard.

"This was a mistake," he trembled. "We weren't even together." Ben turned to Jade for a female perspective. "Am I being a total creep?"

Jade went to respond before Peyton interrupted, "It's not creepy. It's so sweet!" she shrieked, jumping up and down once more. "True love divided by realms of existence."

"I never said I loved her," Ben protested. "I never got the chance to find out." Looking at the door to the coffee shop filled him with dread. "Jade, thank you for doing this, but we should go. When Tom and I tried this, things went pretty badly."

"You mean on the Motorwagen?" Jade scoffed. Tom looked over at the mere mention of their failed escapade. Jade grabbed Ben by the shoulders and guided him toward the cafe. "There are several differences between then and now. Number one: my wings didn't see their heyday in the 1800s. Number two: if I'm not mistaken, not only did you see this girl, but it also happened to be in the very same spot where you died." Ben nodded sadly. "But best of all," Jade continued, "we Guardian Angels can manipulate the situation."

"Manipulate how?"

"Our job is to watch over and guard. So occasionally, that means we may have to push things in the right direction. A symbolic gesture here, a bit of happenstance there. Nothing too obvious to give the game away but just enough subtlety that the spiritually minded know they're in safe hands." Jade smiled at Ben and discreetly pointed at Tom. "So if Eddie the Head here causes any trouble, I can fix it." Tom hadn't heard Jade's dig at all. He was too busy scanning the veranda of the coffee house that overlooked the River Wear.

"Hey, dude!" Tom called to Ben. "Isn't that Lucy sitting with the blonde girl outside?" Ben scanned the various tables scattered across the balcony. Sure enough, Lucy and a friend sat with a beautiful view of the sedate river to their left. The coffee house was a hot spot for university students and tourists who were drawn to the outdoor area so close to the Wear. Today the veranda was quiet, with only a handful of groups enjoying the nice weather. Ben felt an initial pang of relief that Lucy was ok after seeing her so frightened following their last visit. However, as Ben walked closer, the first thing he noticed was how tired she looked. Lucy's eyes, red and heavy, gave away a string of sleepless nights. Usually animated and bubbly, she sat stoically in her chair as her companion tried her best to lift her spirits.

"I don't know why this has affected me so much," Lucy mumbled. Her tone was dull and monotone, almost as if she was the one who had died.

"Because it's so incredibly sad!" her friend exclaimed in sympathy. "It was so sudden. It's all over the local papers. Hell, it makes me sad, and I never met him." Ben stood motionless. He felt completely paralysed. Even after reading the tributes to him at the crash site, he'd never expected his death to have such a huge impact.

"I was so angry when he didn't show up," Lucy confided to her friend. "He was probably on his way to meet me when that maniac hit him." Tom noticed a sharp pang of guilt. There was no way Lucy knew that he was responsible for Ben's death, but that somehow made it worse. "Who drives away after hitting someone with their car?"

"They'll find him," her friend reassured her. "Someone must have seen him drive away." Ben glanced down at a newspaper open on the table next to him. One of the smaller headlines on the open page read, "DURHAM HIT AND RUN: POLICE APPEAL FOR WITNESSES." A jarring screech brought Ben's attention back to the conversation as Lucy's friend pulled her chair out and stood up. "I think you need something stronger than coffee," she advised her grieving friend. "I'm going to use the toilet, and when I come back, we'll get some lunch and a bottle of wine. What do you say?" Lucy didn't reply. Her friend slipped away, leaving Lucy alone at the table. But she wasn't alone for long.

"Oh my goodness, I'm sorry. I don't mean to be a bother. I overheard you from the next table," came the eloquent voice of a skinny, well-dressed man. "Did you know Benjamin May?" Somewhat startled by his approach, Lucy tentatively answered him.

"Yes, I knew Ben." No sooner had the words left Lucy's mouth, the stranger grabbed the previously occupied chair and sat in front of her.

"My name's Giles," he announced somewhat snootily. "I can't believe he never mentioned you. Benjamin and I were best friends." All three of Ben's companions looked at him in disbelief.

"I've never met this guy before in my life!"

"He never mentioned you either," Lucy told Giles suspiciously.

"Oh, what was he like?" grinned Giles. "He loved a bit of mystery, didn't he?"

"Sorry, where did you know Ben from?" asked Lucy. Anyone with an ounce of common sense could hear the irritation in her voice.

"We were old uni chums," replied Giles obliviously. "Lived in dorms together in the old castle there." While some students did reside in dorm rooms in the historic Durham Castle, Ben had never been one of them, and Lucy was unconvinced. Giles stuck out his bottom lip, the start of a terrible impersonation of someone who cared. "Hun, Benji wouldn't want you sat here feeling sad. He'd want you on the bevvies living your best life!"

Watching this slimy display made everybody's skin crawl. Ben's expression hadn't changed. While it was torturous seeing Lucy so sad, who was this stranger to claim they knew what he would want?

"What's this dude's game?" asked Tom. Almost as if to answer Tom's question, Giles gently tried to grab both of Lucy's hands, only for her to brush them forcefully away. Giles persisted, causing customers from other tables to start looking at them.

"Now we know," Jade replied, turning to Ben. "That parasite is using your death to try and get in her pants!" Ben watched the events play out in front of him. All he wanted to do was to interject and ask this pathetic excuse for a man to leave Lucy alone. He lunged forward instinctively, but Tom intervened, blocking Ben's way with his scythe. Tom hadn't forgotten Ben's interaction with the glass bottle on their last trip. A repeat performance would be catastrophic.

"Not this time, dude," Tom warned. Ben was shocked. He had never heard Tom speak in that way before. "There's nothing you can do."

"Well, there's something I can do!" shouted Peyton, who flung her arms in the direction of the river. In reaction, the steady flow of water running past the cafe grew turbulent directly below the veranda. On what was still a pleasant spring morning with a slight breeze, an enormous wave rose out of the river, frothing furiously and heading straight for the cafe. The wave's crest crashed violently on the fence posts on the very edge of the balcony. Foam and water sprayed over the side, with every last drop landing on a hapless Giles, who was soaked from head to toe.

Sitting just inches away, not a bead of water came close to touching Lucy. Her side of the table and her clothes were completely dry. Giles leapt out of his seat in shock, freezing from the barrage of river water that had drenched him. The few other patrons in the cafe who hadn't noticed Giles's advances earlier were now looking firmly at the table. No one could comprehend how a wave so gargantuan could rise up and only catch one person. Peyton coyly looked away, knowing full well that Jade was staring daggers at her. While she had meant well, creating a concentrated tsunami in the north east of England was atypical of how a Guardian Angel was supposed to look out for someone.

"My bloody phone," whinged Giles. "Mummy had just paid that off for me!" Finally, Lucy lost her patience. She wanted to leave an increasingly bizarre situation, so she challenged Giles with the truth.

"You didn't even know him at all, did you?"

"What do you mean? Of course I knew Brian!" Knowing he'd slipped up, Giles snatched his soggy belongings and stormed off. He parted by shouting, "You're probably a frigid bitch anyway!" to the disgust of everyone present. Missing everything, Lucy's friend emerged from inside to see where she once sat, saturated with water. She ran to Lucy, narrowly avoiding slipping on the wet decking as an elderly couple filled her in on what she missed. Lucy stood up, apologetically made her excuses and left for home.

Ben watched Lucy run across the cobbled footbridge. For the second time, he had been forced to watch her, scared and confused. Ben started to wonder if his death may have been the best thing for Lucy and whether he should stay away altogether. Seeing the torment on his face, Jade leapt into action, dealing first with her headstrong apprentice.

"Stay in this cafe until we get back," she hissed through gritted teeth. "Don't move a muscle!" Knowing she had messed up, Peyton nodded. "Tom, would you please stay with Peyton?" Jade asked. After seeing Tom's interaction with Ben just before the wave crashed, she had developed a measure of respect for him. "There's something Ben and I need to do." Tom noticed the way Jade was addressing him had changed.

"No worries, dude. You got this."

With that, Jade grabbed Ben and took flight. She knew that the debacle at the cafe couldn't be the last time he saw Lucy. He may not have worked it out himself, but Jade had been a Guardian Angel long enough to know love when she saw it.

"I think I can fix this, but I'm going to need you to tell me the truth about something that happened back there," said Jade cautiously.

"I'll tell you anything," Ben answered.

"You moved forward to do something when that idiot got handsy before Tom stopped you. But you're dead. You wouldn't have been able to do anything anyway." Ben tried his best to explain what had happened the night the Motorwagen broke down. He told Jade all about kicking the glass bottle and how Lucy had seen it smash. As he relayed the experience of watching her walk away, they both spotted Lucy reaching home and letting herself in. An idea started to form in Jade's mind, but she didn't want to share it until she was sure. "So you have no idea how you could kick that bottle?" Jade confirmed.

"Not a clue," replied Ben. It now felt like the right time for Jade to share her plan.

"I think I might know how you can check on Lucy and use this power you have to your advantage."

Lucy stood in the bathroom, trying to wash the morning away. Her experience at the cafe had been humiliating, yet she couldn't help but loathe herself. One time she would have seen a predatory cretin like him off with ease. But she felt stuck. Stuck in a cycle of guilt, loss and hopelessness. Everywhere she went, there seemed to be reminders of

Ben's passing. The last thing she needed today was someone trying to profit from it. She dried her face and walked across the landing to her bedroom. Lucy flopped headfirst onto her bed, closing her eyes, hoping she might get even a second of sleep. Then she opened her eyes.

Next to her, on the same pillow she lay on, Lucy could see a ticket. She always saved her ticket stubs from every concert she'd been to and added them to a collage on her wall. However, that wall was on the other side of the room, and no tickets appeared to have come loose. Her hands shaking, Lucy picked up the ticket off the pillow and looked closer. Lucy had left her ticket for the show they missed that night amongst the tributes to Ben at the crash site. Yet here in her room was a ticket to that very same show. It made no sense. It shouldn't be. But Lucy couldn't be happier that it was. A tear rolled down her face. Lucy lost all concept of time as she sat with the ticket in hand. Then, for the first time in days, she smiled. She didn't feel alone, if only for a minute.

19

Everyone was exhausted as they arrived back into the AfterLife. Ben came back lighter than he left, with his unused concert ticket sitting in Lucy's room. He and Jade had agreed it was an understated way of reaching out to her, and with any luck, it may negate the impact of the less subtle interactions he and Peyton had had with her in recent days. Nonetheless, with his hand in the empty pocket where it used to be, Ben already missed that ticket. While neither he nor Lucy had made it to the show, the tickets felt significant somehow. They had felt important enough for Lucy to leave hers at the same site Ben had died. The resonance of that act led Ben to react with that same sentiment. It comforted him to know she may have found some solace from this, but should he never see her again, the only tangible thing he had to remember her by had gone.

Despite the chaos she had caused earlier that day, Jade agreed that Peyton would become Lucy's Guardian Angel. However, Jade put an important caveat in place that she would accompany Peyton on initial visits to ensure she could handle it. This was her way of being able to look out for Ben as much as it was for Lucy. She knew he had a difficult road ahead. This small gesture could help while Ben focused on his upcoming appeal. The Angels arrived at the Reaper high-rise, ready to part ways. While Peyton fumbled over an apology which Ben kindly accepted, Jade took a moment to speak with Tom alone.

"Be sure to let us know when the appeal is, and I promise we'll be there," Jade vowed.

"Of course, dude. I think Ben would like you both to come," replied Tom. Jade walked Tom out of earshot of the other two before continuing their conversation.

"After we left, I took Ben to Lucy's house," Jade began tentatively. "In her room, he could touch anything. As Guardian Angels, we can do stuff, but there are limits. Ben could have done anything any living person could do. You've seen it haven't you?"

Tom nodded, "That's why I stopped him in the cafe. I don't know the limits of what he can do."

"No one does," Jade replied ominously. "If we can get the Council of Reapers to understand that, he might have a shot of winning this thing and going home." In a remarkable U-turn since their initial meeting, Tom clenched his bony hand into a fist and stuck it out for Jade in a sign of respect. Jade responded with a fist bump, and the two parted ways. Both Guardian Angels flew off back to Borrowed Heaven, leaving Ben and Tom to head to Tom's flat in an effort to call it a day. As they saw Winston waiting impatiently at Tom's front door, both knew the day was not over yet.

Tom was very familiar with the boil. His lackadaisical attitude and poor diary management meant that Tom was almost an expert at aggravating it. Situated above Winston's right eyebrow, the boil was no bigger than a skin tag on an average day, yet each time Tom arrived at the Pathway late or somehow unprepared, that innocuous little boil would grow larger and redden in shade. It would start with the cocked eyebrow pushing it upward and adding pressure to the area. The more stressed or anxious Winston felt, the angrier and blood-red the boil became. Today was different. In all the years he'd known Winston, Tom had never seen the boil so big. It looked fit to burst!

"The service documents are missing," Winston said as the trio sat down in Tom's apartment.

"They're missing?" Tom replied. "Surely they can just write them up again? Either my bus is a write-off, or it isn't," he reasoned. Winston's boil throbbed as he took a deep breath. He turned to Ben.

"My boy, there are some here in the AfterLife who do not want you to leave," Winston sighed. "I was afraid this would happen."

"You were afraid the documents would go missing?" Ben asked, more confused than ever.

"No. Yes. Well, not exactly," Winston answered, continuing to make little sense. A sombre expression flashed across his face. "After your initial hearing, Grim and I had words. He will do anything to make sure you won't win this appeal. Grim's always been a stickler for law and order, and I figured he would use bylaws and constitution to have his way. He knows it all like the back of his hand." Winston looked down dejectedly. "But I have reason to believe that he has those documents, and he doesn't intend for anyone else to see them." Tom understood the gravity of Winston's words. Grim may be intimidating and forceful but to call him dishonest or deceitful was a huge accusation.

"How do you—"

"I sat all day waiting for those papers to arrive from the Depot," Winston interrupted, unaware that Tom had spoken. "In the end, I got fed up with waiting, so I went over to speak to the engineers. They told me the bus had passed its service."

"So, do we even need the papers, Winnie? They said it was fine. Not the news we wanted, but Ben may still have a good case."

"It wasn't what they said," Winston replied in a hushed tone. "Something happened to those men." Winston's eyes darted across the room, ensuring they had total privacy and no windows or doors were open. He leaned forward. "Every last one of those engineers looked like they had had their soul sucked out of them. Grey husks of what they used to be. Their eyes were dead." He stared past Tom and Ben as he relived the moment in his mind. "All they kept saying was, 'the school bus has passed with flying colours.' I asked for the report, but it was like they hadn't heard me. The Depot of the Dead is usually such a jovial place, but those men have been tainted somehow."

"By Grim?" Tom asked slowly. Winston hesitated for a moment, then nodded sadly.

"I don't want to believe it's Grim," he continued, "but at this moment, I don't feel I know him anymore, and I certainly don't know what he's capable of. Keeping you here in the AfterLife is one thing, but he's practically exorcised those poor men. I can't even begin to fathom what happened there today."

A silence hung over the room as all three contemplated what this meant for each of them. For Winston, a friendship that spanned centuries hung in the balance. A partnership built on mutual respect and trust. If Grim had committed the acts Winston believed he'd carried out, then there was no going back. Even if he hadn't, Winston's trust for his long-time companion was fractured, perhaps irreparably. Tom was less sure what this meant for him, but he knew it couldn't be good. Just because the bus had "passed with flying colours" didn't mean he was off the hook. A Reaper without a licence wasn't going to get far in the AfterLife, and from his brief interactions with Grim, he wondered if that was just how he wanted it. Things, meanwhile, felt hopeless for Ben. For reasons he could not comprehend, the most powerful being in the AfterLife had an axe to grind and was determined not to let him go back to his life. The alternative was too dark to think about.

"I spoke to the secretary at City Hall," Winston finally said after several minutes of contemplation. "I've brought opening statements for your appeal forward to tomorrow morning." A rush of panic jolted through Ben's chest.

"Tomorrow?" he stuttered. "Why would we want to bring it forward to tomorrow?"

"Because Grim has had us on the back foot every step of the way," Winston replied. "He caught us at the Depot when the bus was towed back. He was in control during the meeting at City Hall. He's even manipulated his way into getting his hands on that report. But we can take him by surprise. There's no way he will be ready to start your appeal tomorrow."

"But WE aren't ready to start my appeal tomorrow!" Ben cried.

"And that's why we stay up all night and ensure we're ready." Winston countered. "I've placed a confidant at the Pathway. Grim never sets foot near there, so we should be safe for me to stay and help." He pulled out his BlackBerry from his coat pocket and started tapping furiously. "The first thing you need is some legal representation," he muttered as he continued to tap. "You can represent yourself, but the Council will look more favourably on a legal advocate." Tom's mind cast itself back to the car crash he had been late to weeks earlier, leading to his first audience with Grim and the Council of Reapers.

"I know just the dude!" Tom yelled as he leapt up in excitement before running out the door, pumping his fists as if this would increase his momentum. It did not, but it was arguably the most use the Rock 'N' Roll Reaper was going to be at this point in the evening.

"So," Winston said, now he and Ben were alone. "Tell me everything about the moment you were struck down by that bus." Ben relayed the final moments of his life in meticulous detail, and while he did, Winston continued to tap his device to the point of surrender. As the evening rolled by, they discussed Ben's two visits out of the AfterLife. Winston took down reams of notes as Ben detailed kicking the bottle in frustration and how Lucy had noticed. He disclosed that he and Tom had been to Borrowed Heaven and that the Guardian Angels had taken them to see Lucy. This led to Ben explaining how he took the ticket still on his person from the moment he died and left it in Lucy's bedroom as a sign that he was okay. Upon hearing this disclosure, Winston stopped typing and looked up with genuine astonishment.

"My boy, all the laws of life, death and planes of existence should make what you've just told me physically and cosmically impossible." He paused once more, filled with emotion. "If we can prove the things you have told me here tonight, there's not a member of that Council that could overrule you going home. Not even Grim himself." Winston's tone had turned despondent upon mention of Grim. He looked sadly at his feet as they dangled off the end of Tom's sofa, a good couple of feet from touching the floor.

"Tom told me how close you and Grim have worked together," Ben shared in response to Winston's sadness. "Why would you want to help me over him?" Winston looked back up at Ben, almost as if he himself had asked the same question countless times in his head. He took his time to give a considered answer.

"When Tom brought you to the Pathway, I knew something was different," Winston admitted. "The AfterLife has worked so well for thousands of years because it is efficient and just. There is no agenda. Death is nothing personal or discriminatory. It happens to us all. I knew your death was an anomaly. I have been through millions of records, and you were not there. I know this shouldn't have happened. I believe Grim knows this too, but he's so consumed with keeping the AfterLife and his image chaste that his actions are making it the very thing he's fighting against." Winston's eyes started to well up. "I'm doing this for you because it's right. But I'm also doing it for my friend. I fear he will never see it that way." Winston took a handkerchief from his breast pocket and subtly pretended to blow his nose while wiping the tears from his eyes. Ben smiled at him, pretending he hadn't noticed.

"I hope he understands," Ben said.

"Me too."

20

"**G**entlemen of the Council of Reapers, my name is Claude Bostwick representing the AfterLife in this case of The Anomaly vs The AfterLife." Ben didn't like Claude already. The weathered skeleton had a pompous air about him, overinflated with self-importance. He wore a resplendent business suit in a vain attempt to detract from the precariously balanced toupee on the top of his skull. It was clear to anyone in the Council room that Claude thrived on attention and drama.

"You will hear a lot of conjecture over the coming days," Claude continued. "You will hear this Anomaly's counsel attempt to suggest that his death was an injustice." Claude turned to look directly at the Council, an assembly of former Reapers dressed in fine regalia. "I died once. Gentlemen of the Council, did I wish to expire the moment I did? I did not!" he yelped, wagging his finger in defiance as a lady in the gallery shrieked in shock. "I was two bites into a freshly prepared turkey club sandwich at my local yacht club! It was delicious! The taste still lingers to this very day." Claude spun round on his Cuban heels and motioned towards Ben. "But did I, with the taste of turkey, bacon and disappointment in my mouth, claim that my death was an injustice? Sirs, I did not." As Claude continued to address the Council, Ben was distracted by an unpleasant scraping noise. Looking across at Tom in the seat next to him, Ben noticed the Reaper grinding his teeth in

119

disgust at Claude's preaching to the Council. Simply put, Claude was not a likeable man.

Claude concluded his opening statement. "I will prove to the esteemed Gentlemen of the Council that the Anomaly has an ego so out of control that he believes he is above the efficient and flawless experience that is death. Thank you, and adieu for now." Claude returned to his seat, and many of the Council murmured in approval and talked amongst themselves. As the scattered conversations continued, Tom looked at the gentleman next to him.

Barry Forster had first met Tom several weeks earlier, shortly after the nasty car accident that ended his life. Like many, Barry had not lived a life deemed worthy of an eternity in Heaven or damnation in Hell. Therefore his death so far had consisted of sitting around the AfterLife trying to find some way to pass the time. While he was a name partner at his law firm before he died, Barry's area of expertise had been family law, and he had spent most of his career handling divorces and prenuptial agreements. As Barry sat watching a skeleton give an opening statement more impressive than anything he'd seen on *Suits*, he suddenly felt very out of his depth. Regardless of their legal experience, no lawyer on Earth would have felt comfortable arguing against the fact that someone was dead. Yet, for some reason, Barry had felt obligated to help Tom out when he had burst in on him late last night. Barry felt his legs wobble as he stood up and cleared his throat in a futile effort to silence the Council. The murmurs continued, and Barry tried again to catch their attention. His attempts were to no avail, but a stern voice burst through the chatter.

"Let the defence speak!" Ben looked into the gallery recognising the voice to be Jade's. Scanning the front row, he caught the gaze of a figure with a glimpse of red hair peeking out of a cowl. They nodded gently in his direction. Ben felt comforted by the fact that Jade had kept her promise to come to his appeal. It made sense that she didn't want to bring attention to herself. However, the individual next to her was less than subtle.

"Yeah! Shut up, you bunch of douchebags!" cried the familiar voice of Peyton as her cowl fell off the back of her head and draped over her shoulders. The Council gasped and complained in response. Ben couldn't help but stifle a laugh.

"Quiet in the gallery, or this will become a closed session!" Grim shouted, ever-present at his seat at the head of the Council. He turned his attention to Barry. "Where are our manners? Please begin." Barry gulped and stepped out to address the room.

"I am Barry Forster," he began, as rows of Reapers looked back at him. "I'm a lawyer ... well, I was a lawyer, but now I'm dead, so who knows, really." An awkward silence fell over the room. One Council member picked what was left of his nose in boredom. Barry gestured towards his client. "This man is also dead ... I mean, what I meant to say was he shouldn't be," Barry hesitated as he tripped over his words. "That's right. He shouldn't be dead, so that's what we'll try and prove." Winston placed his head in his hands as Barry lost all semblance of authority and control. "So just to surmise, dead ... sorry! Shouldn't be dead. Evidence to be confirmed!" Barry turned back to his seat dejectedly as Tom offered a supportive hand on the shoulder. Before anything else could transpire, Claude stood up once more to address Grim and the Council.

"This is highly irregular, but I do hope you will indulge me," Claude gushed. "As we know, today's proceedings were brought forward quite suddenly at the request of the plaintiff. Since we have acquiesced to this, I would like to make a request of my own to call our first witness here and now." In an attempt to salvage some dignity, Barry stood up.

"The defence was under the impression that the Council would not cross witnesses until tomorrow, sirs," Barry objected.

"You've had your request for an expedited hearing," Grim replied condescendingly, "I don't believe it would be unjust to call just one witness this morning." Claude smiled knowingly at Grim.

"Thank you, sir," Claude replied. "I would like to call the Gatekeeper of the Pathway, Winston Aloysius the 1st to the stand." The gallery gasped. Winston glared at Grim from across the room. He had seen Claude's cheeky grin, and it couldn't have been more evident that this was his plan all along. Winston rose to his feet and whispered something to Tom as he did. Tom immediately walked towards the gallery while Winston tried his best to make himself comfortable in the Hot Box. "Permission to treat the witness as hostile?" With his request granted, Claude began his cross-examination.

"Can you please confirm to the Council you are indeed Winston Aloysius the 1st?"

"That is correct, sir."

"Of course, it is," Claude replied. "We all know the great Gatekeeper of the Pathway. The man that all Reapers meet after every excursion. Could you please tell the Council how long you have held the position of Gatekeeper?"

"From the very beginning," Winston responded. "As I'm sure everyone in this room knows, Grim and I established this AfterLife together. He reaped, and I checked everyone in."

"Thousands of years in one place must get very tiring, does it not?"

"It's been arduous, yes, but I'm committed to my duty."

Claude wandered closer to the Hot Box. "Prior to the day of the Anomaly's expiration, how many times had you left your post outside the Gates of the AfterLife?"

Winston hesitated. He knew this didn't look good. "Rarely, sir. Perhaps two or three times. Short of an emergency, I had never left my post before that day."

"And why did you do so on this occasion?" Claude challenged.

"Tom Hudson brought Ben to me at the gates," Winston explained as Tom slipped out of the Council room with Jade in tow. "It was long agreed that any Anomaly would require me to review our database. I was following protocol."

"Did you follow protocol when you failed to inform our esteemed Grim Reaper of this Anomaly?" sneered Claude. "The same Grim Reaper you just said established this entire AfterLife in collaboration with you!"

Winston looked over again at Grim, remembering that his initial plan had never been to deceive him. "My intention was to build a full picture of what happened before I presented it to Grim," Winston replied. "I booked Tom's bus for its MOT in the hope of getting some kind of understanding. This has been an unprecedented situation."

"Oh, I see!" exclaimed Claude, adopting a submissive stance. "Well, that makes absolute sense, doesn't it?" Claude once again spun on his heels and started to walk away from the Hot Box. Suddenly he turned back around. "Just one question ..." he began. Ben couldn't believe what he was witnessing. Surely there was no way that this pretentious, jumped-up shyster was pulling a Columbo! "When you helped the Anomaly abscond with his Reaper back to the scene of his death, was that you 'building a full picture' of the situation?" challenged Claude, placing great emphasis on ensuring his air quotes were perfect. The gallery chuntered in disgust.

"That's not true!" Winston thundered, outraged at the very accusation. "In fact, I was the one who brought them back!"

"But you didn't tell your esteemed confidante, did you, sir?" Claude motioned grandly over to Grim, his words dripping in sycophancy. Grim's face may not have been visible, but Winston could tell he was enjoying every second of his discomfort.

"I didn't get a chance," Winston insisted. "Grim was at the Depot the very moment I arrived back with the—"

Claude cut in, "And you didn't have a chance beforehand?" he asked. "You didn't have a chance the very moment that Mr Hudson brought this Anomaly to your Pathway and kickstarted this very chain of events?" Claude paced in front of the Hot Box like a shark circling its prey. "I put it to you that you kept the secret of the Anomaly to yourself to deceive this Council and its glorious leader."

"No."

"To conceal the fact that your Reapers and the Pathway are out of control."

"No!"

"And you have become too old and too aloof to restore order."

"No!" shouted Winston, drawing gasps across the room. Even Grim sat upright in his chair, surprised at his associate's outburst. Before the Architect could react, a timid and uncertain voice rang out across the chambers.

"Objection!" Barry stuttered, "Counsel is testifying." Grim cast his gaze towards the late lawyer, chuckling at his brief burst of courage. Barry shook in the presence of the ruler of the AfterLife, who stoically looked across the room. All eyes were fixed on him as they waited for his decision. Grim never felt more powerful than when a captive audience hung on his every word. He leaned forward and grabbed his gavel for effect.

"Overruled!"

21

After Claude's evisceration of Winston on the stand, the crooked lawyer returned to his seat satisfied with his day's work. While he had nothing against Winston personally, Claude hoped a good showing in front of Grim would be his ticket into the Council of Reapers. Rest assured, he had more dirty tricks up his sleeve to ensure the day was won.

Ben looked at Winston sitting dejectedly in the Hot Box. This had been nothing short of a public assassination in front of his friends and peers. Ben couldn't help but feel responsible for his friend's anguish, even if the hearing had descended into farce. This was supposed to be an appeal, an opportunity for Ben to argue against his premature entry into the AfterLife. Instead, it felt more like an inquisition, as if he was the one on trial. Claude's performance and blatant collusion with Grim proved that Ben would have to fight tooth and nail to return to his life.

A tinny, beeping sound broke Ben away from his thoughts. He could tell the source of the beeping was close by, yet not loud enough to attract the attention of the rest of the room. As it continued, Ben realised the beeps made the unmistakable tune of "The Final Countdown" by Europe. Glancing down at the empty seat next to him, Ben saw Tom's pager. Its digital screen lit up, and Ben pressed the buttons on the front to stop the noise. The message proved Tom hadn't left his pager behind by accident.

Stall them. Coming back!

Meanwhile, Barry tried his best to fix the damage Claude had done. He attempted to rebuild Winston in the eyes of the Council, focusing on his tenure within the AfterLife and esteem amongst his confreres. But every question was met with objection after objection. Grim met each objection raised with a gleeful call of "sustained". After the most one-sided exchange in legal history, Barry returned to his seat defeated. Winston was finally allowed to step down, and Ben could see members of the Council starting to pack up. He knew he needed to find a way to keep the hearing going.

"Well, if that's everything from the so-called defence, we'll reconvene tomorrow morning at 10," Grim sniggered, lifting his gavel ready to bring it down before a voice stopped him in his tracks.

"I'd like to speak." Ben stood before the Council with determination. His throat was dry, and his stomach was doing cartwheels. Ben knew he had to stand up for himself if he ever wanted to feel his heart pound again. The hearing could not be adjourned. Not yet.

"The Anomaly shall not address the Grim Reaper!" shrieked Claude with shock. "This is simply abhorrent." Grim waved his hand dismissively.

"We will bring you to the stand in due course, Anomaly." Anger rose inside Ben. Anomaly. He hated that word. It implied he was abnormal. Peculiar. Wrong somehow. When others used it, it had the power to strip Ben of his identity. When Grim used it, it made him feel worthless. An inconvenience.

"My name," Ben replied, "is Ben May, and I would like to address the Council on my own terms before you question me for your entertainment."

A deathly silence fell over the room. A bespectacled Council member gnawed on a pipe and nodded to himself. Claude gabbled away using words like "impertinence" and "audacity" as he conveyed his disgust at Ben standing up for himself. However, Ben was distracted by unsettling energy from the other side of the room. Watching Grim shift in his seat with discomfort, it was as if the blackness under his cowl grew darker and darker. For a brief moment, Ben became lost in the darkness, with Claude's wittering disappearing into nothing. A feeling of nihilism took over Ben as he saw a small, obsidian spiral form in the centre of the gloom. The only thing that mattered was the darkness, and there was no escape. A rush of fear crashed against the hatred taking over Ben's soul. The room came back into focus. Ben saw Grim clench his left hand furiously and avert his gaze. What Ben had just experienced seemed to have profoundly affected Grim too. Ben watched as Grim composed himself and coughed to clear his throat.

"I apologise," Grim began. While the Council were under the impression that Grim's apology was a further refusal for Ben to speak, Ben sensed that he was apologising for their visceral moment. "You will get your chance to speak when the time is right."

Without warning, the Council room doors crashed open as Tom and Jade re-emerged with a companion in tow. Ben did not recognise the figure but noticed a wry smile spread across Winston's face. Whoever this was, they were bringing good news.

"Oh, what now?" screamed Claude at the intrusion before turning to Grim. "Your Deathliness, this is becoming intolerable!" Grim looked over at the gentleman Tom and Jade had brought into his court. Norman Wells still appeared catatonic after their last meeting, and that could cause a significant amount of trouble. Jade stood before the Council of Reapers.

"We have reason to believe that our esteemed Grim Reaper should not be the one to judge this man's fate." The Council fell into murmurs of shock and uncertainty, except the bespectacled gentleman Ben had noticed earlier, who sat silently in his seat. His interest, however, was noticeably piqued. Tellingly Grim left it to Claude to reply to what Jade had said.

"On what grounds?" Claude huffed.

"He is not impartial," Tom replied in support, "he has some kind of interest in this appeal failing, and we have proof." The Council's murmuring descended into a louder rumble of excitement. No one had ever questioned the ethics of their leader.

"Complete hearsay," spluttered Claude. "The Grim Reaper will rule on this matter. Now piss off the pair of you, or I'm sure he will lock you up for contempt!"

Grim motioned to speak when a member of the Council interjected. "Actually, Mr Bostwick, with all due respect to Grim, I would like to hear this." Ben looked across to see the bespectacled gentleman rise out of his seat. Like the other Council members and Reapers in the room, the gentleman's face was withered down to the bone. But there was no mistaking the air of gravitas emanating from him. He placed his pipe between his middle and index fingers and addressed the room. "If we can't hear from Mr May himself today, then I believe we should hear from our two learned friends here."

"I believe we've wasted enough of the Council's time today, Councillor Cornforth," Grim advised hastily.

"Why not at all," the councillor responded. "I mean, we're all dead, aren't we? We've got plenty of bloody time to kill!" His final comment made way for uproarious laughter across the Council. Grim sat in stony silence. "Let's vote on it," Cornforth continued. "All those in favour of hearing out this grungy Angel and the Reaper in Hawaiian boxer shorts?" While Tom attempted to cover his modesty, hands slowly went up across the Council of Reapers. Among the thirty-nine Council members, a solid majority raised their hands. Claude threw his hands in the air in disgust as Grim clenched his fists once more in defiance.

"Then it's settled!" proclaimed Cornforth. "We'll allow you a couple of minutes to confer with your counsel."

"No need, your grace," Jade replied. "I'll take it from here." Tom gave Barry a sympathetic pat on the back. Even a name partner at Forster Forster and Davis knew when his time was up. Jade continued, "I'd like to call Norman Wells to the stand."

Norman walked stoically into the Hot Box. Ben felt a cold chill as the Depot engineer walked past him and the rest of the group. Ben heard Winston gasp.

"My days," Winston muttered. "He looks worse than I remember." Norman sat in the Hot Box, his grey complexion banishing any light or colour from his features and his face betraying any emotion whatsoever.

"Can you please introduce yourself for the benefit of the Council?" Jade began. Norman stared vacantly back. Any semblance of soul left during his time in the AfterLife was nowhere to be seen.

"The school bus passed its test with flying colours," Norman replied monotonously. The Council and the gallery in attendance looked awkwardly at each other.

"I'm sorry, sir, that's not what I asked," Jade responded. "Can you please confirm your name is Norman Wells?" Silence fell upon the Council room, with everyone waiting to hear his response. The answer was the same.

"The school bus passed its test with flying colours." Cornforth rose from his seat once more to address Norman directly.

"My good man," Cornforth frowned with concern. "Are you feeling ok? Do you need a glass of water?" Norman laboriously turned to face the respected councilman. Though everyone in the room had long since passed, "dead behind the eyes" was the perfect metaphor for Norman's gaze.

"The school bus passed its test with flying colours."

Before Cornforth could speak, Claude gatecrashed proceedings once more.

"Why are we wasting the Council's time with this?" he laughed nervously. "After all, he says the bus passed its examination, which we can explore further in tomorrow's hearing!"

"If what this man says is true, then why wouldn't you want this appeal thrown out right now?" Cornforth asked with suspicion. His fellow Council members voiced their agreement.

"We must do things correctly and by the book now, mustn't we?" Claude stammered as Norman continued to stare absently in the direction of the Council, not having moved an inch since he last spoke.

"You wouldn't even let the appellant speak less than five minutes ago," argued Cornforth.

"Tom Hudson and I have been to the Depot of the Dead," Jade informed the Council. "Every engineer involved in the service of the bus that struck my friend Ben was behaving in the same manner as Norman Wells." As Jade continued to appeal to the Council, Ben began disassociating again. The hateful energy from under Grim's cloak took over Ben, and the darkness threatened to engulf him. The vortex of odium stormed violently inside the black, with Jade's words fading into nothing. Ben tried to look away, but everything inside him kept his eyes firmly fixed. A blood-curdling scream broke Ben from his trance.

"No, please not again, Mr Grim, sir!" shrieked Norman from the Hot Box. He dropped to his knees and cowered as a rush of emotion returned to him. The Council room was in uproar, with everyone wanting their opinion heard. Ben looked over to Winston in time to see a single tear fall down the Gatekeeper's cheek. Ben couldn't imagine the sheer mix of emotions Winston was going through. Tom made his way to the Hot Box and helped Norman to his feet. Norman sobbed, his face falling onto Tom's shoulder and his tears absorbed by the Reaper's cloak. Cornforth stepped out of the Council's seating area and directed his attention to Grim.

"You and I have known each other for centuries, Grim, and I hope

you accept my words in the reverence with which they're intended."
The darkness beneath the pioneer of the AfterLife's cloak had settled
for the most part, but flits of that energy flickered silently. "You are
our glorious leader. Our role model. The reason our deaths have any
purpose," Cornforth continued. "For millennia, you have been our
voice of reason and balance. However, today for reasons that have yet
to be determined, you appear to have some kind of vested interest in
the outcome of this appeal. Tell me you don't, and I will respect you
enough to return to my seat and never question you again." A hushed
silence fell over the room. Albeit with respect and admiration, the Grim
Reaper had been challenged by his Council for the first time. Grim hung
his head in contemplation.

"Councillor Cornforth," Grim replied slowly. "As you have astutely
observed, I indeed have a heavy interest in this case." Ben observed
Winston smile sadly as Grim acquiesced to his long-time colleague.
Perhaps there was hope for their friendship yet.

"Then, by Article 0707 subsection 5, I advise that you step down as
magistrate in this matter, and the Council will vote on an appropriate
delegate behind closed doors following the conclusion of this hearing."
Both Cornforth and Grim stood their ground as yet another anxious
hush befell the room. Grim slowly lifted his gavel without saying a
word, as if he was uncertain what to do next.

"Very well," he said curtly as the gavel hit his desk in front of him.

The room exploded into chatter as everyone in attendance started to
process the events of the hearing in disbelief. Ben stayed in his seat with
his head between his knees, his head still misty from his interactions
with Grim. He felt a bony hand tousle his hair roughly.

"Cheer up, dude," Tom cheered. "There's a chance you might win
this!" he cried as he raised his fingers on one hand into a metal horn
pose Ronnie James Dio would be proud of and high-fived Jade with the
other. Ben's mind was racing, still trying to take in the events of the

hearing, but he took comfort in the thought that things may go his way yet.

22

L ucy sat restlessly, clasping her cup of tea with both hands. It had taken a lot for her to come here, and she still wasn't sure it was even a good idea. Lucy was so consumed with her thoughts she had barely slept all night. She knew she needed to talk to someone and hoped she'd make the right choice.

Jamie sat in front of her, his face pale and sullen. Lucy had only ever seen him in passing the few times she had visited, but it was clear Ben's former flatmate had taken his death very hard. Jamie hadn't been particularly overweight to start with, but it was clear he had lost a few pounds. Unconsciously tapping his foot with apprehension, Jamie stirred a teaspoon in his cup for far longer than he needed before placing it on the table next to him.

"I really appreciate you coming," Jamie mumbled. "I've not had anyone to talk to about this."

"Me neither," Lucy replied. "I hadn't known him as long as you, so none of my friends or family knew him."

"That's Ben, alright. Would rather kick the bucket than meet new people," Jamie joked in a half-hearted attempt to lighten the mood. He winced as soon as the words left his mouth before changing the conversation. "That made him meeting you such a pleasant surprise. He never talks to anyone new. Or he didn't anyway." Lucy smiled at the suggestion she'd been an exception to that rule.

"We just seemed to connect straight away," Lucy said fondly. "To be honest, that's kind of why I'm here."

"Were the two of you—?" Jamie began to ask before he was interrupted.

"No, we were just friends," blushed Lucy as she looked down at her extremely milky cup of tea. She noticed for the first time that her cup had the Guns N' Roses' *Appetite for Destruction* album cover adorning the side. She had no doubt this was Ben's mug when he was alive. "I mean, something might have happened if he ... I don't know," she continued before changing tact. "I just liked spending time with him."

"Me too," Jamie sadly agreed. The conversation stopped for a moment. Lucy took a deep breath and used every ounce of courage she had to explain her true motives for coming to see Jamie.

"So, I want to tell you something, and you're probably going to think I'm crazy, but I need to tell someone otherwise, I think I actually will go crazy, so I'm just going to say it, ok?"

Jamie leaned forward with concern. "Sure thing," he said. "What do you want to tell me?"

Lucy took a deep breath. While others were at the cafe when the wave hit, the whole thing still felt inconceivable. There were no other witnesses to Lucy's strange experiences of the last few days. Talking about it out loud made everything feel all the more real.

"Since Ben died, some weird stuff has happened to me," she began. "What kind of stuff?"

"So I was at the place where he ... you know," Lucy continued, unable to bring herself to say the word. "People had left flowers and cards, but I was the only one there. I turned around to leave and heard this noise. There was a glass bottle in the road that just smashed by itself. Glass flew everywhere." Jamie stared back, confused.

"Maybe you kicked it and didn't realise," he suggested.

"Honestly, Jamie, I was nowhere near it," Lucy insisted. "There was nothing around that could have made that happen."

"So what are you saying?" Jamie asked, more confused than ever.

"Yesterday, my friend dragged me to a cafe in Durham. The one overlooking the river? We were talking about Ben when this creep came over acting like he knew him." Lucy shuddered at the memory of Ben's fake university roommate. "You know how high that balcony looks over the river, right?" Jamie nodded. "I swear to God, a huge wave crashed over the side, but this guy was the only person to get wet. I was sitting at the same table as him and didn't even feel a drop!"

"That's weird?" Jamie said tentatively, unsure as to where the conversation was going.

"And then I got home and found this on my bed," Lucy garbled as she slammed a ticket on the coffee table. Jamie recognised it was for the show Ben was going to the night he died.

"Well, you never used it because you—"

"I left mine with all the flowers where it happened," Lucy butted in. "And Ben had his ticket with him, so how did this end up in my room?" She looked across at Jamie, who had no idea how to respond. Lucy felt a rush of embarrassment. "I'm so sorry. You think I'm crazy. I knew you would."

Jamie smiled sympathetically, his eyes still tinged with bewilderment. "I don't think you're crazy," he reassured her. "But I do think you're exhausted, and perhaps your mind is playing tricks on you. God knows I haven't had a good night's sleep since he died." Lucy sighed as Jamie tried to reason what she knew she'd seen. She may be exhausted and sleep-deprived, but she was certain that the ticket had to mean something.

"Will you at least come with me?" Lucy asked. "I haven't dared to go back yet, but I'll know for sure if it's still there."

"Back to where it happened?" Jamie replied nervously. He had barely left the flat since the news of Ben's passing, let alone visited the hit-

and-run scene.

"I know it's a huge ask," pleaded Lucy, "especially when you don't really know me. But I need to try and find answers to all the questions in my head, and I don't think I can do it alone." Jamie stared at the ticket on the coffee table. He reasoned that if he went with Lucy to the site and showed her she was mistaken, she may get some peace from her mind going into overdrive. As much as he didn't want to stand on the street where his best friend had died, he felt in some strange way that he owed it to Ben to look after Lucy and help her process her grief. He rose to his feet and headed to the hallway to grab his shoes.

"Come on then. If we head out now, we'll get there before it gets dark." With confirmation that Jamie was happy to help her, Lucy felt a pang of nervous energy in her chest. Either Jamie was right, and all she needed was a good night's sleep, or her instincts were correct. However, Lucy knew that created far more questions than answers.

In truth, Lucy needed someone to be with her when she returned to Ben's death place. She had no idea how she would react if going back confirmed her suspicions, and even if it did, what could she do about it? Lucy found herself walking around three paces ahead of Jamie, her mind in another place. With each step closer to the side street, she felt her heart pounding out of her chest. Her mouth began to dry up, and she found herself coughing every few seconds to get rid of the scratchiness at the back of her throat. Lucy replayed the moment she left her ticket with the flowers strewn across the side of the road. She vividly recalled tucking it carefully into a bouquet of lilies so it wouldn't blow away. Lucy reached into her pocket, where the corners of the ticket she found in her bedroom poked gently into her thumb. There was no way these two tickets were the same.

The sun began to set when Lucy and Jamie arrived at the street where Ben had met his demise. Lucy stopped suddenly, her feet frozen to the spot. Now a few metres behind, Jamie quickly caught up and stood next to her. It was difficult for him to comprehend that a perfectly ordinary street he had walked down dozens of times was the site of his friend's passing. Their surroundings were completely innocuous in the dusk of a beautiful spring evening. Cars drove by as people attempted to avoid the rush hour traffic. A young girl skipped with her mother walking home for tea. He looked over to Lucy, who stood shaking, her eyes as wide as saucers as she looked down the road. Jamie followed her gaze and saw a middle-aged man picking up rubbish from the side of the road and placing it in a bin bag he clutched in his right hand. From the few times he had met him, Jamie recognised the litter picker as Ben's father. Walking closer, Jamie heard Lucy whisper to herself. Her voice trembled as she quietly said, "It's gone. It can't be gone."

Gerald picked up the last bouquet and gently rifled through them for a card. He and his wife not only had to deal with their son's passing but were tormented by the fact that it had happened literally on their doorstep. It wasn't until they heard an ambulance outside an hour later that Ben's parents had any idea what had happened. Gerald had been too busy and angry to realise that Ben had died just feet away from his childhood home, and that was a bitter pill to swallow. Since that fateful night, Gerald had sat at his living room window for days as people arrived to leave flowers, cards and their respect at the scene where Ben died. As the week rolled on, the fumes from the cars driving by and the unseasonably warm weather meant most of the bouquets were dying off, and Gerald decided to go outside and tidy up. The petals of the flowers had wilted in the sun, but Gerald felt strongly that the kind words left in each of those bouquets needed to be remembered. He knew in his heart he would never forgive himself for their final conversation, but he could take solace in the outpouring of love from others. Deep in a well of grief and self-loathing, Gerald turned to see Jamie and a young woman walking towards him.

"Ah, Jamie," Gerald tried his best to force a smile and shook Jamie's hand. "Cheryl and I have been meaning to call you," he continued, his eyes shifting back towards his home across the street. Jamie looked across to see Ben's mother standing at an upstairs window inside the house, her face drained of colour and emotion. "As you can imagine, we're both still coming to terms with what's happened."

"Mr May, there's no explanation required," Jamie replied as he continued looking over to the family home. "I can't even begin to imagine what you're both going through."

"I'm so sorry for your loss," Lucy's voice barely managed to squeak out her condolences, but Ben's father gave a knowing nod of gratitude.

"I do hope you and your girlfriend will come to Ben's funeral," Gerald said warmly to Jamie. "You were always a good friend to him."

"Actually, this isn't my girlfriend," clarified Jamie. "This is Lucy. She was a good friend of Ben's too." Gerald shook Lucy's hand and seemed perfectly composed on the outside. On the inside, he remembered the ignorant things he had said to Ben that night when they had spoken about this beautiful young woman for the first time. Why couldn't he have just been happy for his son?

Lucy was similarly distraught on the inside, just like Ben's father. Now Gerald had cleared away all the flowers, she couldn't prove the ticket in her pocket was not the same one she'd left behind. It took everything in her power not to rip the rubbish bag from Gerald's hands and pull everything out until she found what she had come for. Her consideration of such an extreme reaction shook Lucy back to reality. She wondered if Jamie was right and if her mind was playing tricks on her. Ben was gone, and Lucy wasn't ready to move on. She looked down at the kerbside, suddenly bare without the floral tributes and realised that life was ready to move on even if she wasn't.

Gerald and Jamie's conversation faded into the background as, in the corner of her eye, Lucy spotted something wedged in a grated drain just below the kerb. Lucy knelt to retrieve it, and her heart stopped as the distinctive hologram flashed back at her. The words printed on it may have faded, but it was undeniable what this water-damaged piece of paper once was. This was no longer a ticket to a rock show. It was a ticket to the answers she desperately needed.

23

For the first time since his death, Ben was instilled with a sense of hope as he sat with his friends at the Eternal Alcove. What had started as Grim flexing his political muscles had ended in the odds being more weighted in Ben's favour. He felt confident that there was a chance he'd be listened to and, with any luck, be able to go home. However, as if reminding him that he wasn't out of the woods yet, Ben's mind replayed his interactions with Grim in City Hall. Ben had never felt such abject terror, but even hours after the fact, the rush of darkness and the feelings it evoked submerged him as he pictured the black hole permeating from under that hood. While bone-chilling, there was also something peaceful about it. Almost beautiful.

A crash of guitars burst out of the jukebox bringing Ben back into the room. With impressive athleticism, Tom leapt onto a nearby table, his hands too busy playing air guitar to support his landing. Glasses smashed, and patrons muttered disapprovingly, but Tom was too drunk on the spirit of Motörhead to care, growling along with his best impression of Lemmy Kilmister. Even Jade, who usually wasn't impressed with Tom's antics, had a smile on her face.

"Ah, what the hell," Jade said in response to Ben noticing her reaction. "The guy did well today. He deserves to celebrate." She raised her glass of neat Jack Daniels in Tom's direction, much to his approval, before downing it in one shot.

"You both did good," Ben replied with relief. "I really appreciate what you did for me today."

"It was Winston's idea," Jade deflected. "I just did what's right."

"Even so, I want to thank you. I don't even know where I'd be if everybody hadn't been so—" Ben's words were interrupted as Gulliver, the Alcove's ever-present barman, slammed down a cocktail with a live sparkler protruding out of the glass.

"From the gentlemen at the bar," Gulliver announced. Ben and Jade looked over to see a group of four men swaying on their stools while whooping and applauding.

"Woohoo! Go Anomaly!"

"Fight the power!"

"Rage against the machine!" The music from the jukebox scratched to a halt.

"Did someone say Rage Against the Machine?" slurred Tom, misunderstanding the context of the conversation as he tapped the jukebox haphazardly for a track by the LA rock band. "Right on, dudes!" "Killing In the Name Of" blasted across the Alcove while Gulliver presented his latest drink.

"May I present the Molotov Cocktail. One shot of vodka with a dash of 151-proof rum. Perfect for those who like to disrupt the system." Gulliver proudly trotted back to the bar as Ben took a sniff of his drink. It smelt like it could be used to kickstart Tom's bus! While he appreciated free drinks more than protests and verbal abuse, Ben couldn't understand why the attitudes of the AfterLife's residents had changed so dramatically.

"These people hated me a couple of days ago," Ben said to Jade, motioning over at the drunks by the bar. "Why the sudden change?"

"Ben, I don't think you realise how much of an impact your appeal is having here in the AfterLife," Jade replied sincerely. "Most of these people have accepted their fate of an eternity of purgatory. It's one thing for you to appeal your death. It's quite another to get Grim and the Council in a tailspin. This is the most exciting thing to happen here in centuries. Besides, who doesn't enjoy a bit of rebellion from time to time?" she concluded as Tom moshed furiously to Rage's definitive protest song.

"Do you think there's a real chance I'll be able to get home?" asked Ben.

"I don't know," Jade shrugged. "I hope so. I really do. But it's never happened before, and if Grim can do anything to ensure it stays that way, I'm sure he'll do it." Once again, the memory of Grim's darkness took over Ben for a split second, releasing him in time to notice Jade shoving the Molotov Cocktail in his hand. "So drink up! We've got a long road ahead of us."

The door of the Alcove creaked open, followed by a ripple of raucous cheers and clapping. Winston shuffled across the packed room, avoiding eye contact with the patrons of the Alcove. However, he did raise his hand in their direction as a mark of respect. Barely holding on to a mass of files and documents he had pressed to his chest, Winston sat on an empty stool next to Ben and Jade.

"Winnie!" Tom hollered as he spotted the Gatekeeper take his seat. "Welcome to the Alcove, brother!"

"Yes, quite," Winston replied distractedly. After an eternity sitting at the Pathway, Winston had little experience socialising in crowded spaces. In fact, he had never set foot in the Eternal Alcove before. It was as loud and obnoxious as he'd feared. He turned his attention to Ben in an attempt to drown out the heavy metal music and lewd chatter.

"I have some good news, Mr May," he said as he flicked through the various papers on his person. "Councillor Cornforth has confirmed that, as of this moment, he has usurped Grim in presiding over your appeal."

"That's great news!" cheered Jade. "I'm guessing the Council didn't take kindly to Grim's interference?"

"They did not," confirmed Winston. "The Council have questioned several decisions Grim has made over the last few decades, but they can't ignore interference of this magnitude." He laid out his documents on the table and ensured they were in order. "To be honest, I'm relieved. Grim and I haven't always seen eye to eye, but any disagreements between us were always in the name of the greater good. However, even I can't condone the depths my old friend has sunk to this time."

"It almost sounds like you want to see Grim lose," Jade replied. Winston didn't respond immediately, his awkward pause doing a better job of relaying his true feelings than any words could.

"I just want the truth to be known," Winston finally conceded. "And if that gives Grim a little humility, then so be it."

The mention of Grim put Ben on edge. After spending most of his adult life afraid of death, Ben's fear of Grim made sense. That fear had never abated from their first meeting at the Depot of the Dead. Again, it was their time in the Council room he kept replaying. Ben knew he needed to speak to Winston about it. Ben saw his opportunity as Jade returned to the bar for another drink.

"Does he always do that?" Ben asked. Winston shared a look of confusion.

"I'm sorry, my boy, I don't follow."

"Whatever happened to that engineer. You thought Grim had done something, and that poor guy was terrified on the stand." Winston adjusted his glasses.

"Truth is even I don't know the full extent of what Grim is capable of. I didn't want to believe he was responsible for what happened to Norman, but today's events confirmed my worst fears."

"Something happened in the chambers today," Ben confessed. "Something with Grim." A flash of concern etched across Winston's face.

"I don't remember you being left alone with him."

"I wasn't." Ben took a deep gulp of his Molotov Cocktail. "It started when I stood up to him. The room seemed to get darker. It was as if everything dark in the universe was concentrated underneath Grim's hood. It was like watching a black hole burst into life in front of me, and I felt like it was sucking me in. But then Tom and Jade burst in, and it was like I fell out of a trance or something." Winston didn't say a word. His eyes, however, relayed great unease. "It happened again when the engineer took the stand. His screams broke me free that second time."

"I was worried about this," Winston grumbled, almost to himself.

"So this has happened before?"

"Just once," Winston's eyes darted to Ben's drink. "May I?" Ben happily let Winston take a swig of Gulliver's concoction. The one sip he had tried felt like it had stripped the lining inside his mouth. Winston downed nearly the entire glass whole and composed himself.

"It was a couple of centuries ago. With the global population increasing exponentially, the AfterLife was facing a serious overpopulation crisis. An emergency meeting was held with representatives from Heaven, Hell, and ourselves here at the Pathway. It was one of the few times I was pulled away from my post before your arrival. Grim believed that we should use the influx to increase the number of Reapers collecting the dead."

"But others disagreed?"

"Someone present at the meeting suggested a system of reincarnation. Rather than keeping everyone in the AfterLife, we could send a surplus back to live again. Of course, there were so many variables to consider, but Grim was dead against it." A glassy look crossed Winston's eyes, and he downed the remains of Ben's cocktail. "It was like watching a storm at sea and being unable to intervene. It just got darker and faster and ever so violent. That poor man backtracked instantly. Reincarnation was never mentioned again, and Grim got his way. Within two years, the ranks of the Reapers doubled." Winston glanced over at Tom as the inebriated Reaper moshed so hard that his skull went full force into a table of drinks in front of him. "It was inevitable that the standard we'd come to expect from our Reapers dropped somewhat."

"I can relate to giving in," Ben admitted. "I want nothing more than to go home, but at that moment, it was as if none of that mattered. Nothing did."

"I don't think it's a conscious response," Winston suggested. "If Grim did that on purpose, I fear he would have used his power far more often than he has. It's as if it is a manifestation of his innermost fear and anxiety that he can't control." Anxiety? Ben thought to himself. Grim? The thought that Grim was anxious by Ben's very existence felt hugely ironic. "My advice is to be very careful, my boy. Be on your guard. If it happens again during this appeal, try to bring yourself back to the room. Be in the moment." Ben nodded.

Jade returned to the table with four glasses of bourbon. Placing three down on the table, she held one in the air and waved it temptingly to catch Tom's attention. Sure enough, Tom bounded across the bar like a lovable sheepdog, tripping over at least two bar stools as he went. Jade passed Tom a drink before raising another in her right hand.

"To Day One. Grim Reaper 0 - Benjamin May 1!"

"Actually, I'd like to propose an alternative toast," Winston replied before the deed was done. "Jade, you spoke very eloquently in front of the Council. I feel you would be a far better representative for Ben than that oaf we had today. What do you say?" Jade tried to play it cool but couldn't help but flash a subtle smile.

"Thank you, Winston. It would be my honour. That is if Ben agrees, of course."

"Right now, I couldn't think of anyone better," Ben grinned as Tom began to make unspeakable noises into a nearby bin.

"That's the good thing about being a skeleton," gagged Tom. "Only dry heaves, dudes!" Winston grabbed the glass from Tom's bony hand and downed the contents himself.

"And no more drinks for you, 2112! You're on the stand tomorrow morning."

24

Ben sat quietly in the grand Council room moments before his appeal was due to start officially. While yesterday had been eventful, its initial purpose had merely been for each side to give prepared opening statements. Everything else which transpired had been highly unusual but had it not happened, the small but significant sense of hope in his heart wouldn't be there. Jade, Winston, and Tom were huddled around next to the Hot Box. Ben couldn't make out what they were saying but took a moment to chuckle at his motley crew of a legal team. Tom looked nervous, while Ben could hear Winston chuntering away in his usual, formal tone. Out of respect for her new position as Ben's counsel, Jade was not wearing her familiar Reaper hood and cowl, meaning her sharp, red hair was on show. Instead, the Guardian Angel had opted for a smart suit jacket, which, while baggy, hid her wings from view. Seeing Jade look so formal was strange, but Ben understood that she was taking her new role seriously.

Two small-looking gentlemen grappled with an ornate, gold frame as they walked it to the front of the room where Grim had sat the day before. With a series of grunts, groans and the odd swear word directed at each other, the pair hung a majestic oil painting above the judge's bench. Cornelius Cornforth looked regal as his image surveyed the Council room. Holding his pipe in one hand and using the other to stroke his chin, Cornforth did not look as intimidating as the other Reapers whose paintings lined the walls of City Hall. Cornforth looked austere, even trustworthy, or at least as trustworthy as a skeleton with bushy eyebrows and a moustache could look. Ben still hadn't worked out how so many of the Reapers and Council members he'd met managed to have such glorious facial hair.

A bang of Cornforth's gavel abruptly ended Ben's admiration of the painting as he saw the man himself was now sitting directly below it. Everyone rose at the councillor's request, at which point he invited them to return to their seats.

"Now, to say yesterday's proceedings in this room were eventful would be an understatement," Cornforth began. His words caused a burst of chortles and guffaws to echo across the auditorium. "I would like to confirm for the benefit of the Council Charter and our esteemed guests in the gallery that our honourable Commander in Chief Grim has relinquished his authority in presiding over this issue. Therefore I have been granted a full judicial remit to hear this case and rule accordingly." Cornforth turned to the front row of seats where Grim sat next to Claude Bostwick and his team. "I would like to thank Grim for being so gracious and exercising such wise judgement on this occasion." Grim stayed seated but bowed his head disingenuously. "Now, before I call our first witness for today, does anyone have any pressing matters to bring to this Council?" Before the words had even left Cornforth's mouth, Claude shot out of his seat so quickly that his bones began to chatter.

"The defence is proposing a change in legal counsel!" Claude shrieked. "And what is more; it's an angel." The word "angel" rolled out of Claude's mouth as if he had hacked it up with a side of phlegm, causing the Council to murmur away much as they had the day before.

"The defence?" Cornforth boomed with mock surprise. "Good sir, I wasn't under the impression this young man was on trial. The purpose of this hearing is to ascertain if Benjamin May died in the manner everyone else in this room did or whether, as he claims, this was not his time, and we should reverse his expiration. While the Council has never overturned a death before, Item 347 of the Reaper's Constitution entitles Mr May to this appeal. It makes no stipulations as to who chooses to represent him."

"But a woman has never addressed the Council in the hallowed chambers of City Hall, let alone dictated to them!" thundered Claude. "In fact, Item 16 of the same Constitution you dote on so much clearly states a woman is prohibited from joining the Council of Reapers, and that will almost certainly apply to Angels."

Jade stood to address Cornforth and the Council, happy to stand up for herself. "I'm not asking to join the Council. I'm simply wishing to support my friend in presenting his appeal."

"See? She's at it again."

"Silence!" roared Cornforth with a crash of his gavel. "Item 16 is woefully outdated in these progressive times. I mean, it's a real sausage fest at the Council bar. However, even ignoring that, I see no issue in this young lady representing Mr May. Oh, and Mr Bostwick, if you disrespect my authority or Angels again in MY court, I will throw this case out in favour of the appellant." Claude sat down, grumbling to himself, defeated by the fair ruling of Cornforth. Jade turned to Winston, who had made his way next to Ben during the legal tussle. The Gatekeeper winked back.

"With all due respect to Winston Aloysius the 1st and Norman Wells following their testimonies yesterday," Cornforth continued, "I would like to hear from someone who was actually present at the death of Benjamin May. That is why I have requested Thomas Hudson, Reaper number 2112, to take the stand this morning."

A blinding spotlight lit over the Hot Box to reveal Tom was already there. Cornforth may have been more interested in fairness, but he also seemed to revel in the drama. As Tom swore on a dusty, hardback copy of the Reaper's Constitution, he repeated the unsettling vow.

"I shall speak only in truths or let me reap the Earth until I am no more than dust." It was Jade's opportunity to speak first.

"Mr Hudson, how long have you been reaping here in the AfterLife?"

"Must be over 70 years now, dude ... I mean, ma'am," Tom replied. Jade nodded in appreciation at the Reaper's formality.

"You must have reaped thousands of people in that time."

"Hundreds of thousands," Tom confirmed. "Especially since I got the bus."

"Would you be happy to refresh the Council's memory of how vehicles of the AfterLife work when you're reaping?" After Jade asked the question, Tom got a dreamy, faraway look on his face.

"It's nothing but road, man. You're picking up someone on the other side of an eight-mile traffic jam. There's nothing to it, bro. You glide on through, and the most anyone would feel is a shiver." Some of the Reapers shared the same wistful look as Tom. It had been many years since most had roamed the Earth.

"But you've been having some problems with your bus lately, right?" Jade continued.

"I mean, none of them are perfect. I guess that's the problem in only working with stuff that's already a write-off," Tom reasoned. "But yeah, it kept breaking down. I was late to reap, dudes. But I spoke to Grim about it, who was totally chill and said he'd get it fixed."

"Was it fixed before you ran into Ben that fateful night?"

"Na, the Depot hadn't looked at it yet."

Jade's conversation with Tom continued for several more minutes. The Council listened, astounded at the advances in technology which allowed Tom to use his pager to receive live information about his next collection. The days of quill and parchment were nothing but a distant memory. Winston too found himself somewhat impressed at Tom's knowledge of his vocation when he usually appeared utterly useless at it. After Tom explained his passengers would each be assigned a unique ID number he received by page, Jade had her killer question.

"What ID number was Ben that night, Tom?" Despite a full rundown with Jade and Winston beforehand, Tom seemed genuinely confused by the question.

"He didn't have one. I didn't even get a page."

"So, how did you know he needed reaping?"

"I didn't," Tom replied. "First I knew, he was going full force into the grille of my bus. There was no ID. Even Winnie couldn't find him."

"And how many times had this happened before you started having problems with your bus?"

"Err ... none? It's impossible!"

Jade smiled and even had a slight skip in her step as she returned to her seat and confirmed she had no more questions. Tom went to leave the Hot Box, forgetting that Claude still had his opportunity for a pound of flesh. The devious lawyer started innocently enough.

"Mr Hudson, I'm sure you must feel so guilty at hitting this poor man with a 15,000 lb school bus," sneered Claude. Even his attempts at empathy were insincere.

"Well yeah, dude," Tom replied. "Wouldn't you? He came out of nowhere. I feel I owe it to him to help in any way I can."

"Any way I can ..." repeated Claude, swishing the phrase around his mouth like a vintage Merlot. "Would that include lying to our esteemed Council here today?"

"Lying?" Tom cried. "I would never—"

"We already know your character, but for those within the Council not in the know, let me enlighten them." Claude turned to the Council, enjoying their full attention. "You have already established that tardiness is a significant issue of yours—"

"Because my bus kept breaking down."

"Last night, I heard you were in a dreadful speakeasy, completely intoxicated and making a show of yourself."

"Objection!" Jade interjected immediately. "How is this relevant to—"

"And shortly after Mr May's death, you commandeered our Architect's Motorwagen and took it for a joy ride back to the scene of his death, didn't you?" Claude slammed his fist down on his desk with unabashed glee.

"It wasn't like that," Tom replied with gritted teeth. A look of pure malice flashed across Claude's face. He turned to address Jade.

"This all speaks to the character of your witness, Little Miss Angel. How can we trust the word of a drunken little fibber to tell us what happened that night? How can we trust a man who tried to flee and leave his fellow man behind in the midst of the biggest war the world has ever seen?" The room fell into a stunned silence. Tom looked crushed at the words that had left Claude's mouth. The Reaper tried to collect himself.

"My death has nothing to do with this," he eventually retorted shakily.

"If you have the cowardice and disrespect to leave your friends and comrades to die, why should we have any respect for your words here in this room today?" Claude hissed. Jade had seen enough.

"Objection," Jade said once again. "Counsel is testifying and argumentative!"

"Yes," frowned Cornforth. "Yes, he is." He took a long draw from his pipe. "But the appropriation of the Motorwagen is something this Council takes very seriously. If I may, Mr Bostwick, I would like to speak with Mr Hudson directly about this matter?" Claude grinned from ear to ear and returned to his seat. The slight sense of hope Ben could feel was rapidly starting to diminish. All of a sudden, Cornelius Cornforth was beginning to look quite intimidating after all.

"Now, Mr Hudson," Cornforth began. "Why did you take the Motorwagen into your possession and abscond with both the vehicle and Mr May?"

"I wasn't trying to steal it or anything, dude. I mean, sir," Tom rambled. "It was just to try and get some closure for Ben. We wouldn't have even been gone a day if not—"

"A day, you say?" Cornforth butted in. "How long were you gone?"

"Well, the car only goes a few miles an hour, so it took most of the day to get there," Tom explained as he struggled with the mental arithmetic. "Then it broke down, and we waited ten hours for the RRA." Cornforth immediately looked towards Ben in complete astonishment.

"For the love of death!" exclaimed Cornforth as he spoke to Ben directly. "Are you telling me that you left the AfterLife for over twenty-four hours? Show me your fingernails!"

"M-my fingernails?" Ben stuttered, tentatively holding up his hands for the benefit of Cornforth and the Council. The entire room gasped in shock as Ben held up what seemed to him like completely normal, albeit bitten, fingernails. Even Claude showed surprise with his eyebrows raised so high they were in danger of leaping off his skull.

"And you feel alright, boy?" Cornforth asked with genuine intrigue. "You still seem to have plenty of colour in your cheeks, that's for sure."

"Alright as I can be," confirmed Ben. "Can I ask what's going on?" Cornforth spent several seconds eyeing Ben up and down before answering.

"When one passes over to the AfterLife, the atmosphere where we once lived is no longer hospitable for us," Cornforth explained. "That means, as Reapers, we make the ultimate sacrifice in gathering the dead in exchange for our flesh. Every member of the Council you see before you spent enough time outside of the AfterLife that we became nothing but bone. It's wise we got out when we did. Beings like your angel friend transcend the Earth. It is those who roam it who suffer its effects." Cornforth raised his left hand and looked at it thoughtfully. "In my first twenty-four hours outside of the AfterLife, I lost two fingernails, and my left foot started to go a strange colour. Anyone who has ventured out will tell you similar tales. Mr May, for you to have spent so much time outside of the AfterLife after your passing and there be no physical ill effect is extremely unusual. I need some time to consider the implications of this and would like to end the hearing for today."

With a bang of his gavel, the Council was dismissed.

25

The spectators in the gallery made their way out of the boardroom, their chatter fading to a whisper as they disappeared. The room that had moments earlier been a hotbed of chaos and controversy now sat eerily quiet. Ben looked across to the Hot Box. Tom had not moved since Claude blindsided him during his unjust interrogation. Even when Cornforth had taken over proceedings, Tom had engaged in conversation but looked straight ahead the whole time. The Rock 'N' Roll Reaper was a far cry from his usual, animated self. Staring into the distance, he didn't appear to have noticed the room empty moments earlier. A haunted expression was etched across his face, haunted and lost.

"Things got pretty intense for a minute there," Ben said. Tom jumped at the sound of his friend's voice. The Reaper was so absorbed in his own thoughts he hadn't even noticed him walk over. Immediately, Tom reverted to playing the joker.

"Aww, he's a total douche, dude," he replied. "CorCor saw right through him."

"CorCor?" Ben asked, puzzled.

"Cornelius Cornforth! I'm giving CorCor a test drive. Do you think he'll like it?" Ben looked back at him. Tom no longer had eyes to speak of, but there was no hiding the pain he was trying to mask with his questionable comedy.

"What Claude said to you—" Ben began.

"He has no idea what he's talking about," Tom quickly butted in.

"What he did was beyond the pale. I'm sorry I put you in that position."

"Dude, none of this is your fault," Tom reassured. "That's why we're here to make things right. It's been a long time since anyone has thrown that in my face." Tom shuffled in his chair, idly chasing a dust bunny on the floor with his sandal. "For the record, what he said isn't close to being true." Ben pulled up a chair next to the Hot Box and sat down.

"I'm in no rush if you want to tell me the real story. Tom looked deep in contemplation before sighing.

"I was only twenty-two when I joined the Army. The minute Britain declared war on Germany, we all had to enlist. I was ready to play my part, but it was scary, you know?" Ben remembered that Tom had previously mentioned his military service, but this was the first time he had openly talked about it. "One minute, I'm your average guy working in the coal mines. Fast forward two years, and I'm fighting for my life in Egypt."

"Egypt?"

"Yeah, dude," Tom confirmed. "We fought in the desert for over two years. It felt so weird being so far from home, but we all knew how important it was. The irony was that Hitler was too focused on Russia. It took him a while to pull his resources into taking us on. But when he did ..." Tom fell silent. Ben couldn't comprehend the things Tom must have seen at war.

"Operation Skorpion, the Germans called it," Tom continued. "Of course, I didn't know that at the time. It wasn't until I met Lemmy that I found out about that."

"As in Lemmy from Motörhead?" Ben asked, astounded.

"Weird, I know," Tom chuckled. "Turns out Lem was a huge history buff. He knew more about my death than I did!" Ben couldn't help but smirk. Even when relaying a harrowing account of war, Tom couldn't help but name-drop.

"They stationed us at Halfaya Pass; we called it Hellfire Pass. We were in the middle of the desert, after all. It was uncomfortably hot most of the time." Tom reached inside his cloak and rummaged in an inside pocket. His hand emerged with a small photograph in its grasp. Tom passed the picture over to Ben. At one time black and white, the two young soldiers in the portrait were difficult to make out. Decades of journeys in and out of the AfterLife had washed away much of the detail. A radiant smile from the soldier on the left gave away that it was Tom. Ben wished the picture gave more clues to how the Reaper once looked.

"That's me and my friend, David," Tom explained, confirming Ben's suspicion. "When the war was over, David was going to get married. I mean, we all had plans, didn't we?" Tom gently took his prized photograph back and stared at it wearily. "The Germans came one morning. We fought hard, but they pushed us out of Halfaya Pass." The haunted expression returned to Tom's face. "Most of us, anyway."

"Neither of you made it out of Halfaya Pass," Ben realised. Tom nodded mournfully in confirmation.

"They got David first. He told me to carry on, to leave him to die. I'm ashamed to say that at first, that's what I did." Tom paused once more as if he was reliving the final moments of his life blow-by-blow. Finally, he resumed his story. "As I headed into the heart of the battle, I realised I couldn't leave my friend behind. Even if it cost me my own life, I had to try. So I turned, and I ran back. I ran as if my life depended on it because I knew his life did."

"You never made it back."

"I didn't."

The pair sat for a moment, neither knowing what to say next. Ben thought back to Tom's exchange with Claude. "But Claude said you left your fellow man to die. Surely what you did was the opposite?"

"Running the opposite way on a battlefield sure doesn't look brave," conceded Tom. "Not even a Reaper can read minds. All my Reaper saw, and all my comrades saw was me running away." Ben couldn't help but feel terrible for Tom. Not only did he lose his life at such a young age, but no one knew the considerable sacrifice he had made.

"Did you ever try to explain your actions?" Ben asked.

"To be honest, I felt like I deserved everyone's contempt," Tom admitted. "After all, I couldn't save David. It seemed easier for the AfterLife to think I was a coward than a failure. I mean, in a way, Claude was right. I did leave my man behind,"

"No," Ben replied forcefully. "That idiot told us he died by choking on a sandwich. He's in no position to judge the way you died." Tom stifled a giggle but wasn't able to hold it in. Before long, he and Ben laughed heavily at the thought of Claude scrambling for help while gagging on his turkey club. Tom noticed Winston, who had respectfully stayed away throughout their conversation, glance over as the pair descended into laughter. He quickly composed himself.

"That's pretty dark, dude. I'm sorry, I don't usually laugh at how people have died."

"I think you've earned it after the way he spoke to you," Ben justified.

"Yeah, maybe," Tom reasoned. "This is why I signed up to be a Reaper," he disclosed. "I may have left David behind, but I can make sure I don't leave anyone else behind ever again." Tom's logic hit Ben like a mallet. Ben realised Tom saw it as his duty to reap as penance for not saving his friend.

"I'd say you've more than made up for it," Ben smiled. "Not that you needed to, in my opinion."

"Thanks, man. Weirdly I'm glad I started reaping," confessed Tom, "or I wouldn't have discovered all the amazing music that came after I was gone. I'm sure it would have made its way here eventually, but by getting out of the AfterLife, I'd hear a bit of Bowie here, some Sabbath there. There was nothing like that when I was growing up. It just speaks to me, you know?" Ben did know. It made all the sense in the world.

"If I was going to be hit by a bus that ripped through planes of existence and killed me before my time, I'm glad that the driver was at least listening to Scorpions when it happened." It took Tom a moment to register Ben's joke. Amongst all the drama of appeals, Motorwagens and inappropriate cocktails, Tom couldn't recall a point where Ben had come close to making light of his death. Ben looked at Tom kindly. "Thank you for trusting me," he smiled. "I'm sorry you weren't able to save your friend."

"Perhaps I'll get it right the second time," Tom replied.

Sensing it was now appropriate, Winston approached Ben and Tom to join the conversation. The Gatekeeper patted Tom on the back in support.

"What that parasite said has nothing to do with me," Winston said, "but for what it's worth, I never took stock in what people said about your death."

"Thanks, Winnie."

"However, your time management leaves something to be desired," Winston muttered, a genuine gripe that he hoped would lighten the mood.

"Dude, if I get my licence back, I'll be the first in the queue every shift," the tardy Reaper promised.

At the other side of the boardroom, the entrance door creaked open to reveal a short, gangly man pushing a trolley crammed with cleaning supplies. The cleaner parked the trolley in one of the aisles and draped a duster over his shoulder. Grabbing a bottle of polish from one of the shelves, he grumbled to himself about running late, oblivious to anyone else being present. Catching Ben and company in the corner of his eye, he huffed impatiently.

"Come on. Time to get out of here. It's Game's Club in the boardroom this afternoon. The Council are having a Mancala tournament!"

"Apologies," replied Winston. "We're just leaving."

"Thank goodness," moaned the cleaner. "This bloody appeal. The crowds outside have made me late. I've had to battle through everyone just to clock in."

"Crowds, you say?" Winston asked with surprise.

"Oh yes," came the reply. "It seems like the whole AfterLife, and his dog are out there. City Hall still needs to be polished."

"He's right, you know," a familiar voice rang through the empty boardroom. "The crowd bit; I couldn't care less about this place." Jade leaned against the door frame leading back to the winding corridors of City Hall. "I don't think I've ever seen so many people." Ben felt physically sick. The thought of hundreds of people waiting for him was the stuff of nightmares.

"No chance of waiting until they get bored and go home?" Ben gulped.

"Whatever you do, you can't stay here," whinged the cleaner. Jade shot him a dirty look that would keep him up for several nights.

"It'll be fine," Jade reassured Ben. "Come on. We'll all head out together."

26

As the morning progressed, hordes of people had gathered outside City Hall to be abreast of Ben's ongoing appeal. There was so much interest in this unprecedented legal battle that the Council had no choice but to set up a wireless telegraph broadcasting the events inside the Council room to the crowd via radio signal. Hundreds of Reapers and residents of the AfterLife listened intently as Tom had been cross-examined and given Cornforth pause for thought. When Ben and the others emerged from the dishevelled City Hall, the gathering met them with monstrous cheers. Still confused by the change in public opinion towards him, Ben waved timidly. Tom leapt onto the scattered remains of the brick wall surrounding the building and raised his fist in the air.

"Your Rock 'N' Roll Reaper is here, dudes!" The cheers from the crowd grew louder and more boisterous. Ben breathed a sigh of relief that he was no longer the centre of attention and watched with amusement as Winston waddled over to stop the Reaper, who was scaling the walls of City Hall with the intent to stage dive off the roof. Amongst the chants of "Do it!" and "Rock and Roll!" a familiar face pushed through the mob.

"Guys, guys!" Peyton squealed. "This is unbelievable!" The Guardian-in-training squeezed amongst the population of the After-Life, inadvertently hitting an unlucky Reaper in the face with one of her wings. Free from the pack, Peyton rushed towards Jade and threw her arms around her. "You were amazing!" she squeaked, her voice getting higher and higher. "It was like watching Michelle Obama." Jade reluctantly gave in to the hug and patted her friend on the back.

"I've had worse comparisons," smirked Jade as she allowed herself to feel a hint of pride in her performance. "I was pretty good, wasn't I?"

"Good?" Peyton beamed. "You were like Hillary Clinton!" Jade's smirk settled into an ugly scowl.

"I think I preferred your first example," she snorted as she broke free from Peyton's vice-like grip. Unperturbed, Peyton turned her attention to Ben for another warm embrace.

"So Lucy found your ticket," she teased. Ben felt a rush of excitement. In all the drama of the last couple of days, he had completely forgotten Peyton had been watching over Lucy. He had so many questions.

"Is she okay?"

"She's fine! Although she is a bit freaked out by all the weird stuff that's been going on."

"You mean like the massive tidal wave that appeared completely out of nowhere?" Jade sniped. Peyton blushed. She was still hugely embarrassed at her emotions getting the better of her like that.

"Yes, that. But also, Lucy went back to where you died and now has both tickets." Ben's heart sank. His intention in leaving his ticket behind was to let Lucy know he was okay. It seemed as if every interaction they'd had since his death had only done more to scare her. Peyton noticed the worried expression on Ben's face. "Ben, that's a good thing!" Ben struggled to agree.

"How so?"

"Lucy was already wondering why all this stuff was happening. She'd even spoken to your friend Jamie about it. Now she has both tickets, and she knows the truth. She knows it was you!" Peyton swooned, convinced that this was the most romantic chain of events she'd ever witnessed. "That's why I'm here," she continued. "She's going to see a medium. Tonight!"

"This is perfect," Jade told Ben. "If she's seeing a medium, we can get a message to her." As she spoke, an idea began to formulate in her head. "In fact, if we play our cards right, she might just be able to help with your appeal without even knowing it." Winston returned to join the conversation at the perfect time, dragging Tom like a naughty schoolboy behind him. "Right, guys," Jade announced. "We're off to see Otis!"

Otis Rickenbauer lived at the very edge of the AfterLife, where the planes of life and death met the closest. The rise of the living's obsession with communicating with the dead coincided with the emergence of Spiritualism in the 19th Century. The initial use and then denouncement of Ouija boards led to individuals claiming themselves to be mediums, a conduit between those across realms of existence. Rickenbauer had dedicated his death to receiving these messages and helping those in the AfterLife to converse with loved ones they'd left behind. While his intentions were pure, time had left Otis obsessed with his pursuit. The Council of Reapers did not recognise his discipline; consequently, Otis was often mocked and discredited. As his reputation fell into disrepute, Otis had been left well alone by most for decades.

Ben's popularity outside City Hall had meant one Reaper had been more than happy to lend his minivan on his day off. While nowhere near the size of Tom's bus, it had comfortably sat Ben, Winston, Peyton and Jade in the back while Tom got behind the wheel for the first time in several days. The journey had taken several hours, but any hope of a nap was lost as Tom howled along to one of his many heavy metal mixtapes.

Upon their arrival, Otis's control tower loomed over the barren landscape. Tom's bones cracked as he climbed out of the driver's seat and stretched. He craned his head upward to take in the full 500ft structure.

"It's gonna take us ages to get up there, dudes," he moaned.

"Not to worry," chirped Peyton as she unfurled her wings. "We'll have you up in a jiffy!"

The ascent was nowhere near as pleasant as the journey over Borrowed Heaven. Ben made the mistake of looking down to see Winston quickly shrink to the size of an ant as he dutifully waited with the van. Ben closed his eyes tight. He started to feel dizzy, and the sky spun around him. The musty smell of the AfterLife only increased with the altitude. At least Tom's screaming seemed more warranted this time. The Angels landed near the top of the structure, directly in front of the door to Otis's control room.

"Is someone there?" came a voice from inside. "Come in, come in!" Walking in, Ben's eyes took some time to adjust to the dark. A dimly lit bulb sat on a table in the centre of the room where a scruffy-looking gentleman was seated. He looked around the room skittishly, his curly hair flapping around erratically as he did. On desks littered across the room, dozens of clunky devices were clicking away to themselves. Had there been just one, Ben might have been able to establish a pattern, but with so many clicking at the same time, he could barely hear himself think. The man stood up to greet his guests, picking up the bulb from his desk to light the way. Coming closer, Ben could see this man was wearing glasses with the thickest frames he'd ever seen. Amongst the tuft of messy hair sat a chunky pair of goggles, the straps for which hung loosely under his chin.

"Otis Rickenbauer?" asked Ben.

"The one and the same," he proclaimed, motioning for Ben and his friends to sit. "I hope your journey wasn't too arduous."

"Nothing that a seasoned driver like me couldn't handle," replied Tom, but something had already diverted Otis's attention. His head darted in every direction in response to the machines around him continuing to click at different frequencies. Under his breath, he started to mutter seemingly random numbers.

"83. No, 79. Back to 82."

"Everything okay, dude?" asked Tom with concern.

"Smashing!" Otis replied manically, shuffling back to his seat. "Gosh, it's so great to have company. It's been a long time since my control room was this full." Continuing to mutter numbers to himself, Otis pulled off his glasses and breathed heavily on each lens before rubbing both with the sleeve of his jumper. "How can I help you fine fellows today?" Jade explained the purpose of their visit and Ben's hope to get a message to Lucy, with Peyton excitedly chipping in behind her.

"And you're sure Lucy will visit a medium tonight?" Otis asked. "92, 89, 94."

"Positive," beamed Peyton.

"Then, my friends, I'm happy to report I'll be able to help you." Otis stood up and surveyed the machines dotted around the room. "We'll just need to find the right telegraph, is all."

"The right telegraph?" repeated Ben. "Are these machines how you communicate with—"

"Morse code, my lad!" boomed Otis with pride. "If it's good enough for the navy, by gum, it's good enough for me."

Otis relayed how his system worked. Each telegraph was designed to send and receive messages in Morse code. The telegraphs picked up messages from mediums on the other side and relayed them in the clicks and ticks that rang out across the control room. If the right person had come to Otis's tower and picked up the message, they would reply there and then, which would be communicated back by the medium. However, it wasn't the most flawless system. Otis didn't like to admit it, but the use of Morse code could often lead to mistakes and messages getting lost in translation. This issue caused both Otis and the mediums he communicated with to be taken far less seriously in their respective planes of existence. Trying to monitor one hundred telegraphs alone exacerbated those mistakes and had caused Otis to become slightly peculiar. Ben had several questions but settled for the most pressing one.

"How on earth are we supposed to know which machine my friend will come through on if she comes through at all?"

"Well, I count five of us," Otis replied. "I propose we take twenty each and keep an eye on them all until she comes through."

"But I don't know Morse code," Ben groaned.

"No matter. Your name would always come through first. We're lucky your name is Ben. One guy who came here many years ago was called Alessandro. We were waiting half an hour for the machines to spell that one out!" Otis guffawed at the memory of his long-named client. Ben groaned, making no attempt to hide his frustration.

"Trust me," whispered Jade. "This is the best chance of reaching Lucy. It's going to work." Ben took a deep breath and apologised to Otis.

"I'm sorry. What do I need to do?"

After a brief lesson on spelling his name in Morse code, Ben and the others were each assigned twenty of the telegraph machines. Rather than trying to learn the entire alphabet, it made more sense to learn "Ben" and to ignore any machines spelling something different. Minutes passed as each device pipped away with messages for people other than Ben. Messages for Bethany or Bella would briefly induce a sense of euphoria before the sinking realisation that it wasn't to be by the third letter.

Ben's eyes grew heavy as the clicking continued. Initially irritated by

Otis's eccentricities, Ben now understood him much better. An eternity alone with these machines was enough to drive anyone mad. Fighting to stay awake, Ben stared at the telegraph in front of him. It had been hours since this mind-numbing torture began, and he was certain his mind was playing tricks on him. Every click started to sound like his name in Morse code. Those three simple letters. B E N.

⁻... . ⁻.

Ben jolted upright, the incessant tapping from the telegraph now music to his ears.

"Hey guys!" he yelled. "I think I've got something." Otis reached Ben first and grinned from ear to ear upon hearing the correct code.

"Grab a seat, my friend," Otis said as he pulled his goggles over his chunky frames. "I'll take it from here."

27

Lucy and Jamie sat quietly as they waited for Astrid Winter to re-emerge from the kitchen. A quick internet search had found Astrid to be the only medium in the city who happened to be free that evening. While Jamie had been dubious about seeing a psychic at all, much less that night, Lucy didn't want to wait. Rather than force her to go alone to a complete stranger's house, Jamie put his scepticism aside.

Astrid flounced in from the kitchen with two cups of tea that she placed in front of her visitors.

"I also do tea readings, so we can get to that after the important stuff," she said proudly. Jamie rolled his eyes. "Now, before we begin, I must warn you that messages or images can sometimes come through a bit hazy or perhaps make little sense to me personally." She looked intensely at Lucy with her round, hazel eyes. "Remember, these messages are for you, so I may need you to help me fill in the blanks." Jamie scoffed, prompting a sharp jab from Lucy under the table. Astrid continued regardless. "Is there anyone you are hoping to connect with tonight? The spirit world is a crowded place, so we need to make sure the right person comes through."

"My friend Ben," Lucy replied without hesitation. "He died earlier this month."

"Ah, a new soul," Astrid said knowingly. "I'm sure you have a lot of questions."

"And I'm sure you've already got the answers you need," snorted Jamie with disdain. Astrid shifted her focus towards Ben's former flatmate.

"You seem cynical about what we're doing here."

"You're right," Jamie told Lucy mockingly. "She is psychic!" Astrid did not seem angry or offended by Jamie's mistrust of her gift.

"All I ask is that you approach this with an open mind and, as I say, help me piece things together when they're hazy." Jamie was still unconvinced, but a stern look from Lucy kept him firmly in his seat.

***

Otis tapped like a man possessed at the telegraph that had spelt out Ben's name seconds earlier, taking brief pauses to allow the machine to tick back just as furiously. No one else in the room had any idea what any of the noise meant, but the eccentric seemed to know what he was doing.

"There's two of them there!" Otis reported back breathlessly. "The Lucy girl you spoke of, and a man called Jamie. He's very sceptical about it all." Ben couldn't help but smile. It meant a lot to him that his flatmate was trying to reach him, even if he did think it was a total con. "Quick, Ben, tell me something only he would know." Ben thought for a moment.

"Well, I guess when we were kids, we used to pretend we were the Mario brothers," Ben admitted. Tom stifled a laugh. Video games hadn't made their way to the AfterLife yet, but he'd been on enough reaping expeditions to know who Super Mario was. Otis's finger was a blur as it tried to break the land speed record for typing. Tom leaned over to Jade, who was watching intently.

"I bet he was Luigi!"

***

"Ben was your brother."

"No," replied Jamie flatly. "No, he wasn't." Momentarily shaken by her error, Astrid tried to regroup.

"But he was like a brother to you, wasn't he?" she said with a lack of conviction.

"I guess?" Even Jamie felt a bit sorry for her at this point.

"Perhaps he saw you as his brother. You two were very close. I'm feeling a lot of love coming through at this moment."

"We lived together," Jamie conceded. "He was a good friend."

"You got into a lot of scrapes together, didn't you?" Astrid laughed warmly. Jamie thought back to how difficult it was to get Ben to leave the house, let alone get into any kind of trouble. His negative view of mediums was in no danger of being shaken.

"Not really. That doesn't sound like Ben at all." An awkward silence fell over the room. Astrid closed her eyes and tried her hardest to focus on the message coming through.

"Must be particularly hazy tonight," she said nervously, keeping her eyes shut and tapping her fingers on the table.

***

An eyebrow arched quizzically above Otis's goggles as he read back the reply he'd received from Astrid.

"He's not convinced at all," he said with confusion. "He seems to think that you claim to be his brother!"

"That's because you're typing too fast!" Jade snapped. "How can you get it right when you're going at a breakneck speed? You need to slow down." Otis took great offence to being challenged in such an outright way.

"Young lady, I have been doing this for over one-hundred years," he retorted pompously. "I don't come to your work and tell you how to watch over people. Anyway, it's not my fault. This medium is obviously half-baked. A complete ninny!"

"If it's not going well with Jamie, why don't we concentrate on Lucy?" Peyton suggested. "After all, she is the one who wanted to try this."

"Good idea Peyton. Let's try something a bit easier, so Otis's finger doesn't drop off," Jade quipped. "What was that band you were going to see together on the night you got run down?"

"Black Stone Cherry," Ben replied. "She'd definitely know it was me then." Otis mouthed the band name to himself three times before tapping it with authority on the telegraph.

***

"I see an image coming through," whispered Astrid. "This may be for you, Lucy, but I cannot be sure." Lucy could suddenly feel her heart in her throat. The last few days had been the strangest of her life. The glass bottle flying through the air. The incident at the cafe. The ticket on her bed. But the moment she had seen her weather-worn ticket on the ground earlier today, she resolved there could only be one answer. This had to be Ben trying to reach her. As Astrid opened her eyes, Lucy took a deep breath and waited for Ben's message.

"I'm seeing a blackberry," Astrid announced. "Does a blackberry mean anything to either of you?" All the nervous energy inside Lucy drained away, and the familiar feeling of despair returned. She looked down dejectedly and thought about what a fool she'd been for considering something so absurd. Seeing Lucy's reaction to Astrid's fruity vision, Jamie rose to his feet.

"I'm sorry, I can't sit through another minute of this," he said crossly. "We're here grieving for our friend, and you're just making fun of us and profiting from our pain." He turned to Lucy. "Stay if you want, but I'm going to wait outside."

***

The latest reply from the telegraph provoked a visceral reaction from Otis, who started pulling at his hair and yelling in frustration.

"Who said anything about a blackberry!" he repeatedly screamed as he banged his head on the desk.

"You're typing too fast," Jade insisted once again. "They're not getting any of our messages. It's all just complete nonsense."

"I'm trying my best!" cried Otis, decidedly overwhelmed by the situation. "It's been a long time since anyone has asked this of me. It's not easy being alone." Otis's outburst of anxiety and emotion resonated heavily with Ben. Throughout his life and even at times since his death, the panic had consumed Ben and taken over his entire body. Jade's tirade of abuse towards the sensitive operator had left him close to hyperventilating in his seat. Ben knew what he had to do. He walked slowly over and pulled up a chair next to him.

"Otis," Ben began softly. "I want you to take a deep breath in through your nose, okay? Now hold it for just a few seconds." Otis obliged, counting to five in his head before breathing out through his mouth as Ben instructed. "You're doing great, Otis. A good friend told me to do this when I was scared, and it really helped me." Ben caught Tom's gaze and nodded. He hadn't forgotten the Reaper's support on that first bus journey to the AfterLife. Tom smiled and gave Ben a thumbs-up for a job well done.

After a few more deep breaths, Otis composed himself and reached for a handkerchief from his breast pocket. He looked down at the telegraph standing there motionless on the desk. The control room felt somewhat hushed despite the rest of the machines in the room still noisily tapping away. Otis's eyes started to well up.

"I'm so sorry," he whispered, his voice cracking against his resistance to start crying. "I've blown it. I've bloody blown it!"

"We don't know that yet," Ben replied. "Now take another deep breath and type out exactly what I say."

***

Lucy rifled through her purse to pay Astrid her fee and try to put the entire evening to the back of her mind forever. Placing the notes on the table next to the medium, Lucy couldn't help but see the troubled look on her face.

"I didn't mean to upset your friend," Astrid mumbled. "Please take your money back. I did nothing to help you tonight."

Lucy left the money on the table and smiled half-heartedly. The only person she blamed for how she and Jamie were feeling was herself.

"You keep it," Lucy replied. "Weirdly, tonight might actually have given me some closure." Lucy pulled on her jacket and placed her hand on the door, ready to leave the room. This may not have been how she expected the night to end, but the trail had truly run cold. Ben was dead, and the strange events that had occurred since were pure happenstance.

"You have two tickets."

Lucy stopped dead in her tracks. Her entire body froze to the very spot she was standing in. She presumed she had misheard what Astrid had said.

"What did you just say?"

"I see two tickets. Ben says you have them." Lucy slowly turned around and walked back to her chair. Sitting down in front of Astrid once again, Lucy placed her hand into her jacket pocket and, with her entire body shaking, clasped the two tickets tightly.

"You didn't see these?" Lucy asked cautiously. "You didn't know they were here?" Astrid looked back at her with confusion.

"See what, my dear?" Lucy lifted her hand out of her pocket and placed the two tickets on the table in front of her. One was worn and faded from its exposure to the elements, the other looking as new as the day it was printed. Astrid gasped, confirming that this wasn't some sick ploy to torment her. Lucy picked up the second ticket that had started this entire journey.

"I found this on my bed," she told Astrid as a tear rolled down her face.

"I know," Astrid replied emotionally. "He says he put it there." The next few minutes raced by as Astrid confirmed all of Lucy's suspicions. Ben had been there each time she suspected he had been. Astrid was also able to relay that Ben had never meant to frighten her, and he just wanted to ensure she was okay. Lucy wiped the tears out of her eyes and sat silently as she took everything in. After a short time, she noticed Astrid was silent too. The medium winced and rubbed her temples. Lucy asked if she was alright.

"I'm fine, dear," Astrid groaned. "I've never had messages come through so vividly before. It's taking its toll."

***

On the opposite plane of existence, Ben, too, sat with tears in his eyes. Thanks to Otis and his army of Morse code telegraphs, he had finally spoken to Lucy and put his worries about her to rest. He reflected on the trouble he had gone to since his death to keep her safe and well. On his previous adventures with Tom and the Guardian Angels, Ben had never gone looking for other important people in his life, such as Jamie or his parents. Only one person had been on his mind, and he had gone to great lengths to see her. Today alone, he had travelled for hours to the very ends of the AfterLife just to get a message to her. Ben thought about the appeal to quash his death and return to his life again. He decided there and then in that dark, drab control room that if he were lucky enough to be reunited with Lucy, he would tell her exactly how he felt. He could finally admit that he loved her and knew he would use the strength of that love to triumph over even the darkest of forces in the AfterLife. A contented hush fell over the control room. The machine began to tap once more. Otis transcribed it for the group.

"She's about to leave now. Is there anything you'd like to say before we say goodbye?" Ben gave thought to how he wanted to leave things. Before he could respond, Jade spoke up first.

"Ask her if she can make sure she's at home this time tomorrow night." Jade looked across at Ben for approval. He had no idea what she was planning but knew by now that he could trust her completely. With a nod from Ben, Otis resumed typing, taking his time to ensure he made no mistakes. Jade stood next to Ben and told him that her request would make much more sense in the morning. Ben had no doubt she was right but couldn't wait to find out why.

28

C laude was conspicuous by his absence upon Ben's arrival in the boardroom the following day. The slimy lawyer representing the AfterLife wasn't sitting in his usual seat facing the Hot Box, and a quick scan of the room left him nowhere to be found. Ben spotted Tom breathing a sigh of relief. Tom may have been his usual cheerful self for most of the previous day, but Ben knew Claude's words had gotten to him. Although there was one less person in the room, the spectators in the gallery more than made up for Claude's disappearance. Ben's appeal had become the talk of the AfterLife, with many wondering if the unthinkable might happen. Is it possible that someone would overturn their death and get a second chance at living their life?

Cornforth marched into the boardroom and took his seat to start proceedings.

"You may notice that Mr Bostwick is not in attendance today," he announced. "I did not feel he was adding any value to these proceedings and have banished him from entering these chambers. I believe rather than this becoming a witch hunt, we will benefit more from an honest reflection from all parties." The Council of Reapers voiced their agreement. "I wish to learn more about Mr May's interactions outside the AfterLife. However, first, another matter requires our attention, and for that, I call our Architect, Mr Grim, to the stand."

Gasps filled the boardroom, with everyone turning to face the First Reaper. Grim sat still. Negative energy seemed to seethe from under his hood. Ben purposefully avoided looking directly at him but felt a sudden chill in the air.

"I'm right here, Counsellor Cornforth and happy to answer any questions you have." The tension was palpable.

"With all due respect, sir, I would like to do this by the book," Cornforth replied firmly. "Could we please continue this conversation once you have entered the Hot Box?"

As he walked toward the Hot Box, Grim's towering presence took over the boardroom. From where Ben was sitting, Grim's raven black cloak obscured his feet, giving the impression he was floating. A Council member presented Grim with a copy of the Reaper's Constitution. The Architect looked at it with disgust.

"Surely you don't expect ME to be subject to such archaic traditions?" Grim asked in disbelief. Winston stood up to address his long-time partner.

"These traditions are ones you created, old friend. Even you must adhere to them." Grim smouldered with resentment as he placed his hand on the Constitution and spat out the sacred vow he had written.

"I shall speak only in truths or let me reap the Earth until I am no more than dust."

"I appreciate your cooperation," Cornforth told Grim with appreciation. "Now, sir, could you please inform the Council when you were first made aware of Mr May?"

"A Council member made me aware of the Anomaly on the morning my Motorwagen was stolen," Grim replied. A jolt of hatred shot through Ben. Being called an 'anomaly' didn't get any easier, and he appreciated that Cornforth was consciously avoiding the word. "There had been a commotion at the Pathway," Grim continued. "Many Reapers saw the Anomaly and his Reaper conversing with the Gatekeeper. It's not every day our Gatekeeper leaves his post." Winston's cheeks shone red with embarrassment.

"We heard from Winston Aloysius the First on the opening day of this appeal," Cornforth reminded Grim. "That was the day you presided over this matter. Do you remember what he said?"

"I believe there was some excuse or other," Grim recalled dismissively.

"Allow me to refresh your memory, sir," Cornforth replied and clicked his fingers. On command, a decrepit skeleton creaked and cracked from the back of the room all the way to the area where Cornforth proudly sat. After passing over a yellowing piece of paper, the skeleton dragged himself back to the recesses of the boardroom and resumed writing furiously with an inked quill. Cornforth read back Winston's very words from just days earlier.

"My intention was to build a full picture of what happened before I presented it to Grim. I booked in Tom's bus for its MOT in the hope of getting some kind of understanding."

"He can claim that was his motive, but they are merely hollow words to me," sneered the Architect.

"Is that why you collected the results of the bus's service yourself?" Grim paused for a moment at Cornforth's question. "And do remember, sir, you are under oath."

"I can confirm I attended the Depot of the Dead and spoke to the engineers completing the service," Grim confirmed, choosing his words very carefully.

"And did the bus pass?" Cornforth asked sternly.

"You heard the man on the stand," Grim answered evasively. "He told us several times that the bus indeed passed its service."

"Yes, we certainly did hear from Mr Wells," argued Cornforth. "We also saw him cower at your very presence. I ask you again, sir. Did the bus pass its service?" Anticipation in the boardroom was at an all-time high. No one had ever spoken to Grim in this manner, yet it was clear to anyone watching that the President of the Council had something to hide.

"I don't know," Grim said slowly.

"I sense you are being obstructive," challenged Cornforth.

"If you wish for me to stick by the very pledge I wrote, then I suggest you accept my answers in the spirit they have been offered today."

"Why is it so important to you that we do not know the outcome of this service?" Cornforth glowered at his superior. Any pretence of cordiality had long since evaporated.

Ben felt the room close in again as Grim struggled to contain his anger and distress. Ben closed his eyes and tried to push back against the onslaught of darkness seeping into his soul. As the blackness threatened to overwhelm him, he felt a skeletal hand grasp his own.

"Deep breaths, dude."

The fusty air of the boardroom filled Ben's lungs before he breathed it out, Grim's influence disappearing with it as he did. Ben heard the Reaper rant and rave as he fought against the sickness.

"I graciously agreed to you overseeing this appeal. However, I am still the Architect of the AfterLife, and I reserve the right to terminate this cross-examination," Ben opened his eyes to see Grim exiting the Hot Box and storming towards the door leading to his quarters. "You may be sitting at my bench, but that does not make me accountable to you!" he raged. "I shall return to my chambers and mercy to any soul who follows me!"

Grim's slam of the door reverberated around the boardroom. Seconds passed without a sound. Appearing unruffled by their exchange, Cornforth turned his attention to the Council.

"I put forward that Mr Hudson's bus is reassessed while this Council continues with further business. All those in favour?" A sea of hands rose gradually across the Council, some with authority, others with timidness at the thought of going against their leader. Eventually, every Council member showed their support for Cornforth's motion.

"Aye!" Cornforth asked for any further business, at which point Jade confidently rose to address him.

"Councillor Cornforth, I would like to make a suggestion if you'd let me," the Angel said gracefully. Cornforth nodded in approval. "I'm sure it wasn't lost on the Council during Tom's testimony that my client was able to stay outside of the AfterLife without any ill effects. However, I also appreciate that our claim may be hard to believe for some. How long do you think the service on Tom's bus will take?"

"I wouldn't expect the results until tomorrow at the earliest," Cornforth replied.

"In that case, why don't you see for yourself?" Jade proposed. "Come with us back to Ben's life. You can see first hand he doesn't decay as you'd expect the dead to. Surely it's better to see the evidence for yourself than take our word for it?" The idea appeared to intrigue Cornforth, who sat back and nibbled on his pipe as furiously as ever.

"It's been a long time since I set foot outside the AfterLife," the councillor admitted. "I'll be honest; I'm not sure how much time I'd have left!"

"We still have some of those suits!" piped up a Council member. "They're cumbersome, but they protect from the atmosphere."

"I must admit the idea of getting back out there one more time is exhilarating," Cornforth sighed, his words full to the brim with nostalgia. Remembering the kaleidoscope of colour and light that bridged the two planes of existence together, Cornforth looked at Tom with almost childlike innocence.

"Is the journey as wonderful as I remember?"

"Dude," Tom smiled, "it's even better."

"Then it's settled!" Cornforth cried enthusiastically. "We shall adjourn for today and meet at the Pathway in one hour." The excitable Cornforth forgot to bang his gavel to end the hearing, instead sprinting full pelt out of the boardroom to prepare for his voyage.

As the Council and the gallery filtered out of the boardroom, Jade gathered her friends around. Winston looked particularly impressed.

"A brilliant suggestion, young lady. It seems I made the right decision in choosing you... not that I'm trying to claim this is all down to me or anything," the Gatekeeper stuttered, trying not to offend.

"Relax, Winnie! We all know that's not your bag," Tom laughed. "It's gonna be a snooze fest, though, right? Stand around for a few hours to watch someone NOT decompose."

"Actually, I thought we could pay Lucy another visit while we were there," Jade casually suggested. "After all, we did promise."

"But why would the Council care about going to see Lucy?" Ben asked.

"Well, that's just it," Jade replied cryptically. "They're coming to see what you don't do outside the AfterLife. I say it's the perfect opportunity to show them what you can do." Ben finally put the pieces together. If Cornforth saw him communicate with Lucy, that was far more powerful an image than his skin not dropping off. Ben remembered Jade's words in Otis's control tower.

"This was your plan all along, wasn't it?"

"I'm not a Guardian Angel for nothing, you know!" Jade teased. She quickly turned and headed for the door. "I'll meet you all at Lucy's house. Peyton's done such a good job watching over her; she will want to be part of this. See you there!"

Jade left Ben, Tom and Winston alone in the boardroom. Ben tried not to get his hopes up, but he could feel the excitement build inside him.

"Do you guys think I actually have a chance to go home?" he asked with trepidation. Winston looked at Ben with complete sobriety.

"My boy, the day I met you, it seemed absolutely improbable. However, if things go your way today, there's a genuine possibility that you will be the first person ever to get a second chance."

29

The air in the AfterLife felt particularly cold as Ben and Tom waited for the expedition that would accompany them back into Life. Tom insisted that it was just like any other day and that the weather never changed, but Ben was unconvinced. Ben tried to ignore the chill catching the back of his neck and making him shudder and instead concentrated on seeing Lucy again. Then it dawned on him. If things didn't go his way, this might be the last time he ever saw her. While Jade and Winston were extremely optimistic, Ben couldn't shift the image of Grim storming out of the boardroom from his mind. Ben could save a child from a burning building in front of Cornforth's eyes but was the councilman any match for Grim in terms of rank or sheer power? Ben resolved he had to make this visit count. Regardless of whether he impressed the Council or not, this may be his only opportunity to say goodbye.

Ben's worrying was cut short by a guffaw of laughter that brought him back to the AfterLife with a jolt. Tom, who had previously stood right beside him, was now doubled over, holding where his stomach used to be and pointing back towards the Pathway. Ben looked back to see three figures emerging from the mist. The murky aura of the Pathway made it hard to pick out detail. Still, with the trio wading ever closer, he started to make out that all three were dressed in identical canvas body suits, balancing cumbersome copper diving helmets on their heads. The weighted boots appeared to make walking a significant challenge for all three men, who would occasionally grab one another for balance. Against the hazy backdrop, it looked like the trailer for some terrible B-movie.

"Are those the suits the Council were talking about this morning?" Ben asked. Tom took a moment to collect himself from his convulsions of laughter.

"Oh yeah, dude," the Reaper replied in between cackles. "They'll need them to survive the journey back."

"But you don't wear one of those," replied Ben with confusion.

"They're long retired now, but they were out there reaping long before I was born, let alone dead," Tom explained. "It's not a career you can do forever. Even I'll have to stop eventually. Everyone has their last reap, and after that, the diving suits are the only way to protect yourself."

"So, if you've seen those suits before, then what's so funny?" Ben's question caused Tom to start howling once again.

"Look at Winnie!"

Ben turned his attention back to the advancing diving crew. Now much closer, Ben realised there were, in fact, four members of the party. Reaching waist height of his three colleagues, a much shorter, plumper diver walked in front of them. With a helmet that looked far too big for his dumpy, little frame, Ben could see Winston's distinctive face peeking out of the faceplate. Close enough to hear Tom's childish reaction, Winston's expression was not a cordial one.

"Winnie, you look so cute I just wanna eat you," Tom teased in a babyish voice.

"I'll remind you I am still the Gatekeeper of the Pathway, and I would appreciate some respect!" came the curt reply from beneath the copper helmet.

"You didn't wear that when you picked us up last time," Tom continued, trying his best to stifle another fit of laughter.

"That was my first time out of the AfterLife, and I am lucky I was in and out as quick as I was," argued Winston. "I'm not taking any chances, so be as immature as you like. It will be me who has the last laugh."

"Quite right," muttered one of the full-size divers in agreement.

"Don't make me regret suggesting you for this assignment," Winston grumbled as he threw a leather wallet in Tom's direction. Ben could spot excitement spread across Tom's face as he caught the wallet with ease.

"We're going to need transportation for this expedition," Cornforth's voice boomed from one of the helmets. "Back in the day, we reaped with horse and carriage. We wouldn't know a handbrake from a bone break!" The party burst into guffaws of their own.

"You're the most experienced driver out of all of us," shuddered Winston, recalling what an unreliable Reaper Tom had been in the past. "In fact, let me rephrase. You are the only one of us who can drive. We need you to give us safe passage out of the AfterLife." The expression on Tom's face morphed from excitement to exhilaration, clutching his precious Reaper's licence in his hands for the first time in what felt like an eternity. The irreplaceable rush of being out on the open road was just moments away.

"I must say I'm excited too, young man," Cornforth confessed. "It must have been over 350 years since I last got out there. The Great Fire of London it was. They had us all on overtime for that humdinger." From below Cornforth's thigh bone, Winston gave the councillor a gentle tap to get his attention. Tom ground his teeth together to avoid further laughter at the Gatekeeper's expense.

"The engineers at the Depot of the Dead have secured us a vehicle that should happily fit all six of us," Winston informed Cornforth and the group. "The Angels are going to meet us there. They have their own means of travel as we know."

"Then to the Depot we go!" proclaimed Cornforth before laboriously shuffling ninety degrees in his diving suit and setting off at a snail's pace. Ben politely waited to walk behind the procession when he spotted Tom take flight like an Olympic sprinter, racing towards the Depot.

"I'll meet you guys there. I'm gonna need my tapes," he looked toward Ben. "Are you coming, dude?" Ben willingly followed, deciding that rummaging through Tom's music collection had to be infinitely better than walking in slow motion with three and a half deep-sea divers.

Presuming Tom was heading back to his flat, Ben was surprised to see the Reaper lead him directly to the Depot of the Dead. It turned out that while Tom had an extensive music collection at home, all his cassettes were still aboard his confiscated school bus. Tom rushed through the gaggle of Reapers, all getting ready to leave or just returning with a fresh intake of souls to check in. Barely keeping up, Ben noticed Tom scan the sea of skeletons with confusion before quickly spotting something and advancing straight through the crowd with intent. Ben failed to keep up as Tom disappeared behind one of the bus terminals. The Reapers penned in around him and began to notice who they were knocking shoulders with.

"Hey, it's Ben!" cried one.

"Vive la résistance!" rallied another. Seeing they were blocking his way, the Reapers parted to form a path for Ben to catch up with his friend. Appreciative of the gesture but mortified at the attention, Ben modestly thanked the gathering as they chanted the word "Anomaly" in unison. Suddenly, Ben didn't seem to have such a problem with that word after all.

Ben rounded the corner, and Tom's bus came into view. Looking at the vehicle that ended his life with such nostalgia and fondness felt strange. It was clear the Depot engineers had given Tom's pride and joy a good clean as well as the all-important second service that was currently underway. Tom stood clutching a stack of cassettes, chatting with one engineer while a pair of feet stuck out from below the front bumper of the bus. The chants of "Anomaly" behind Ben began to patter out, leaving him able to hear Tom's discussion with the engineer.

"Is that a new grille on the front, dude?" Tom asked giddily. "It's gnarly, man!" Ben looked over at the front of the bus. Sure enough, a brand-new chrome grille sat proudly in place.

"Sure is," confirmed the worker. "Seemed a good opportunity to fix 'er up." He waved toward a pile of exterior vehicle parts piled up in the corner of the work area. "All that time on the road, these things drop to bits, and they're pretty banged up when they get here, as you know! I'm pretty sure we changed both bumpers on yours last time. It's hard to find the right parts for a beautiful vintage like this, but we've got plenty of stuff that fits. Just means your baby is getting souped up every time she comes here."

"Damn straight," Tom replied, staring at his bus with love.

"Does Grim know you do that?" Ben interjected. "Use random parts to fix the vehicles up?"

"Absolutely," the engineer cheerfully shot back. "Anything that makes the Depot more efficient!" Ben looked back at the bus and its shiny new grille with the front bumper inches below it. How significant was it that a broken-down bus designed to transport the dead had been modified? Before he could think further on it, Ben heard the engineer greet the Council, slowly trudging closer in their deep-sea gear. "Ah, Councillors! The VW Type 2 is all ready for you." He chucked the keys to Tom. "Be careful with her, mate. I went to Woodstock in that."

Both Ben and Tom turned to face their new ride. The classic Type 2 with flowers boldly painted across the sides and roof of the van was the quintessential hippy dream. Tom looked slightly dejected. Ben imagined going from the power and oomph of the bus to the flower-power mobile was a bit of a downgrade for his friend. Undeterred, they followed the rest of the party, climbing aboard their vehicle for the day.

Without debate, Cornforth claimed the front seat, stretching his legs for the long journey ahead. Tom turned the key in the ignition, causing the van to purr into life. Ben found himself squashed between the two other Council members in the back. Both men scrambled to find their seat belts, causing them to bash Ben in the head with their helmets accidentally. Sitting directly across from them, Winston kindly patted the seat next to him, encouraging Ben to move over.

"I hope you don't get sick travelling backward," Winston said affectionately.

"Better than getting a concussion!"

"Aww, man," Tom groaned from the driver's seat. "The tape deck's jammed. What's the point of adding a tape deck to this hunk of junk if it doesn't work?" he lamented.

"We could listen to whatever's stuck in the player," suggested Ben. Tom sighed with resignation and pressed play. The pleasant opening riffs of Cliff Richard and the Shadows' "Summer Holiday" breezed through the van's tinny speakers. Tom looked to his passengers in the back.

"This isn't going to work," whinged the Reaper.

"Nonsense," countered Winston. "I think it's jaunty. Let's go!"

With Winston's command, the van steadily chugged out of the workshop and through the Depot of the Dead. Noticing Ben was inside, the Reapers stopped in their tracks and moved aside for the vehicle to make its way to the exit unobstructed. While a couple of the Reapers couldn't resist singing along with Cliff Richard's ode to the perfect vacation, the rest of the rabble resumed their chanting from earlier. Winston cocked an eyebrow in surprise at the reception Ben was receiving from the residents of the AfterLife but chose not to acknowledge it openly. The van reached the exit of the Depot and the chanting dissolved into respectful applause that Ben could hear until the Reapers were nearly out of sight.

Ben wasn't the only one to hear the applause. Grim had a perfect view of the Depot of the Dead from his chambers and walked to the window when the chanting started. With no doubt that the rapturous reception was for the Anomaly, Grim felt the rage cascade inside of him and threaten to overwhelm him completely. A quill in his hand crumbled to dust as he clenched his fist. His loathing resentment rolled over him, consuming his mind with one menacing thought.

It's time to remind everyone why they call me the Grim Reaper.

30

"If there's one thing to take away from all your training, remember this. Rooftops are the perfect place to catch some sun." Peyton took note of Jade's advice as if it were one of the Ten Commandments. The two Guardian Angels had just arrived at Lucy's house, and Jade was not afraid to stretch out across the roof and make herself at home. The sun beamed over the street with only a couple of wispy, inoffensive clouds joining it in the sky. "They'll be here soon," Jade advised her protege. "Might as well chill out until they get here."

Guardian Angels had a much easier time journeying to and from the AfterLife than the Reapers. Soaring hundreds of feet in the air, Angels could avoid the toxic atmosphere that perished the flesh and bone of their harvesting rivals. As if that wasn't enough, Angels spent their time in Borrowed Heaven attending classes focused on physical and mental wellbeing and engaging in various spa treatments considered mandatory. As a result, Guardian Angels experienced no ill effects from going on assignment. The fact was that Angels were simply far more resilient when it came to venturing outside. Jade could happily have laid on that rooftop all day without the slightest of repercussions.

"Ooh ooh, I think they're here!" Peyton announced with a high-pitched squeak. This is so exciting!" Sure enough, as Jade looked down, she could see Tom and Ben emerge from a van with Winston and the Councillors, who looked dressed to explore the Lost City of Atlantis.

Usually unfazed by most things, Jade couldn't help but feel a pang of nervous energy in her chest. She knew in her gut that what happened here today had the potential to change the AfterLife forever. Jade took a deep breath and glided down to greet the arrivals.

"How does it feel to be back, Councillor?" Jade asked Cornforth, spotting a wondrous expression on his face.

"It all looks very different," he admitted. "Things have certainly changed a lot in 350 years."

"We'll keep you right, CorCor," replied Tom, seizing the opportunity to test out his nickname for the distinguished councilman. The looks of disgust from the other councillors confirmed it hadn't landed well.

"So what's the plan?" Cornforth piped up. "Stand here and wait until the boy's not decomposing?"

"Well, that's one option, but I have another idea," Jade replied. "You see, Tom, Peyton, and I have all had some very eventful experiences with Ben here, and I thought rather than tell you it would be easier to show you." Cornforth couldn't help but look enthralled.

"I'm game. How about you boys?" Cornforth's two peers murmured in agreement. Jade motioned to Ben and took him to one side.

"Are you ready to go in?"

"I think so," Ben replied. "I didn't expect there to be so many of us."

"Pretend that we aren't here. Lucy's expecting you this time, so hopefully, she won't be so scared." Jade shot a dirty look at Tom and Peyton, who were already heading to the front door to let themselves in. Stopping dead in their tracks, Jade turned back to Ben and smiled. "I'll deal with everyone else. You'll know what to do."

However, in Ben's mind, that was the problem. Standing inside Lucy's house, Ben had no idea what to do now he was there. Lucy's experience with the medium may have gone well, but that was entirely different to this. Any time he had been close to Lucy since his death, it had gone horribly wrong. Whether this was his ticket to a second life or his chance to say goodbye, Ben didn't want to unsettle Lucy any more than he already had, and certainly not at the expense of his own freedom.

A quick scan downstairs found no sign of Lucy, so the search continued upstairs. Cornforth and his friends foolishly went first, causing a gridlocked procession up the staircase. Ben and the others stood impatiently as the Council of Reapers plodded up each step as if they were exploring uncharted waters. *Pretend the rest aren't here. That's going to be easy,* Ben thought to himself, waiting impatiently for the retired Reapers to get to the top of the stairs and onto the landing. On Jade's orders, Tom and Peyton stayed with her downstairs until the bottleneck on the staircase resolved itself. Glancing back down at them, Ben noticed Tom admiring a photograph on the wall of Lucy posing with Dave Grohl from Foo Fighters. Taken after a concert, the nicest guy in rock had his arm around Lucy, whose bedraggled hair gave away several hours in a mosh pit. Tom nodded approvingly to himself.

Once the Council members had navigated the stairs in their deep-sea gear, the rest, including Ben, followed suit. While Lucy did well to afford a two-bedroom house on her own, it was nonetheless a modest size. Ben stood with seven other people on Lucy's compact landing; the Council and Winston in their clunky suits, Tom and two Angels, who, while petite, had quite a significant wingspan. This didn't feel like the intimate moment Jade had suggested it would be.

"Right," Jade barked, breaking the inane chattering of the Council. "We need to make some space to show you what Ben can do," She pointed at the two Council members who had accompanied Cornforth on this expedition. "You two can back up into that room behind you."

"But that's a toilet!" one protested.

"We'll leave the door open for you," Jade responded with authority. "Peyton, Tom. I'm going to need you guys to wait at the top of the stairs. Just for now." The pair obliged, leaving much more room for herself,

Ben, Winston and Cornforth, who remained on the landing. "Now, Ben, which room is Lucy's?"

"This one," Ben replied, looking straight ahead. Lucy's bedroom door was ajar, and now the area around him had cleared. Ben could see her for the first time since they'd entered her home. Lucy sat cross-legged on her bed with both gig tickets laid out in front of her. Nervous energy spilt out of the room. In the past, Lucy had had no idea he was there watching over her. This time she was waiting for him.

"What are we standing here for?" Cornforth spluttered. "Let's go inside!"

"Not yet," Jade insisted, noticing some hesitance from Ben. "What's the matter?" Ben didn't respond. Jade's question had hit hard. Something felt different, but he couldn't put his finger on it. The rest of the expedition respectfully gave Ben time to piece his thoughts together. The silence gave him his answer.

"There's no music," Ben realised. "She always has music on." He looked across to another room on the landing and smiled. "You were right, Jade. I know exactly what to do."

Rather than join Lucy in her bedroom, Ben walked into her spare room that boasted her massive music collection, the same room they had spent night after night playing their favourite albums for each other. Jade followed Ben into the room, and Winston ushered Cornforth to do the same.

Ben stared at the hundreds of records on the shelves dominating the room. Ben had felt such peace the last time he had been here, and that same feeling washed away the nervous energy he'd felt moments earlier. His eyes scanned Lucy's collection until he found the record he was looking for. Ben heard a soft gasp from Cornforth as he pulled his album of choice from the shelf.

"How is that even—" hushed Cornforth in astonishment.

In the next room, Lucy continued to sit on her bed, staring at the tickets in front of her. Following her experience with Astrid, she decided not to tell Jamie about what happened after he left. It was hard enough to believe, without having to convince others. From the moment Astrid had told her to stay in the following night, Lucy had gone straight home and waited. She hadn't dared answer the phone or look out the window for fear of missing something. Instead, Lucy had sat in her room, looking at those tickets and waiting. The hours had drifted by in complete silence.

Suddenly the silence was over. Acoustic guitar drifted quietly into the room. Lucy checked her phone to make sure it hadn't set itself off by mistake. As she sat and listened, she realised the music she could hear was coming from the next room. Her heart pounded as she climbed off her bed and walked warily towards her spare room.

Lucy hadn't touched her record player in days. She was sure she had unplugged it the last time she'd used it. Yet somehow, "Fire and Rain" by James Taylor crackled through the speakers as her precious copy of *Sweet Baby James* spun on the turntable. Her eyes welled up, staring at the record, the words meaning more to her than they ever had before. Lucy caught the chair behind her as her legs began to give way, and she sat with tears streaming down her face.

Emotion fell over everyone in the room. Although hard to make out inside a diver's helmet, Jade thought she could detect a sniffle or two from Cornforth. She couldn't help but hold back a tear or two herself. As the second verse began, Jade noticed Peyton step into the room.

"Watch this," she mouthed so as not to spoil the moment and motioned toward the window. On command, raindrops began to hit against the window, loud enough to be noticed but not so loud as to drown out Lucy's favourite song. The tears Jade was trying to hold back started to fall. She nodded at Peyton in approval. Her trainee was beginning to get the hang of this.

Ben hadn't noticed any of this. Instead, he was focused on the moment, watching Lucy listen to the song that meant so much to her. The other times he'd been near her, she had left with fear or confusion in her eyes. Lucy may have sat there in tears, but Ben could see no fear in her eyes. He realised Lucy must be experiencing a rush of feelings, but the one he could see in her eyes was happiness. As the song faded, Ben remembered what Lucy had told him the first time they had listened to it together.

"One day, you'll listen to this song and kick yourself for not realising sooner how perfect it is."

Oh, how right she was.

Lucy sat in total exhaustion with the end of "Fire and Rain" bringing silence back to the room. Before the next track on the album could start, Lucy noticed the needle carefully lift and place itself back to the side where it belonged. After flying glass and mini tsunamis, nothing surprised Lucy anymore, but it did make her wonder. Was Ben there in the room with her? Battling every instinct that made her feel stupid or crazy, Lucy wiped her tears and cleared her throat.

"Thank you, Ben," she whispered. "I miss you." Ben choked up at Lucy's heartfelt words. Cornforth, Peyton and Jade filed out of the room. Ben watched Lucy take *Sweet Baby James* from the record player and examine the disc intently. Knowing how much her words had meant to him, it broke his heart that she couldn't hear the words he was about to say.

"I miss you too."

Ben walked out of the room with his head hung low. He'd never expected the night's events to have such a strong impact on him. Ben took a moment to look back into the room and saw Lucy still looking at the vinyl record. He was in no rush to look away in case this was the last time. A familiar, bony hand clasped his shoulder.

"Don't worry, dude. No matter what happens next, you're coming back. I promise."

31

The mood on the journey back to the AfterLife was one of quiet reflection. Every passenger inside the VW had a unique perspective of what had taken place in Lucy's spare room. Edging closer to the AfterLife, Cornforth wasn't afraid to open the faceplate on his helmet to have a puff of his pipe. The comforting smell of tobacco and patchouli wafted across the van as Tom continued to drive the group home. Ben couldn't help but wonder what the esteemed councillor was thinking. No one had said a word since leaving Lucy's house, but Cornforth's focused nibbling on the mouthpiece of his pipe gave away that he was deep in thought. Winston too looked submerged in contemplation. For the most part, the Gatekeeper stared straight ahead, completely lost in his own worries and anxieties. Then at seemingly random intervals, he would look down at his watch and tut to himself. It was unclear to Ben whether Winston was in a rush to return to the AfterLife or whether he was hoping their journey would last an eternity.

"Summer Holiday" had long worn out its welcome, so the group had reached an unspoken consensus for the journey to continue without music. While the slight purring of the VW's engine was pleasant enough, it did little to shift the air of tension in the cab. Ben had never enjoyed silence and found the lack of conversation rather unsettling.

He was about to break the ice when he noticed gentle humming coming from the front seat. Ben turned around to a face full of smoke from Cornforth's pipe. He tried his hardest not to cough, determined to hear more of the crooning that had caught his attention. Sure enough, Tom was the source of the noise, singing the same song Ben had chosen to play for Lucy moments earlier. Ben smiled to himself. "Fire and Rain" may not have the usual heavy metal trappings that Tom favoured on a long drive, but the Reaper had obviously developed a soft spot for it.

Ben looked out the window in time to see the Depot of the Dead emerge into view through the thick smog of the AfterLife. Usually bustling with Reapers and their passengers, the Depot was, for some reason, completely empty. Noticing many abandoned vehicles as they passed, Ben sensed something did not feel right. The inoffensive smell from Cornforth's pipe seemed to grow in intensity and take on a far less pleasant odour. As the stench overwhelmed Ben's nostrils, he heard Tom cough and splutter at the wheel. Tom addressed Cornforth in the passenger seat, still keeping his eye on the road.

"Hey, CorCor, any chance you could put the pipe away?"

"I'm not smoking my pipe, old boy," came the reply from inside Cornforth's helmet. Ben continued to stare out of the window at the deserted Depot. The typical gaseous environment of the AfterLife did appear more intense than he remembered. In fact, the fog seemed to be getting thicker by the second. Even with his fog lights on, the mist was so thick it had reached the point that Tom could no longer see well enough to drive. The Reaper had no choice but to park in the middle of the Depot. Both Ben and Tom continued to choke on the fumes polluting the van.

"Can't you smell that, Winnie?" coughed Tom. Like the Councillors, the Gatekeeper was still sat in full diving gear, his helmet protecting him from the vapour.

"I'm afraid I don't," began Winston. His expression changed

dramatically upon looking out the window. "Oh my goodness," he exclaimed. "That's smoke. I think there's a fire!" Pure fear flashed across the faces of the Councillors. Not one made any advance toward moving out of their seats. Tom, in contrast, leapt from the driver's seat and out of the van, hoping to find the source of the smoke. Several tense seconds passed before Tom flung open the side door of the VW.

"I can't see any fires around here. I think the Depot is safe," Tom confirmed, holding his cloak over his mouth. Winston breathed a sigh of relief.

"Is anyone hurt out there?" he asked with concern.

"It's hard to see Winnie. It doesn't look like there's anyone here," Tom replied before adding, "It should be safe to come out." One by one, Ben, Winston and the Reapers clambered into the gloom. As they looked around, the Depot looked even more desolate than it had from the safe confines of the van. Tears streamed down Ben's face as the smoke spilt into his eyes. Squinting slightly, he noticed flames dancing in the distance.

"Over there," Ben pointed, choking on the smoke that continued to billow up his nose and down his throat. His eyes adjusted, and the flames came further into focus. Ben felt a deep sense of dread rise from the pit of his stomach. "Is that where I think it is?" Tom looked across the Depot in alarm.

"Dude, I sure hope not!" The Reaper sprinted in the direction of the fire. Knowing there was no chance of Winston and the others keeping up, Ben gave chase, pursuing Tom through the winding streets and alleys near City Hall. Following Tom through a familiar side street, the smoke got thicker and thicker. Sensing Ben was behind him, Tom held out a hand to ensure he didn't lose him in the mist. Although billows of smoke impaired his vision, Ben could still hear hushed chattering the further down the street he ran. Through the smog, Ben could make out scores of people sitting in groups in front of a smouldering building.

The flames they had seen were now extinguished, with three skeletons manhandling a giant hose to put the fire out.

With the blaze under control, the atmosphere started to clear, confirming Ben's fears. The Eternal Alcove was no more. The once nondescript building was now a shell, and the other buildings nearby were also fire-damaged. Ben turned to Tom, who looked shell-shocked at the Alcove's demise. Tom caught the attention of an important-looking man with a clipboard who was surveying the damage.

"We got a page that the Alcove was on fire at around 1800 hours," explained the gentleman. "With all the alcohol in that place, it didn't take long for the fire to get out of hand."

"Do you know how the fire started?" Tom asked. Ben didn't get an opportunity to hear the answer. Instead, he was distracted by a restrained sobbing coming from a gathering of skeletons behind him. Ben turned around to see Gulliver weeping into his hands. Usually immaculately dressed, Gulliver's waistcoat was sodden with ash, and even his skull had a murky, grey complexion. Sat around him were three other skeletons, all much smaller than him. While hard to tell when they were comprised entirely of bone, Ben guessed they were almost certainly children. Ben took a seat next to the barman.

"I'm so sorry, Gulliver," Ben sighed. Gulliver lifted his head from his hands and turned to Ben. The darkness where his eyes once were tinged with anguish.

"I reaped for years," Gulliver replied. "I had to take my children out on the road because I couldn't get anyone to watch them." He looked at his kids, who nestled into him sadly. "Their beautiful faces withered away because no one would help us. The Eternal Alcove was supposed to be our fresh start. I wouldn't have to sacrifice my children or myself anymore." Gulliver's teeth gritted together, his grief making way for anger. "He couldn't even give us that!"

"He?"

"Grim!" Gulliver wailed. "He was no help to us when I was forced to expose my family to the outside. Then he comes to my place of work, my home and destroys it." Tom immediately darted around upon hearing Gulliver's version of events.

"Grim did this?" he gasped.

"I've never seen him like that," Gulliver continued. "I didn't think he even knew about the Alcove. He walked into the bar in this rage, so full of hatred. I couldn't even look straight at him." Gulliver grabbed his smallest child and covered the pits where their ears once were on both sides of their skull. "My spirit bottles started exploding. Cocktail glasses on the bar started flying all over. I couldn't even tell you where the fire started. The next thing I know, the whole place is engulfed in smoke. I ran upstairs to grab the children, but there was so much smoke we had to escape out the back window."

"Why would he do such a thing?" asked Ben in shock.

"I don't know," Gulliver sniffed. "I mean, we're all dead, aren't we? It's not as if the fire could kill us, but it could damn sure turn my death upside down." He looked down at his monogrammed apron. "We have nothing left. We have nowhere to go. Grim has taken everything from us!" Tom knelt next to Gulliver and wrapped an arm around him.

"You can stay with me tonight, Gully," Tom kindly offered. He looked at Gulliver's young family. "You all can. Stay as long as you need until you're back on your feet." Gulliver sobbed happily.

"Oh, Tom, I don't know how to thank you!"

"I've spent plenty of lock-ins passed out in the Alcove. It's the least I can do." Tom fished out a set of keys from his cloak pocket and handed them to Gulliver. "Mine is apartment 0001 on the ground floor of the Reaper high-rise. Get yourself back for a shower and some rest. Ben and I will join you soon."

Gulliver gratefully rounded up his rabble of children, and together they made their way out of the dusky side street. The barman looked back at where the Eternal Alcove once stood one last time before sadly turning around and walking away. Ben couldn't help but feel responsible for the decimation of Gulliver's home.

"I should have accepted my fate," Ben said as Gulliver's family disappeared in the distance. "Grim is angry at me. This is my fault."

"That is not true," replied Tom firmly. "You didn't ask for any of this. Grim is a cold-hearted, evil man."

"He isn't evil!" a voice protested. Winston had finally caught up after stripping out of his diving suit and was only now witnessing the extent of Grim's destruction. "Grim is scared. Scared of what it could mean if you win this appeal. Scared of what that means for his vision of the AfterLife. A man with that much fear can be a very powerful man." Tom felt compelled to speak.

"I'm sorry, Winnie, I know he's your friend, and you have known him for a long time, but I don't think he's that same person anymore. You've said yourself that you're scared at the lengths he is willing to go to. Look around you, dude. He did this." Winston observed the carnage with a desperate look in his eyes. Ben fell silent. He couldn't begin to imagine the torment Winston was going through.

"I believe there is a way back for him," Winston confessed. "However, that's my cross to bear, not yours." He looked at Tom. The conflict was etched across his face for all to see. "What we can both agree on is that right now, Grim is a dangerous soul. This isn't just about the appeal anymore, my boys. The entire fate of the AfterLife hangs in the balance."

32

Councillor Cornforth invited the boardroom to sit, signalling the beginning of another day of evidence for Ben's appeal. The mood of everyone present was particularly sombre following the events of the previous evening. Word had spread across the AfterLife about the fire at the Eternal Alcove, and the rumour and innuendo were sky-high. Many had heard Grim started the fire but refused to believe it. Always a symbol of stability and authority, it was inconceivable that Grim could do something so awful. Yet the appeal had pushed Grim to the edge on more than one occasion. He wasn't the same Architect everyone knew and respected.

Cornforth began to address those present when the doors to Grim's chambers creaked open. A dramatic hush fell over the room, with every last person watching Grim saunter into the gallery and take a seat. Jade leaned over to Ben.

"What a bastard," she hissed. "I can't believe he has the gall to waltz in here after what he's done." On Ben's other side, Tom stared daggers at the Architect. After spending half the night comforting Gulliver and his family, Tom understood more than most the true impact of Grim's actions. Ben noticed Tom's fists clench before Winston looked at the Reaper and mouthed a stern warning.

"No."

Cornforth was unfazed by Grim's arrival. Picking up where he left off, he even made a point of greeting his superior.

"Thank you for making yourself present for these proceedings, Mr Grim, sir. I have some information I trust you will find most enlightening." Grim sat eerily still, giving no indication he was rattled or concerned.

"I look forward to it," he replied calmly. Cornforth shuffled through some papers on his desk and pulled out a scruffy-looking sheet from the middle. He held it up and stared at it closely.

"The results from the bus's second service have come back," he grumbled, "but for the death of me, I don't know what all this mumbo jumbo means. Do we have someone who can break this down into layman's terms for me?"

"I could take a look, sir," came a voice from the gallery. Norman Wells rose from his chair, looking gaunt and pale but on the mend since the last time he'd appeared in the boardroom. "That's if it pleases the Council?" Cornforth nodded in agreement. Ben noticed Grim flinch for the first time since he'd sat down. Practically a zombie when he last gave evidence, Norman was far more in control of his faculties this time. Cornforth invited Norman to approach his bench and handed over the oil-stained sheet of paper.

"Amazing things, these automobiles, but well beyond my time on Earth," Cornforth explained. "What exactly does all this mean?" Norman looked over the document meticulously, uhm-ing and ah-ing as he read.

"Yes," he finally said. "My memory's a bit hazy. I've not been well since I serviced this vehicle. However, I seem to recall our findings were the same." Tom glared at Grim once again. It was no secret why the engineer wasn't his usual self.

"The last time you addressed this Council, you advised that the bus involved in the collision had passed its service," Cornforth replied. "I understand this may have been under duress, but I must ask, do you stand by your statement?" After some consideration, Norman gave his answer.

"Yes, sir, I do. As memory serves, this vehicle met the standards of the Depot of the Dead's MOT examination." Ben felt instantly deflated. He knew that the outcome of the service was an integral part of his defence. With the wrong result, his extraordinary feats outside of the AfterLife may not be enough proof that he should go back.

"May I please address Mr Wells?" Jade asked out of nowhere. From his seat in the gallery, Grim shot the notion down.

"Mr Bostwick has been prohibited from engaging further with this appeal. Therefore you being here is frankly superfluous."

"Once again, I feel the need to respectfully remind you of my authority in this matter," Cornforth warned. "Please do not undermine my jurisdiction, or I will have to ask you to return to your chambers!" All eyes were on Grim for his reaction. In all his years as the Architect of the AfterLife, nobody had openly challenged him like this. Grim sat still, bristling with fury but did not say another word. Satisfied he had quelled Grim's attempts to usurp his command, Cornforth answered Jade's question. "Young lady, if you wish to ask Mr Wells a few questions, now is the time." Jade nodded and turned her attention to Norman, who stared back nervously.

"There's nothing to be scared of," Jade said softly. "I'm not looking to disprove anything you've said. I was hoping to take further advantage of your expertise." Norman smiled apprehensively. "So, to confirm, both your service and the one requested by Councillor Cornforth deem the bus passed. Is that correct?"

"Yes, ma'am."

"And what does it mean to say that it passed?"

"As I told Councillor Cornforth, it means that the vehicle met the standards of the Depot of the Dead's MOT examination," Norman confirmed.

"Were there any advisories or recommendations?" Jade asked.

"I'm not quite sure what you're getting at," Norman admitted timidly. Jade sensed Norman's anxiety rising.

"Norman, no one's out to get you," she reassured the engineer. "I want to ensure I fully understand these services' results. I'm a Guardian Angel after all, we don't rely on vehicles to get around." Norman relaxed, showing some colour in his cheeks for the first time. "When I said recommendations, all I meant was, was there anything wrong with the bus that wouldn't cause it to fail but should be monitored?"

"Ah, I get it!" Norman replied confidently. "We call them Future Guidance, although some stuff we fix on the fly. Speeds things up a bit, you know."

"Was there any Future Guidance on Tom's bus?" Jade asked. Ben felt a sharp series of nudges in his side from Tom.

"They changed the bumpers!" Tom whispered excitedly.

"Well, that bus is a beaut, but the bumpers aren't the original ones," explained Norman. "At some point on a previous service, we've replaced the originals for some reason. The problem is we've had to use whatever we can find. There's no guarantee they were the same ones. In fact, I'd argue it's next to impossible."

"And why's that?" Jade's questions appeared to be leading somewhere that concerned Grim as Ben witnessed him shuffling awkwardly in his seat.

"A vintage model like that bus is in short supply." Norman consulted the notes one more time. "It looks like they replaced the front grille too. We considered doing that during our service but added it as Future Guidance."

"So this bus has bumpers from a different vehicle and a front grille from somewhere else," Jade summarised. "Over the years, it's almost certainly had a new tyre or two, maybe even some bigger work like a new exhaust pipe. If what was once a defunct, vintage model of an

American school bus is now an assortment of all different parts from all kinds of vehicles, is it really the same bus anymore?" Norman appeared deep in contemplation. The entire boardroom hung on his response.

"I guess it isn't, ma'am."

"And if it's no longer a defunct model of a bus we thought it was, does that affect its viability to transport the dead safely?" Norman slipped into deep thought once more.

"Very possibly." The Council descended into frenzied chatter. Cornforth banged his gavel furiously.

"Order Council! Let's show some decorum."

"One final question, if I may," Jade continued. Cornforth nodded in approval. "Mr Wells, where did this practice of using random vehicle parts start? Was this something the Depot of the Dead engineers began off their own backs?" Norman shuffled nervously.

"I don't feel comfortable saying," he mumbled, paying close attention to his shuffling feet.

"Mr Wells, I can assure you there will be no repercussions to you or your colleagues," Cornforth promised. All you have done today is help us with our enquiries." Norman glanced over at Grim, who continued to seethe in the gallery. Norman gulped before coming clean.

"It came as a direct order from Mr Grim in the name of efficiency and order."

"Thank you so much, Norman," Jade smiled. "You did great! No further questions."

Norman scuttled back to his seat in the gallery, attempting to avoid the gaze of Grim. Ben looked over at the Architect, who was extremely close to losing his composure. While Grim had yet to explode the same way he had previously, Ben was still swept into a sea of discontent, feeding off the bleak aura radiating from him. Lost in the dark, another jab to the ribs brought Ben back to reality.

"It's your turn, dude." Ben scanned the boardroom and saw all eyes were on him. Cornforth looked back at Ben with anticipation. Making a concerted effort to avoid his eyes shifting back to Grim, Ben made his way to the Hot Box. Ben closed his eyes and took a deep breath. Cornforth began in a manner which took Ben by surprise.

"My boy, I would like to start by offering you my most sincere gratitude." Ben wasn't sure what to say.

"You do?"

"Absolutely," confirmed the councillor as he turned to address his peers. "Taylor, Grantham, and I witnessed something extraordinary on our expedition with this young man and his Reaper yesterday. The man you see before you was able to ..." Cornforth paused to find the right word, "manipulate the environment in ways I have never seen a dead person do. He used this ability to send a message to a loved one right before our eyes. It was beautiful. It was poignant and made me wish the relationship between the living and the dead was a stronger one. I feel truly privileged to have been there." Grim continued to glower from his seat in the gallery. Ben tried his best to ignore him.

"Thank you, sir," Ben replied. "It was a special moment for me too."

"When did you learn you could interact with the living world in such a way?" Cornforth asked directly.

"It was during our first trip back in the Motorwagen. I kicked a glass bottle in frustration. Not only did it smash, but my friend Lucy noticed it." Cornforth seemed to prepare himself for his next question, almost as if he seemed nervous.

"We've seen once already during these proceedings the importance of sensitivity when discussing one's death," he eventually said. Tom hung his head sadly, remembering the vicious lengths Claude had gone to when he was in the Hot Box. "I ask this with great respect Mr May, and only because it is imperative to your case. What do you remember of your death?" Ben relayed every detail of that transformative moment. The sudden pressure he felt in his side. The unbearable pain as he heard his bones crunch. The sheer force of being thrown several feet down the road but not seeing so much as a bicycle to collide with. Cornforth listened, enthralled by every word. Discussing his death in such vivid detail left Ben feeling dejected and low. He held back tears as he described the sting of the rainwater against the blood and wounds across his body. Cornforth raised a hand, inviting Ben to stop.

"I can't help but notice a parallel between yourself, a man who is almost a patchwork of life and death, and the very bus that hit you; a jigsaw of parts from all kinds of vehicles." The power of Cornforth's words felt like an uppercut to the jaw. "Does that make any sense?" Before Ben could answer, Grim leapt out of his seat.

"I've entertained this circus for long enough!" Grim growled, his voice thundering around the boardroom. Council members cowered as their glorious leader unleashed a diatribe of hatred and bile. "Councillor Cornforth, I conceded to you overseeing this appeal, but I can see this was a terrible decision on my part. It is time for the Anomaly and I to have a little chat!"

33

Cornforth rose from his seat at the bench, incensed by Grim's sudden outburst in front of the entire Council of Reapers. This wasn't the first time the two had been at odds, but everything seemed to have been building up to this one momentous confrontation.

"I have tried my best to respect your sovereignty throughout this entire process, but your actions are no longer becoming of the leader of our Council," Cornforth boomed at his superior.

"My actions?" scoffed Grim. "Your residence over this matter has been nothing short of a joke! You have shown blatant bias towards the Anomaly on more than one occasion, but it was your dewy-eyed speech about the relationship between the living and the dead that made me want to vomit." Grim's voice took on an echoed roar as he struggled to keep his vitriol inside. "You don't have the balls to preside over such an important hearing, so I will now resume control of my Council." A bitter chill filled the entire boardroom. Without taking his eyes off the Architect, Cornforth called out to the Council of Reapers.

"In the spirit of preserving the honour of this Council, I implore any of you that wishes for our leader to address Mr May to raise their hand." As the words left Cornforth's mouth, Grim directed his attention towards the panel of Reapers who had observed the appeal from the very start. Slowly but surely, a smattering of hands started to rise, some out of loyalty, others out of fear. When Grim saw that just over half the

Council were sat with a hand in the air, he seized his opportunity.

"It's settled!" he gloated infuriatingly. "Don't you just love democracy?"

Ben had stood quietly during Grim's clash with Cornforth. It took everything in Ben's being to push away the hate and loathing oozing from beneath Grim's cloak. Standing face to face with the Grim Reaper, Ben realised he was the personification of everything he'd ever feared. He had found the strength to withstand him once before and knew he had to do it again.

"Let's get one thing out of the way, Anomaly. No one has ever disputed the fact that your expiration was premature," Grim sneered arrogantly. "However, I have heard nothing over the last few days to suggest that I should rule to have your death reversed. I've heard sob stories, and I've seen the truth bent to cast myself as the villain. What I haven't seen is any tangible evidence that I should overturn millennia of law and tradition to give you your life back." Ben did not answer straight away. Instead, he took his time to consider every word Grim used. Rather than fixating on Grim's negativity polluting the boardroom, he focused on the meaning behind his words and the inflections he used. No longer afraid, Ben knew that the tidal wave of nihilism spilling out of Grim was masking his driving emotion.

"Can I tell you what I can see?" Ben asked firmly, his voice unwavering. "I see fear. I spent my life and most of my death terrified of you and what you represent. But as I stand here talking to you right now, all I see is someone who is just as scared as I am."

"Scared?" roared Grim. The familiar spirals of darkness faded into view. "What do I have to be scared of?"

"You don't know," Ben retorted. "You called me an Anomaly the first time you met me. That means I am different. That means I defy everything you have ever known about this world you have created. I make you feel uncertain and out of control, and that scares you more than anything."

"Shut up!" Grim yelled, his voice reverberating again across the boardroom. "I'm warning you. You've seen what I am capable of!" Tom leapt out of his seat.

"We saw the fire!" he yelled, buoyed by Ben's lack of fear. "You ruined Gulliver's AfterLife just to send a message."

"You're damn right I did!" shouted Grim, owning up to the blaze. "You and the rest of you ingrate Reapers need to remember who is in fucking charge!" The louder Grim raised his voice, the heavier it crashed around the room, screeching and distorting in everyone's ears. The Architect's chosen phrase of "ingrate Reapers" had caused pandemonium across the Council in attendance. The cacophony of noise was jarring for Ben, but he remained focused and steady. Grim's fear continued to manifest stronger than ever, the darkness spilling into black clouds that collected around the ornate chandeliers above. However, Ben was not phased. He saw the petulant display for what it was, fear at its most pure and violent. Ben started hearing the Council of Reapers complaining through the wall of noise.

"Ingrates, are we?"

"Grim did set the fire!"

"How dare he speak to us that way!" Cornforth tried to make himself heard amongst the chaos.

"The Architect of the AfterLife has shown that he no longer has the faculties to preside over this Council," he declared. "I propose a vote of no confidence in our Grim Reaper. All those in favour?" The same Reapers who had raised their hands minutes earlier did so again. However, their hands rose this time in defiance of their ruler rather than fear. Within seconds every member of the Council had their hand aloft in favour of ousting Grim there and then. Grim howled with fury as thunder began to rumble from the clouds his torment had created. With an order from Cornforth, four burly skeleton guards rushed toward their usurped leader and attempted to restrain him.

"Don't fight them," pleaded Winston to his long-time partner. "Please calm down before it's too late." Grim didn't hear a word as he grappled with the security and tried to stand his ground. Without warning, a flash of light lit up the entire room. Ben looked up to see a bolt of lightning had emerged from the darkest cloud that hovered just below the beams across the ceiling. As quickly as it arrived, the bolt struck Cornforth on the centre of his head, dropping him to the floor. Winston and a Council member ran to Cornforth's aid, but he lay motionless atop the steps leading to his bench. The commotion in the boardroom ground to a halt. The only sound that Ben could hear was a crash of thunder from above. The rumbling began to diminish as the security guards finally overpowered Grim and dragged him from the boardroom. The clouds drifted away and followed Grim out the doors, which slammed heavily, announcing his exit.

Ben sat in the Hot Box, completely stunned by the events of the last few minutes. Cornforth still hadn't moved, and more Reapers had gathered around in an attempt to resuscitate him. Tom sat down next to Ben and joined him in the Hot Box.

"Well, that escalated quickly," the Reaper gasped in shock.

"What will happen to Cornforth?" asked Ben with concern. "Is he going to be ok?" Tom looked over at the fallen councillor.

"I don't know. Who knows what Grim is capable of."

Seconds felt like minutes as Winston, and various members of the Council attended to the fallen Cornforth. Jade also volunteered her services as everyone attempted to bring the councillor back to consciousness. Besides the guarded discussion of the Council, who were trying in vain to resuscitate Cornforth, no one in the boardroom uttered a single word. Jade stood up to walk back to Ben and Tom in the Hot Box. From where Ben was sitting, he caught a glimpse of a gaping hole in Cornforth's skull, smouldering with smoke. Jade approached the Hot Box with a grave expression on her face.

"It's not looking good," she said, her voice full of woe. "I think he's gone."

"Gone?" Tom exclaimed. "He's already dead!"

"I don't know what to say," replied Jade, trying to understand the situation herself. "He's not moving. Nothing's working." Tom tried his hardest to contemplate Cornforth's fate. It was well established that too much exposure outside the AfterLife could cause a Reaper's body and soul to perish. But beyond that, everyone understood that the AfterLife was forever. Was it possible that Grim had put an end to Cornelius Cornforth once and for all? Had Tom just witnessed Cornforth's second death?

After several more minutes of attending to Cornforth's body, Winston stood to one side, allowing four Reapers to respectfully lift the councillor and carry him into Grim's chambers at the back of the boardroom. Winston returned to his seat next to Jade, avoiding eye contact with anyone. Staring aimlessly, he failed to notice Godfrey Marmaduke, one of the most senior members of the Council of Reapers, standing to address the room.

"Esteemed guests, I am Godfrey Marmaduke, and as of a few minutes ago, I became the longest-serving member of this Council." His words took a mournful tone as he acknowledged the departure of his dear friend. "I have never known such a dark day in all my years in this privileged position. I feel compelled to continue the work of Councillor Cornforth, who stood steadfast in the face of corruption and wrongdoing." Marmaduke climbed the steps to the judicial bench and sat down. "All those in favour of exonerating Benjamin Michael May from his death and returning him back to Life?"

Ben could barely catch his breath as he witnessed scores of hands across the Council go up in the air. With no hesitation from a single member, they all voted in favour of Marmaduke's motion. Ben couldn't believe his eyes. He was finally going home. Marmaduke nodded in satisfaction.

"Very well," he announced. "About time justice was served." He turned to Winston, who jumped at the mention of his name. "I trust you have kept the key to the Third Door safe all these years?"

"The Third Door, you say?" Winston stuttered. The poor Gatekeeper had been so lost in his thoughts he had missed the all-important vote.

"Indeed, Winston," replied Marmaduke. "It is you who has it and not Grim, isn't it?" Winston nodded.

"Absolutely. I am the Gatekeeper, after all."

"In that case, I'll leave the particulars to you," Marmaduke responded before looking toward Ben. "Mr May. I must tell you that no soul has ever been given the gift of walking through the Third Door. You must promise this Council that you will never utter a word of your experience to anyone upon resuming your life," he warned. "If we hear of any disclosure of your time in the AfterLife, the Council will revoke your life immediately. Do you understand?"

"I do," replied Ben. "I promise I won't say a word. I don't think anyone would believe me, quite frankly."

"Then, I officially conclude proceedings today. Congratulations, Mr May. You've got your life back!"

With a thump of the gavel, Ben's appeal was over. A roar of approval rang throughout the boardroom, with people in the gallery applauding wildly at the ruling. Ben didn't even get a chance to turn around before Peyton, who had bounded over like an Alsatian from her seat in the gallery, threw her arms around him in the tightest hug he'd ever felt in life or death. Once Peyton released her vice-like grip, it was Jade's turn to congratulate him.

"You did it!" she beamed, extending her arms for a hug of her own.

"No, you did," Ben replied gratefully. "I couldn't have done this without you."

With Ben occupied with the Guardian Angels, Tom noticed Winston was still sitting in his seat, staring into the ether. He approached the Gatekeeper and sat beside him.

"I thought the Third Door was a myth," he admitted, breaking Winston from his trance.

"It's easier that way," he responded distractedly. "The less who know about it, the better."

"Are you ok, Winnie?"

"I don't know," Winston confessed before changing his mind. "I will be. Yes, it'll be fine." Winston got to his feet and began to head out of the boardroom. "Once you've all said your goodbyes, get your bus from the Depot and meet me at the Pathway."

"Don't you want to say goodbye?" Tom asked.

"I will get the opportunity at the Pathway," replied Winston sharply. "There's something I have to do first."

34

The AfterLife didn't look quite so gloomy when Ben stepped outside City Hall for the last time. In reality, nothing had changed, but to Ben, it was as if someone had reimagined purgatory in glorious technicolour. Swarms of people broke into rapturous applause upon the sight of the man who beat death emerging from the innocuous little shack. Tom led Ben through the crowd, who all offered Ben handshakes, pats on the back and kind words.

"You did it, kid!"

"Enjoy your life!"

"Don't waste your second chance!"

This kind of attention would generally be Ben's idea of Hell. However, he was in such a good mood he was more than happy to revel in everyone's good wishes. Reaching the end of the mob, Ben turned around to see Jade and Peyton wading their way through to join him.

"This is amazing!" Peyton screamed with excitement. "You did it, Ben. You freakin' did it!" She wrapped her arms around him with the grip of a boa constrictor. Ben grinned bashfully.

"No, we all did it," he replied. "None of this would have happened without all three of you." As Peyton released Ben from her clutches, he noticed Jade lifting her hood to obscure her flaming red locks. A twinge of sadness pierced through his feeling of triumph.

"Aren't you coming to the Pathway?" he asked.

"I've already gone above my station addressing the Council of Reapers," Jade responded coolly. "There's no way Winston will let me within a hundred feet of the Third Door." Ben looked away in disappointment, hoping no one could see his eyes beginning to well up. "Hey, let's not get too emotional," she continued. "This is what we wanted, right?" Her voice wavered. It caught her by surprise just how difficult she was finding this moment.

"Thank you so much for everything." Ben considered offering Jade a hug goodbye but remembered she wasn't as tactile as her apprentice. He extended his hand for a handshake. To his surprise, Jade rejected it in favour of the warmest of hugs. She ensured she was out of earshot of the others before she shared one last thing.

"Toby knew that you'd win."

"You know Toby?" Ben managed to stutter.

"He would have come himself, but he's not fully trained yet," Jade smirked, knowing what she'd told Ben had likely blown his mind. "Don't worry. He'll let you know when he's with you." With tears in his eyes, Ben watched Jade turn to Peyton and together, they took flight over the murk and smog. Heading back to Borrowed Heaven, Peyton's shrill voice rang across the AfterLife.

"Say hi to Lucy for me."

Both Ben and Tom looked wistfully up in the sky as the Guardian Angels faded out of view. Ben thought about how both Angels had helped him throughout his death. He remembered Jade's covert arrival at the Eternal Alcove and Peyton's not-so-covert tidal wave at the cafe. Then he thought about Jade's final words. The thought that Toby had been watching from afar the whole time was wonderful. On the other hand, Ben felt disappointed at the lost opportunity of seeing his friend.

The Guardian Angels flew out of view, and Ben brought his attention back to ground level. Most of the revellers had moved on from their vigil at City Hall, leaving just Tom and Ben with a smattering of others attending to their own business.

"We've got a bit of time before we meet Winnie," Tom said in an uncharacteristically flat tone. "We can chill at mine 'til then."

The walk to the Reaper high-rise felt awkward somehow. Usually full of enthusiasm and hard to contain, Tom was far more restrained than usual. Even in their most sombre moments together, Tom always had a joke to crack or a tune to hum. This felt different. The minutes passed in silence, and Ben could not understand why Tom was so downbeat. The uncomfortable atmosphere continued all the way back to Tom's apartment, where Gulliver and his children were convalescing. Two of the kids were rifling through Tom's music collection while the third threw himself around the room to Megadeth. Their father had also made himself at home and stood in the kitchen with bottles of spirits in front of him.

"How did it go?" The barman asked.

"We won," Tom replied. "Ben's going home." Ben could hear the happiness in Tom's first statement but couldn't help but notice it was absent from the second.

"Are you ok, Tom?"

"Yeah, dude. Totally fine. Never felt better," the Reaper overcompensated. Ben didn't believe a word of it.

"I think we've been through enough together that we can be honest with each other. You've been quiet since we left City Hall." Realising he'd been rumbled, Tom opened up.

"I'm being so selfish," he began. "It's like, I want you to live, but it's been a blast having you here, so now I'm like wishing you could—" Tom stopped dead in his tracks. "No, man, I'm not even gonna say. I'm not explaining myself properly."

"Maybe this will help," came a voice from the kitchen. Gulliver joined the pair holding two cocktail glasses and a shaker, placing the glasses on the table in the centre of the room. He gave the shaker a theatrical flourish and poured its contents into both glasses. "One ounce of rye whiskey, one ounce of dry vermouth and a final ounce of Campari. I give you the Old Pal!" As always, Gulliver's cocktail was just right for the occasion. Embarrassment flashed across Tom's face. He felt relieved that his skull couldn't blush. With his first sip of Old Pal providing some Dutch courage, Tom tried again.

"What I'm trying to say is that I'm so stoked you get a second chance, but man, am I gonna miss you!"

"I'm going to miss you too," Ben replied. Now it was the Reaper's turn for a hug. Ben contemplated how far they had come since their first meeting. When Tom struck Ben down with his bus, both were filled with confusion and fear. Since then, Ben had explored so many facets of the AfterLife, and Tom had been the one person who had been there for the entire experience. As a Reaper, Ben thought Tom had been the perfect guide most of the time. "So what will you do now?" Ben asked. "I bet you can't wait to get back on the road reaping.

Tom walked over to his wall of fame on the other side of the room. He stared proudly at the litany of legendary rockers he'd provided safe passage to over the years. After a moment of contemplation, he gave an answer that caught Ben off guard.

"Actually, I think I might retire,"

"Retire? But I thought you loved your job?"

"I do," Tom reasoned. "But look at me. I've not got much time left out there, do I? One too many trips back, and I'll be nothing but dust. Plus, there are a couple of seats going on the Council. Maybe I'll shake things up a bit." Ben laughed, surprised at the prospect that Tom may venture into AfterLife politics. "Plus, I've got one more journey in me," Tom continued, "so I have to make sure I make it."

"Which member of Metallica is it then?" joked Ben, assuming Tom wanted to add to his impressive gallery before he traded his scythe for a pipe and slippers.

"Ben, when the time comes, I want to be your Reaper," Tom pledged. "After everything that's happened, I can't imagine anyone else bringing you back here for the real deal. What do you say?" Tom's request deeply touched Ben. He had come to know the Reaper pretty well since his death, and he had never seen him so serious about anything. When Tom disclosed the details of his own death, it had been an intense conversation where the Reaper exposed his most significant weakness. Tom was coming from a position of strength this time with his respectful yet confident wish to be Ben's Reaper.

"I can't think of anyone I'd rather see when my life ends," Ben smiled, joking. "Besides, it can't go any worse than the first time!"

"Well we've had a dress rehearsal now, dude," Tom laughed. "Maybe you'll not freak out so much next time."

Gulliver poured another drink as Tom regaled Ben and his lodgers with his best reaping stories. Tom's tales of meeting his musical heroes were trumped by Gulliver, who claimed that back in 1912, he had arrived in Paris just in time to see a man jump from the Eiffel tower wearing a parachute made of cloth. Even the Rock 'N' Roll Reaper had to concede that the story of the Flying Tailor was a great one. Ben, conversely, tried his best not to vomit at the thought of the poor Frenchman hitting the Parisian pavement. A clock struck the hour on Tom's mantlepiece, and all conversation abruptly stopped. Tom glanced over at the time.

"I think it's time to go. Winnie will be at the Pathway by now." Seeing Tom struggle to hide his sadness at the thought of him leaving, Ben noticed his own mixed emotions. After all the struggle and turmoil involved in appealing his death, Ben never thought in his wildest dreams that any part of him would be sad to return to his everyday life. Watching Tom disappear into his bedroom to gather his scythe and sandals was bittersweet. Seconds later, the Reaper emerged without his trusty blade, holding a Polaroid camera.

"Ok, get over here, bro," ordered Tom beckoning Ben toward him with a bony finger. He tossed the camera to Gulliver, who haphazardly juggled with it until it settled in his grasp.

"This is your camera?" Gulliver teased. "Even my camera is more modern than this." Tom looked back, almost offended.

"The Model 95 Gully! The first ever Polaroid camera, and it hasn't failed me yet." Tom flashed the metal horns and draped his arm across Ben's shoulder. Gulliver dutifully took a photograph that Tom inspected. No one said a word as the image emerged on the photographic film. Dissatisfied, Tom shook his head and asked Gulliver to try again. The second attempt was more to Tom's liking, and an inane grin spread across his face as the photograph came into view. "Perfect!" he cried, heading over to his wall of fame. Tom carefully moved photos around to make room for his snapshot with Ben.

"I don't understand," said Ben. "I thought your wall of fame was just for rock stars?"

"Rock and metal," corrected Tom, surveying the wall for the perfect space. "Ronnie James Dio invented the metal horns. Eddie Van Halen could tap a guitar with two hands. Cliff Burton made bass solos cool!" Tom looked fondly at each musician's photo as he praised them. "But I can't think of anything more metal than being the first person to die and get a second chance at life." Tom stuck Ben's photograph pride of place in the centre of the wall of fame. Ben felt humbled at Tom's display of love and respect. Gulliver sniffled at the back of the room, coming as close as any skeleton has to shedding a tear. Tom held his hand out to Ben for a fist bump which he accepted.

"Come on, dude. It's time."

Ben said his goodbyes to Gulliver and the children. He looked back at his photo on the wall of fame, took a deep breath and headed out the door.

35

Winston hobbled down the long flight of stairs, deep into the bowels of City Hall, his chest tightening with each laboured step. All he had ever wanted was an eternity sitting at the Pathway. He hadn't asked for any of this. Winston couldn't ignore that he had grown fond of Ben and knew in his heart that he deserved to live his life. However, watching his oldest friend descend into madness so publicly had not been easy. Winston had never condoned Grim's actions but understood the motive behind them. Candles that adorned each step flickered and shone brighter the further Winston descended the staircase. The exquisite oil paintings that dominated City Hall's upper floor were nowhere to be seen. Instead, the damp-ridden stone walls seeped with moss between each brick, a mildewed scent taking over at the lower steps.

Very few people were aware of the dungeon that sat directly below the boardroom in City Hall. Only the most senior members of the Council of Reapers were privy to its existence, and far fewer had clearance to access it. Winston hadn't ventured into the dungeon for thousands of years, but it was as rank and melancholy as he remembered. Reaching the bottom step, he felt his chest tighten to a level that he was unable to exhale. In contrast to the dozens of candles on the staircase, the dungeons themselves only had scattered lighting, making it very difficult to see. Winston squinted in the darkness, trying to make sense of his surroundings.

As his eyes adjusted, Winston realised that it wasn't just the darkness obscuring his vision. Masses of thick vapour spilt out from the end of the corridor. Smoke invaded Winston's nostrils, and he coughed hoarsely, his bark echoing across the dungeon. Momentarily, the haze subsided. Winston stood still. He tried to call out, but the tension in his chest forbade him from doing so. Unable to react, the Gatekeeper remained frozen to the spot as the billows of mist resumed. Winston took a moment to collect himself and fought through his trepidation to speak.

"Grim? Are you there?"

His voice trembled so timidly it had barely made an echo, but it was enough. The vapour ceased for a second time, leaving Winston to see a closed cell at the end of the corridor. Cautiously, Winston walked toward the cell. Although walking softly, his footsteps rang loudly across the entire bullpen. A voice called out from the shadows.

"Winston? Is that you?"

The pressure in Winston's chest felt heavier than ever. He had never been so conflicted. Edging closer, Winston saw a cloaked silhouette huddled in the cell furthest away from him. Winston grabbed a candle from a few feet away, precariously close to burning out but enough to provide some light. The dim candlelight was enough to reveal the Architect of the AfterLife shaking and convulsing in the far corner of the cell. Cowering on the end of a bench that stretched the length of the enclosure, it was jarring for Winston to see Grim look so vulnerable, a shell of the man he'd known for centuries.

"Can I come in?" Winston asked. Grim's head turned to face the Gatekeeper, the abyss beneath his hood vibrant against the dingy backdrop of the dungeon.

"Why not?" he answered. "I clearly have no authority left, so do what you like." Winston tentatively stepped into Grim's cell, so bitterly cold that a shiver raced down his spine. Grim's gaze followed the Gatekeeper, the pitch black within Grim's cowl more intense and desolate than ever. Staring deep into the void, everything in Winston's soul ached to help his friend.

"What happened back there?" Winston asked, his voice brimming with desperation.

"I don't know," replied Grim. "I've always been able to control it. It seems as of late that it's controlling me."

"Why didn't you say something? I could have helped!" Grim scoffed at the very suggestion.

"Helped?" he scolded. "You kept the Anomaly from me in the first place! You were too busy making friends with Angels and that pathetic excuse for a Reaper." The atmosphere began to thicken as Grim worked himself into a frenzy. "How could I have possibly come to you?"

"Because it's always been you and me," Winston said sadly. "I only kept Ben's death a secret because I wanted to know the gravity of the situation before I involved you, and I regrettably had to oppose you when I realised you would go to any measures to bury this."

"Wouldn't you?" yelled Grim, the ether intensifying to match his anger.

"Not at the cost of a man's life and the integrity of what we built together," argued Winston. Grim looked away and clenched his fists, making a concerted effort to quell the emotions raging inside him. The vapour yielded.

"How is Cornforth?" Grim asked, staring at the floor of the cell. Winston sighed.

"He's gone."

"Pity," Grim replied flippantly. "That wasn't supposed to happen."

"And that poor engineer? That was an accident too?"

"Indeed," Grim lied. Winston breathed a huge sigh of relief.

"Oh, thank goodness!" he started to babble. "I didn't want to believe you would go out of your way to hurt anyone, even when under such immense pressure. I'm sure we can straighten this out with the rest of the Council once Ben has gone through the Third Door and—"

"The Third Door? Are you telling me those idiots have overturned his death?" Grim snapped.

"The evidence was overwhelming," Winston stammered. "Even you know deep down that he was never meant to die."

"I bet you're loving this," snarled Grim. "You sat with the Anomaly and his motley crew of friends through the entire thing. This is exactly what you wanted."

"No, it isn't!" Winston shot back in defiance. His tone took Grim by surprise. The Architect remained silent to allow his oldest confidante to say his piece. "I sit at the Pathway day after day, year after year, and I feel fulfilled. I don't crave excitement or drama, yet unfortunately, that is exactly what the last few days have been full of. I admit I've grown fond of the boy and am pleased he will get a second chance, but I also have faith that the institution we created together will withstand this one unfortunate breach. I can resume my duties at the Pathway, and we can learn from the mistakes we have made."

The pair sat in the quivering light of the candle, mere minutes from burning out. Neither said a word as they considered the future of the AfterLife, both sharing a mutual desire for things to go back to the way they were. Deep in thought, Grim began to shudder once more. Gentler than his previous convulsions, it still caused the Architect to let out an anguished wail. Winston instinctively reached out for Grim's hand, clutching it tightly to guide him through the pain.

"Did you mean what you said?" Grim asked as another wave passed over him. "That you believe we can come back from this?" Winston nodded.

"I really do. First thing tomorrow, I'll speak to the Council about reinstating you. Godfrey Marmaduke stepped in after Cornforth's demise. He's always admired you."

"That was before I struck a Council member down," Grim retorted.

"Look at you. It's obvious to anyone you're not yourself. What happened in that boardroom was a horrendous accident." Grim didn't respond. "It was an accident, wasn't it, Grim?"

"An unfortunate one," he replied.

"Then we will try our hardest to help the Council understand." Winston stood up and began to make his way out of the cell. "I'm going to meet Ben and Tom at the Third Door now so we can put this whole sorry mess behind us." Stepping foot back into the dungeon corridor, Winston heard Grim utter four words that he could never have expected.

"Take me with you!"

"What?" Winston spluttered. "You've been incarcerated, and you're extremely vulnerable. There's no way I can take you to the Third Door."

"Then I guess your words before meant nothing," Grim grumbled.

"What do you mean?"

"You said there was a way back for us," Grim explained. "That what we've built can withstand this sordid event. I don't think that's possible without rebuilding our trust."

"I don't understand," admitted the Gatekeeper.

"In the thousands of years we have worked side by side, not one soul has ventured through the Third Door. If my efforts to maintain that flawless record are for nought, the very least you could do is allow me to be present to ensure all goes to plan."

"I don't know if you are aware," Winston said sarcastically, "but you are currently detained under the custody of the Council of Reapers."

"And what better way to show them I have seen the error of my ways than being present at the Anomaly's homecoming."

"And have you seen the error of your ways?" challenged Winston.

"I stand by my belief that the Anomaly's death should never have been overturned to maintain the sanctity of the AfterLife," Grim conceded. "However, in the spirit of a fresh start, I am willing to bear witness to his safe passage through the Third Door." Winston looked back at his partner in the cell. Every word he'd said to Grim was the absolute truth. He believed Ben's death and subsequent second chance could be overcome. He genuinely hoped the Council would have mercy and reinstate Grim to his rightful place as Council leader and Architect. He wished with every fibre in his being that his eternity would return to normal. Winston reflected on centuries of partnership, and his sentimental side kicked in.

"Oh, alright," he said. "But we'll have to be discreet. Should any members of the Council see us, I can't comprehend what would happen."

"They'll all be in the billiards room getting drunk and playing a game or two," replied Grim. "We'll come straight back after, and no one will ever know I was gone." Treading quietly toward the staircase, Winston advised he had one condition if Grim was to accompany him to his rendezvous with Ben at the Third Door.

"You must keep your emotions under control," he insisted.

"Of course, of course."

"We can't have anyone else hurt, can we?"

"What happened to Cornforth was a one-time thing," Grim replied. "It'll never happen again."

The final candle in the dungeon corridor died out seconds before Grim and Winston reached the staircase. The pairs of candles on each step guided them back up to the hallowed hallways above. The absence of light in the dungeon concealed the fate of the skeleton guards who had strong-armed Grim into the lower echelons of City Hall. In the closest cell to the stairway, all four bodies were piled carelessly on top of each other, with no hint of soul between them. The manifestation of Grim's fear and torment had won out, and despite his promise to Winston, it was only just getting started.

36

Behind the wheel of his pride and joy for the first time in several days, Tom carefully steered the school bus out of the Depot of the Dead and headed straight for the Pathway. The colossal iron gates loomed heavy over the landscape. Even if it weren't such a short drive, there would be no danger of getting lost. Along the journey, scattered witnesses whispered to each other as Tom drove past. Tom reckoned his bus was now the most famous vehicle in the entire AfterLife.

While he was thrilled to be in the driver's seat again, he still had no clue why Winston had asked him to drive his bus to the Pathway. Before this morning, Tom thought the Third Door was a myth, a product of many drunken tales in the Eternal Alcove. The odd inebriated Reaper would claim he had seen it, but their stories never held up to further interrogation. Still, if Ben was to be the first to walk through the Third Door and return to his life, why did Tom need his bus? Rather than confuse himself further, Tom contented himself by wailing along with Styx as "Come Sail Away" thundered from the speakers.

The same thought had crossed Ben's mind. However, after all the things he'd seen since his death, the one thing he had learned was to expect the unexpected. Tom had had no answers as to what to anticipate upon their arrival at the Third Door, and Winston had disappeared seconds after Marmaduke had ruled in favour of Ben's freedom. Ben remembered his flight with Jade and how the clouds had obscured what lay beyond the Pathway. Ben could only presume the Third Door lay behind those gates and that he would be privy to something very few had ever experienced.

Ben felt the bus slow to a peaceful stop. Peering through the nearest window, the intimidating gates of the Pathway shot high into the sky and out of view. The last time Ben had been here, the Pathway had been extremely busy, with dozens of Reapers battling to check in their passengers. On this occasion, there wasn't a soul to be seen. Curiously that included Winston.

Ben turned to ask Tom where the Gatekeeper was when an unearthly screech heralded the opening of the gates. Not expecting them to open of their own volition, Tom reversed the bus back a few metres to allow space for the awe-inspiring gates to swing open. Winston stood pensively at the centre of the entranceway with two distinct lights illuminating him from behind. On his left side, one light was pure and rich. While there was no particular colour to it, what stood out to Ben the most was its radiance. It was flawless.

In contrast, the light on Winston's right was red and harsh. Standing perfectly between both lights, Winston cut an imposing figure despite his limited size. Ben followed Tom out of the bus and cautiously walked toward the light.

"Ben, congratulations on your appeal," said the Gatekeeper. "I apologise for my hasty retreat from the boardroom. There has been much to prepare." Winston embraced Ben and held him tight. Ben felt the Gatekeeper shaking against his body.

"Thanks, Winston," Ben replied. "There's no apology necessary." A disconcerting wind howled through the bars of the gates. The lights emanating from behind were even more intense when they stood beneath them.

"The Third Door is just beyond the entrance," Winston explained. "Tom, can I ask you to return to your vehicle and drive your bus through the gates."

"Sure thing Winnie," replied Tom suspiciously. Heading back to the bus, he glanced over his shoulder to ensure nothing was amiss. Without saying a word, Winston turned his back to Ben and walked deeper into the light, taking great care to ensure he did not veer further onto one side than the other. Ben followed suit, ensuring Winston wouldn't disappear from sight. He could hear the gentle chugging of the bus behind him as Tom guided it into the light.

Ben saw in front of him a large, pristine door reaching about twenty feet into the sky. At the very point where he expected the two lights to meet, there was no light at all. A glass barrier sheltered the door, refracting the light from both sides and sending it bouncing back from whence it came. Ben stood in the knowledge that this had to be the Third Door. A pair of circular lights suddenly appeared on it. Ben turned to see Tom in the bus, its headlights shining onto the door in front of it. Turning off the ignition, the Reaper clambered out of the cab and took in the awesome structure.

"So this is the Third Door?" he said to no one in particular. "What a sight." Winston rifled through his pockets, pulling out all kinds of keys and other essentials. He finally settled on a chunky brass ring with three distinct keys attached. Ben couldn't look directly at the gold key that shone with such intensity that it hurt his eyes. The key next to it was rusty and neglected, but it was the third key that Winston chose. Cumbersome and bronze, there wasn't a single scuff or imperfection on it.

"I could imagine it being a bit stiff," Winston said to Ben. "As I'm sure you know, we have never opened the Third Door." He walked over to the Third Door and attempted to reach the keyhole. His small stature meant he was a good foot shorter than required, and he jumped in vain to use the key. Ben offered his services to lift the Gatekeeper, who sheepishly agreed.

Tom hadn't noticed any of the inconvenience. Usually aloof, Tom had been feeling quite unsettled since Winston had made his speedy exit from City Hall earlier in the day. He understood Winston's integral role in Ben's appeal, but as the pipe dream of a second chance had become a reality, the Gatekeeper had become increasingly more withdrawn. Winston had gone from preparing legal documents and drinking in the Alcove to waiting outside while Ben and the group scaled Otis's control tower. Tom conceded that there was a chance he was in denial about Ben returning home, and his edginess was his mind creating roadblocks to reassure himself it wouldn't happen. Whether that was true or not, Tom knew something did not feel right.

The Third Door swung open, and a vibrant blue hue burst through it. The glow from within shot into the air, and the distinct lights blended for the first time into a breathtaking aurora of violet. Ben watched in awe as patterns of spirals and rays flickered in the sky, the previous segregation of red and white a distant memory.

Tom was captivated, his previous reservations a distant memory. He hadn't even noticed his cowl drop off his skull from craning his neck too far back. Lost in the aurora's beauty, Tom missed Winston's instructions for Ben's safe passage through the Third Door. A sharp jab to the ribs from Winston broke Tom's concentration.

"As I was saying," the Gatekeeper grunted, "the road behind the Third Door is not the easiest to navigate. There are many directions you can take, and it would be easy to get lost forever. All you need to do is ensure you always follow the orb."

"Always follow the orb," Tom repeated to himself. He looked back at Winston in confusion. "What orb?"

"The orb that is making this beautiful light," clarified Winston. "It's beguiling enough, but the road back to the exact moment of Ben's death may be long, so don't take your eye off the road!"

"So I'll go back to the very moment I died?" Ben asked.

"The very second," Winston confirmed, "and being you were on the road at the time, I'd suggest you think fast, or your second life may be a brief one." He ushered Ben over to one side. Ben noticed Winston was continuing to shake nervously.

"Are you ok, Winston?"

"Fine dear boy," he replied. "Now, because you will have returned to the very moment you've died, no one, including Lucy, will have any memory of your death. As the Council requested, it is imperative you never speak of your experience. If you do, I will be powerless to help you. Do you understand?"

Ben and Winston's words faded into the background as Tom spotted sickly, black fumes oozing out from behind the bus. The fumes continued to spill out with more intensity and urgency until they began to interfere with and spoil the stunning display in the sky. After the events he had witnessed in the boardroom that morning, Tom had no doubt as to the source of the smoke.

"Grim?" shouted Tom fiercely. His cry ripped Ben and Winston from their conversation, both noticing the grey whirlpool that had formed in the sky for the first time. Tom stood facing the riptide in front of him. "Come out and show yourself, Grim. I know that it's you!" Emerging from the gloom, the Architect revealed himself, clouds and vapour continuing to pour from beneath his hood. He stumbled into what was left of the light, overpowered by his own vitriol.

"This wasn't what we agreed, Grim," Winston pleaded. "You promised you would observe from a distance." Taking his eyes off Grim for the first time, Tom turned and stared at the Gatekeeper in disbelief.

"You did this, Winnie?"

"He's not a bad man," Winston insisted. "I can help him." He walked over to Grim, who had fallen to his knees and was convulsing on the floor. "Please go, Grim. Now. If you've ever valued our friendship, then please take control of your fear and let Ben go." Grim let out a primal groan and lifted his head, looking directly into Winston's eyes.

"I—"

Before Grim could say another word, two pitch-black thunderclouds flashed from beneath his cowl and struck Winston to the ground. The force of their arrival threw Grim onto his back, and his venom spewed out violently across the entire constellation of light above them. Ben stared up at the ever-increasing vortex the Architect had created. He felt someone grab him from behind.

"Dude, we've got to go!" Tom cried as he yanked Ben off his feet and led him to the bus. As Tom dragged him up the steps, Ben looked back at Winston, a hollow and grey version of who he used to be. Ben implored deep in his heart for Winston to move. He wished for a small twitch or quiver to prove that he was alright, but it was not to be.

The bus lurched forward forcefully just as the smog became thick enough for Winston to disappear behind it. Tom slammed his foot on the accelerator, crashing through the Third Door with mere inches to spare on each side. The orb shone proudly in front of him, guiding the way. However, Tom checked his rearview mirror to see the storm from the Pathway following them at a furious pace. Frantically spinning the wheel to follow the orb, the tempest didn't relent and continued to gain on the bus. Even at top speed, it was inevitable.

Within seconds, shadows drowned out all light, submerging the bus and everything around it. Tom and Ben looked out the front window and watched the once radiant orb of light become consumed by the darkness and fade to nothing. Thunder rolled, and clouds fought for space as the ether nearly burst at the seams. Rain began to fall gently across the bleak landscape. Tom dejectedly stopped the bus, staring at the mist in front of him.

The patter of the rain on the roof was the only sound the pair could hear in between intermittent rumbles of thunder. Ben spoke first, keeping his attention on the raindrops splashing off the window.

"So what do we do now?"

Tom took a deep breath. He felt a slight itching on the little finger on his left hand. Using his thumb to scratch it, he noticed the very tip disintegrate into dust. He hid his hand up the sleeve of his cloak, hoping Ben had not seen it.

"Sorry, dude," Tom replied. "I really don't know."

Epilogue

I t had been thousands of years since she last stood at the Pathway. The AfterLife had run itself for the longest time, and she had been free to attend to more pressing matters. It hadn't rained the entire time, not so much as a drop. But as raindrops fell from the darkest clouds in the sky and saturated the ground, she observed that those times were over.

The downpour grew heavier. Her pace picked up, and with it, her heels kicked up the mulch and sodden Earth beneath her. A few feet away, she could see the gates were wide open, and no one was there to keep watch. A loud bark filled the air, and her dog raced to her through the dense fog. Their eyes locked, and the dog bounded back into the distance without command. She followed in anticipation.

Stepping through the Pathway gates, it did not take long to discover the source of her companion's excitement. The Third Door was open, and the thick impurity unleashed from inside Grim was spilling through it. She looked up at the sky and saw the ooze had blocked out the light. The Architect lay shuddering at her feet, with remnants of gas and vapour still emerging from the darkness beneath his cowl. She heard her dog sniffing with excitement.

"Yield, Garmr," she commanded. Garmr dutifully stepped away. She turned to see the body of her Gatekeeper. Grey and desolate, Winston's body was nothing more than the flesh that was left behind. She placed her good hand on Winston's forehead and focused her thoughts. Colour began to return to Winston's skin, and he gradually opened his eyes.

Winston hadn't seen her in centuries, but in many ways, he thought she looked as beautiful as ever. Auburn hair draped down her left side, brushing against her cheek. The glint in her eye was as intoxicating as ever, even though its presence often assured someone else's downfall. The rain showed no sign of relenting, and the deluge of water soaked her veil, pressing it against the right side of her face in the process. He found it easier to ignore her right side that way.

"Hel?" Winston croaked, trying his best to gather himself. "Did you bring me back?" Hel nodded affirmatively.

"What happened here?"

"Well, it's a long story," stuttered the Gatekeeper as he tried to recount everything that had transpired. He could see Hel's expression did not change, usually an indication that she was bored with the conversation.

"Whose fault is this?" she interrupted.

"Wh-whose fault?"

"Yes, Winston, whose fault is this? Why are the gates open, why is the Third Door open, and why is it raining across my beautiful AfterLife?" Winston froze in fear. Every decision he had made along the way was in an effort to do the right thing. However, as the Gatekeeper of the Pathway, he was accountable for the Third Door and any issues related to it.

"My lady, as the Gatekeeper, it is my responsibility—"

"I'll try again," Hel interjected. "You've brought up responsibility. Who is the one responsible for striking you and leaving your body without its soul here on the Pathway?" Winston hesitated.

"Well, that would be Grim, ma'am, but—"

"Thank you, Winston," Hel turned her attention back to Grim, who still lay on the ground, unable to control himself. He murmured in pain.

Winston wondered if the Architect was even aware of Hel's arrival.

The rain continued to beat down, leaving Grim's cloak soaked through. Hel knelt beside him and slowly removed her veil. The contrast of beauty between both sides was as shocking as ever. The coppery shades of her hair on the left clashed noticeably with the withered, greying black on the right. The knots and tangles encapsulated years of neglect and poor self-care. Beneath it, Hel's smooth skin had faded away, revealing a filthy, rotting skull beneath. Her full, inviting lips, from which she spoke on the left, were diminished to nothing but decaying teeth on the right. Winston's blood ran cold. Thousands of years had not dulled the impact of seeing Hel's bad side. It was as terrifying as ever.

Hel looked deep into the abyss beneath Grim's cowl and smiled affectionately. She ran her perfectly manicured left hand across Grim's hood and stroked it gently. Leaning intimately close, she listened for a moment to Grim's laboured groans, not once averting her gaze. Her right hand perished to the bone, cradled Grim by the back of his head and lifted him with care. Winston could just make out Hel's words as she whispered faintly to the Architect.

"Goodbye, Grim. I knew this day would come."

Hel smoothed out Grim's hood and softly kissed his forehead. The moment her lips made contact, Grim's convulsions stopped immediately, and his head fell back, lifeless in her arms. Suddenly taking flight from his cowl, a murder of crows soared into the troubled sky and followed the vortex flow circling the Pathway. When the last crow ascended to join its brethren, all that lay before Hel and Winston was an empty cloak, dishevelled and messy like clothes on a child's bedroom floor. Garmr inspected it zealously, ruffling his nose into the material to catch Grim's scent. Rolling onto his back, the faithful hellhound made himself comfortable, treating Grim's cloak like his favourite blanket. Hel pulled the veil from under him and draped it across his back. Winston sobbed at Grim's fate as tears flooded his eyes. He looked at Garmr with disdain. Only seconds after Grim's demise, his robe had been reduced to nothing more than a dog's plaything.

Hel walked away from where Grim once lay and approached the Third Door that still hung ajar. She idly watched the remaining wisps of his negative energy float through to the other side and chuckled wryly to herself.

"Has the Anomaly gone through the Third Door?" she asked suddenly. Winston's anxiety rose once more.

"Grim wasn't responsible for that," Winston confessed.

"I know," Hel replied. "Your mistakes are far easier to rectify than his." She surveyed the spoiled atmosphere around her. "At least our old friend has tainted the Third Door too. There's no chance anyone is getting back before I catch them."

"Catch them?" Winston gulped nervously. "I just gave that boy his freedom. I can't renege on the Council's ruling."

"The days of the Council of Reapers are over!" snapped Hel. She took a moment to centre herself and regain her composure. "I am not asking you to help me. All I request is that you walk back through those gates and take a seat."

"And what will happen to Ben?"

"That's no longer your concern," Hel answered gravely. "Now, please return to your post. I have a lot of work to do to clean up your mess."

THE END

Ben and Tom will return in

'Reap Sleep Rock Repeat: Turn To Dust'

About the Author

Mike Norris lives in County Durham with his wife Kayleigh, their daughters Eleanor and Imogen and their three needy cats. This is his first novel. When Mike isn't pondering the inner workings of the AfterLife, he presents the popular podcast 'My Classic Album', where musicians share their love for their all-time favourite album.

Mental health is a huge passion for Mike. After struggling with depression and anxiety throughout his twenties and early thirties, Mike now supports others in his day job as a Senior Psychological Wellbeing Practitioner.

Mike loves rock and metal (he also has a soft spot for the Corrs) and has spent the last 23 years cheering on his favourite professional wrestlers. Buy him a pepperoni pizza and an Apple Tango, and he's yours for the night!

You can connect with me on:

http://www.mikenorrisauthor.co.uk

https://www.facebook.com/mikenorrisauthor

Printed in Great Britain
by Amazon

33198922R00141